SIMON VS. THE HOMO SAPIENS AGENDA

Becky Albertalli

PENGUIN BOOKS

PENGUIN BOOKS

UK | USA | Canada | Ireland | Australia
India | New Zealand | South Africa

Penguin Books is part of the Penguin Random House group of companies
whose addresses can be found at global.penguinrandomhouse.com.

www.penguin.co.uk
www.puffin.co.uk
www.ladybird.co.uk

First published in the USA by Balzer + Bray, an imprint of
Harper Collins Publishers and in Great Britain by Penguin Books 2015
This edition reissued with new material 2018

015

Set in 11.04/17.30 pt by Adobe Garamond Pro
Printed in Great Britain by Clays Ltd, St Ives plc

A CIP catalogue record for this book is available from the British Library

ISBN: 978–0–141–35609–9

All correspondence to:
Penguin Books
Penguin Random House Children's
80 Strand, London WC2R 0RL

Praise for Becky Albertalli

'The love child of John Green and Rainbow Rowell'
Teen Vogue

'I love you, Simon. I love you! And I love this fresh, funny, live-out-loud book' Jennifer Niven, *New York Times* bestselling author of *All the Bright Places* and *Holding Up the Universe*

'Touching and passionate . . . This tender, witty tale normalizes Simon's experience and shows him as completely loveable, with bags of empathy'
Observer

'A radically tender debut . . . Steal this from your teen'
O (Oprah's Magazine)

'Delightfully funny and at times heart-wrenching. Readers will ache for Simon's awkwardness, cheer his small triumphs, but, most of all fall in love with this kid and this remarkable gift of a novel'
Andrew Smith, author of *Grasshopper Jungle*

'Both hilarious and heartbreaking . . . Readers will fall madly in love with Simon'
Publishers Weekly (starred review)

SIMON vs. THE HOMO SAPIENS AGENDA

Becky Albertalli

is the author of the acclaimed novels *Simon vs the Homo Sapiens Agenda* and *The Upside of Unrequited*. She is a clinical psychologist who specializes in working with children and teens. Becky now lives with her family in Atlanta, where she spends her days writing fiction for young adults. You can visit her online at:

www.beckyalbertalli.com

You can follow Becky on Facebook, Twitter (@BeckyAlbertalli), and Tumblr (BeckyAlbertalli).

Also by Becky Albertalli:
The Upside of Unrequited

To Brian, Owen, and Henry,
who are the reason I write love stories

SIMON vs. THE HOMO SAPIENS AGENDA

1

IT'S A WEIRDLY SUBTLE CONVERSATION. I almost don't notice I'm being blackmailed.

We're sitting in metal folding chairs backstage, and Martin Addison says, "I read your email."

"What?" I look up.

"Earlier. In the library. Not on purpose, obviously."

"You read my email?"

"Well, I used the computer right after you," he says, "and when I typed in Gmail, it pulled up your account. You probably should have logged out."

I stare at him, dumbfounded. He taps his foot against the leg of his chair.

"So, what's the point of the fake name?" he asks.

Well. I'd say the point of the fake name was to keep people

like Martin Addison from knowing my secret identity. So I guess that worked out brilliantly.

I guess he must have seen me sitting at the computer.

And I guess I'm a monumental idiot.

He actually smiles. "Anyway, I thought it might interest you that my brother is gay."

"Um. Not really."

He looks at me.

"What are you trying to say?" I ask.

"Nothing. Look, Spier, I don't have a problem with it. It's just not that big of a deal."

Except it's a little bit of a disaster, actually. Or possibly an epic fuckstorm of a disaster, depending on whether Martin can keep his mouth shut.

"This is really awkward," Martin says.

I don't even know how to reply.

"Anyway," he says, "it's pretty obvious that you don't want people to know."

I mean. I guess I don't. Except the whole coming out thing doesn't really scare me.

I don't think it scares me.

It's a giant holy box of awkwardness, and I won't pretend I'm looking forward to it. But it probably wouldn't be the end of the world. Not for me.

The problem is, I don't know what it would mean for Blue. If Martin were to tell anyone. The thing about Blue is that he's kind of a private person. The kind of person who wouldn't forget to log out of his email. The kind of person who might never forgive me for being so totally careless.

So I guess what I'm trying to say is that I don't know what it would mean for us. For Blue and me.

But I seriously can't believe I'm having this conversation with Martin Addison. Of all the people who could have logged into Gmail after me. You have to understand that I never would have used the library computers in the first place, except they block the wireless here. And it was one of those days where I couldn't wait until I was home on my laptop. I mean, I couldn't even wait to check it on my phone in the parking lot.

Because I had written Blue from my secret account this morning. And it was sort of an important email.

I just wanted to see if he had written back.

"I actually think people would be cool about it," Martin says. "You should be who you are."

I don't even know where to begin with that. Some straight kid who barely knows me, advising me on coming out. I kind of have to roll my eyes.

"Okay, well, whatever. I'm not going to show anyone," he says.

For a minute, I'm stupidly relieved. But then it hits me.

"Show anyone?" I ask.

He blushes and fidgets with the hem of his sleeve. Something about his expression makes my stomach clench.

"Did you—did you take a screenshot or something?"

"Well," he says, "I wanted to talk to you about that."

"Sorry—*you took a fucking screenshot?*"

He purses his lips together and stares over my shoulder. "Anyway," he says, "I know you're friends with Abby Suso, so I wanted to ask—"

"Seriously? Or maybe we could go back to you telling me why you took a screenshot of my emails."

He pauses. "I mean, I guess I'm wondering if you want to help me talk to Abby."

I almost laugh. "So what—you want me to put in a good word for you?"

"Well, yeah," he says.

"And why the hell should I do that?"

He looks at me, and it suddenly clicks. This Abby thing. This is what he wants from me. This, in exchange for not broadcasting my private fucking emails.

And Blue's emails.

Jesus Christ. I mean, I guess I figured Martin was harmless. A little bit of a goobery nerd, to be honest, but it's not like that's a bad thing. And I've always thought he was kind of hilarious.

Except I'm not laughing now.

"You're actually going to make me do this," I say.

"Make you? Come on. It's not like that."

"Well, what's it like?"

"It's not like anything. I mean, I like this girl. I was just thinking you would want to help me here. Invite me to stuff when she'll be there. I don't know."

"And what if I don't? You'll put the emails on Facebook? On the fucking Tumblr?"

Jesus. The creeksecrets Tumblr: ground zero for Creekwood High School gossip. The entire school would know within a day.

We're both quiet.

"I just think we're in a position to help each other out," Martin finally says.

I swallow, thickly.

"Paging Marty," Ms. Albright calls from the stage. "Act Two, Scene Three."

"So, just think about it." He dismounts his chair.

"Oh yeah. I mean, this is so goddamn awesome," I say.

He looks at me. And there's this silence.

"I don't know what the hell you want me to say," I add finally.

"Well, whatever." He shrugs. And I don't think I've ever been so ready for someone to leave. But as his fingers graze the curtains, he turns to me.

"Just curious," he says. "Who's Blue?"

"No one. He lives in California."

If Martin thinks I'm selling out Blue, he's fucking crazy.

Blue doesn't live in California. He lives in Shady Creek, and he goes to our school. Blue isn't his real name.

He's someone. He may even be someone I know. But I don't know who. And I'm not sure I want to know.

And I'm seriously not in the mood to deal with my family. I probably have about an hour until dinner, which means an hour of trying to spin my school day into a string of hilarious anecdotes. My parents are like that. It's like you can't just tell them about your French teacher's obvious wedgie, or Garrett dropping his tray in the cafeteria. You have to perform it. Talking to them is more exhausting than keeping a blog.

It's funny, though. I used to love the chatter and chaos before dinner. Now it seems like I can't get out the door fast enough. Today especially. I stop only long enough to click the leash onto Bieber's collar and get him out the door.

I'm trying to lose myself in Tegan and Sara on my iPod. But I can't stop thinking about Blue and Martin Addison and the holy awfulness of today's rehearsal.

So Martin is into Abby, just like every other geeky straight boy in Advanced Placement. And really, all he wants is for me to let him tag along when I hang out with her. It doesn't seem like a huge deal when I think about it that way.

Except for the fact that he's blackmailing me. And by extension, he's blackmailing Blue. That's the part that makes me want to kick something.

But Tegan and Sara help. Walking to Nick's helps. The air has that crisp, early fall feeling, and people are already lining their steps with pumpkins. I love that. I've loved it since I was a kid.

Bieber and I cut around to Nick's backyard and through the basement. There's a massive TV facing the door, on which Templars are being brutalized. Nick and Leah have taken over a pair of rocking video game chairs. They look like they haven't moved all afternoon.

Nick pauses the game when I walk in. That's something about Nick. He won't put down a guitar for you, but he'll pause a video game.

"Bieber!" says Leah. Within seconds, he perches awkwardly with his butt in her lap, tongue out and leg thumping. He's so freaking shameless around Leah.

"No, it's cool. Just greet the dog. Pretend I'm not here."

"Aww, do you need me to scratch your ears, too?"

I crack a smile. This is good; things are normal. "Did you find the traitor?" I ask.

"Killed him." He pats the controller.

"Nice."

Seriously, there is no part of me that cares about the welfare of assassins or Templars or any game character ever. But I think I need this. I need the violence of video games and the smell of this basement and the familiarity of Nick and Leah. The rhythm of our speech and silences. The aimlessness of mid-October afternoons.

"Simon, Nick hasn't heard about le wedgie."

"Ohhhh. *Le wedgie. C'est une histoire touchante.*"

"English, please?" says Nick.

"Or pantomime," Leah says.

As it turns out, I'm kind of awesome at reenacting epic wedgies.

So maybe I do like to perform. A little.

I think I'm getting that Nick-and-Leah sixth-grade field trip feeling. I don't know how to explain it. But when it's just the three of us, we have these perfect, stupid moments. Martin Addison doesn't exist in this kind of moment. Secrets don't exist.

Stupid. Perfect.

Leah rips up a paper straw wrapper, and they're both holding giant Styrofoam cups of sweet tea from Chick-fil-A. I actually haven't been to Chick-fil-A for a while. My sister heard they donate money to screw over gay people, and I guess it started to feel weird eating there. Even if their Oreo milk shakes are giant vessels of frothy deliciousness. Not that I can bring that up with Nick and Leah. I don't exactly talk about gay stuff with anyone. Except Blue.

Nick takes a swig of his tea and yawns, and Leah immediately tries to launch a little paper wad into his mouth. But Nick clamps his mouth shut, blocking it.

She shrugs. "Just keep on yawning, sleepyhead."

"Why are you so tired?"

"Because I party hard. All night. Every night," Nick says.

"If by 'party,' you mean your calculus homework."

"WHATEVER, LEAH." He leans back, yawning again. This time, Leah's paper wad grazes the corner of his mouth.

He flicks it back toward her.

"So, I keep having these weird dreams," he adds.

I raise my eyebrows. "Yikes. TMI?"

"Um. Not that kind of dream."

Leah's whole face goes red.

"No, just," Nick says, "like actual weird dreams. Like I dreamed I was in the bathroom putting on my contacts, and I couldn't figure out which lens went in which eye."

"Okay. So then what?" Leah's face is buried in the fur on the back of Bieber's neck, and her voice is muffled.

"Nothing. I woke up, I put my contacts in like normal, and everything was fine."

"That's the most boring dream ever," she says. And then, a moment later, "Isn't that why they label the left and right sides of the containers?"

"Or why people should just wear glasses and stop touching their eyeballs." I sink cross-legged onto the carpet. Bieber slides out of Leah's lap to wander toward me.

"And because your glasses make you look like Harry Potter, right, Simon?"

One time. I said it once.

"Well, I think my unconscious is trying to tell me something." Nick can be pretty single-minded when he's feeling intellectual. "Obviously, the theme of the dream is vision. What am I not seeing? What are my blind spots?"

"Your music collection," I suggest.

Nick rocks backward in the video game chair and takes another swig of tea. "Did you know Freud interpreted his own dreams when he was developing his theory? And he believed that all dreams are a form of unconscious wish fulfillment?"

Leah and I look at each other, and I can tell we're thinking the same thing. It doesn't matter that he's quite possibly talking complete bullshit, because Nick is a little bit irresistible when he's in one of his philosophical moods.

Of course, I have a strict policy of not falling for straight guys. At least, not confirmed straight guys. Anyway, I have a policy of not falling for Nick. But Leah has fallen. And it's caused all kinds of problems, especially now that Abby's in the picture.

At first, I didn't understand why Leah hated Abby, and asking about it directly got me nowhere.

"Oh, she's the *best*. I mean, she's a cheerleader. And she's so cute and skinny. Doesn't that just make her so amazing?"

You have to understand that no one has mastered the art of deadpan delivery like Leah.

But eventually I noticed Nick switching seats with Bram Greenfeld at lunch—calculated switching, designed to maximize his odds of sitting near Abby. And then the eyes. The famous Nick Eisner lingering, lovesick eyes. We'd been down

that vomit-inducing road before with Amy Everett [...]
freshman year. Though, I have to admit there's so[...]
cinating about Nick's nervous intensity when he lik[...]

When Leah sees that look pass across Nick's fa[...]
shuts down.

Which means there's actually one good reason for being
Martin Addison's wingman matchmaker bitch. If Martin and
Abby hook up, maybe the Nick problem will just go away. Then
Leah can chill the heck out, and equilibrium will be restored.

So it's not just about me and my secrets. It's hardly about
me at all.

2

FROM: hourtohour.notetonote@gmail.com
TO: bluegreen118@gmail.com
DATE: Oct 17 at 12:06 AM
SUBJECT: Re: when you knew

That's a pretty sexy story, Blue. I mean, middle school is like this endless horror show. Well, maybe not endless, because it ended, but it really burns into your psyche. I don't care who you are. Puberty is merciless.

i'm curious—have you seen him since your dad's wedding?

I don't even know when I figured it out. It was a bunch of little things. Like this weird dream I had once about Daniel Radcliffe. Or how I was obsessed with Passion Pit in middle school, and then I realized it wasn't really about the music.

And then in eighth grade, I had this girlfriend. It was one of those things where you're "dating" but you don't ever go anywhere outside of school. And you don't really do anything in school either. I think we held hands. So, we went to the eighth-grade dance as a couple, but my friends and I spent the whole night eating Fritos and spying on people from under the bleachers. And at one point, this random girl comes up to me and tells me my girlfriend is waiting in front of the gym. I was supposed to go out there and find her, and I guess we were supposed to make out. In that closed-mouth middle school way.

So, here's my proudest moment: I ran and hid like a freaking preschooler in the bathroom. Like, in the stall with the door closed, crouched up on the toilet so my legs wouldn't show. As if the girls were going to break in and bust me. Honest to God, I stayed there for the entire evening. And then I never spoke to my girlfriend again.

Also, it was Valentine's Day. Because I'm that classy. So, yeah, if I'm being completely honest with myself, I definitely knew at that point. Except I've had two other girlfriends since then.

Did you know that this is officially the longest email I've ever written? I'm not even kidding. You may actually be the only person who gets more than 140 characters from me. That's kind of awesome, right?

Anyway, I think I'll sign off here. Not going to lie. It's been kind of a weird day.

—Jacques

FROM: bluegreen118@gmail.com
TO: hourtohour.notetonote@gmail.com
DATE: Oct 17 at 8:46 PM
SUBJECT: Re: when you knew

I'm the only one? That's definitely kind of awesome. I'm really honored, Jacques. It's funny, because I don't really email, either. And I never talk about this stuff with anyone. Only you.

For what it's worth, I think it would be incredibly depressing if your actual proudest moment happened in middle school. You can't imagine how much I hated middle school. Remember the way people would look at you blankly and say, "Um, okaaay," after you finished talking? Everyone just had to make it so clear that, whatever you were thinking or feeling, you were totally alone. The worst part, of course, was that I did the same thing to other people. It makes me a little nauseated just remembering that.

So, basically, what I'm trying to say is that you should

really give yourself a break. We were all awful then.

To answer your question, I've seen him a couple of times since the wedding—probably twice a year or so. My stepmother seems to have a lot of family reunions and things. He's married, and I think his wife is pregnant now. It's not awkward, exactly, because the whole thing was in my head. It's really amazing, isn't it? Someone can trigger your sexual identity crisis and not have a clue they're doing it. Honestly, he probably still thinks of me as his cousin's weird twelve-year-old stepson.

So I guess this is the obvious question, but I'll ask it anyway: If you knew you were gay, how did you end up having girlfriends?

Sorry about your weird day.

—Blue

FROM: hourtohour.notetonote@gmail.com
TO: bluegreen118@gmail.com
DATE: Oct 18 at 11:15 PM
SUBJECT: Re: when you knew

Blue,

Yup, the dreaded "okaaay." Always accompanied by arched eyebrows and a mouth twisted into a condescending little butthole. And yes, I said it, too. We all sucked so much in middle school.

I guess the girlfriend thing is a little hard to explain. Everything just sort of happened. The eighth-grade relationship was a total mess, obviously, so that was different. As for the other two: basically, they were friends, and then I found out they liked me, and then we started dating. And then we broke up, and both of them dumped me, and it was all pretty painless. I'm still friends with the girl I dated freshman year.

Honestly, though? I think the real reason I had girl-friends was because I didn't one hundred percent believe I was gay. Or maybe I didn't think it was permanent.

I know you're probably thinking: "Okaaaaaaay."

—Jacques

FROM: bluegreen118@gmail.com
TO: hourtohour.notetonote@gmail.com
DATE: Oct 19 at 8:01 AM
SUBJECT: The obligatory . . .

Okaaaaaaaaaaaaaaaayyyyyyyyy.
(Eyebrows, butthole mouth, etc.)

—Blue

3

THE SHITTIEST THING ABOUT THE Martin situation is that I can't bring it up with Blue. I'm not used to keeping secrets from him.

I mean, there are a lot of things he and I don't tell each other. We talk about all the big things, but avoid the identifying details—the names of our friends and anything too specific about school. All the stuff that I used to think defined me. But I don't think of those things as secrets. It's more like an unspoken agreement.

If Blue were a real junior at Creekwood with a locker and a GPA and a Facebook profile, I'm pretty sure I wouldn't be telling him anything. I mean, he is a real junior at Creekwood. I know that. But in a way, he lives in my laptop. It's hard to explain.

I was the one who found him. On the Tumblr, of all places. It was August, right when school was starting. Creeksecrets is supposed to be where you can post anonymous confessions and secret random thoughts, and people can comment, but no one really judges you. Except it all kind of devolved into this sinkhole of gossip and bad poetry and misspelled Bible quotes. And I guess it's kind of addictive either way.

That's where I found Blue's post. It just kind of spoke to me. And I don't even think it was just the gay thing. I don't know. It was seriously like five lines, but it was grammatically correct and strangely poetic, and just completely different from anything I'd ever read before.

I guess it was about loneliness. And it's funny, because I don't really think of myself as lonely. But there was something so familiar about the way Blue described the feeling. It was like he had pulled the ideas from my head.

Like the way you can memorize someone's gestures but never know their thoughts. And the feeling that people are like houses with vast rooms and tiny windows.

The way you can feel so exposed anyway.

The way he feels so hidden and so exposed about the fact that he's gay.

I felt strangely panicked and self-conscious when I read that part, but there was also this quiet thrum of excitement.

He talked about the ocean between people. And how the whole point of everything is to find a shore worth swimming to.

I mean, I just had to know him.

Eventually I worked up the courage to post the only comment I could think of, which was: "THIS." All caps. And then I wrote my email address. My secret Gmail account.

I spent the next week obsessing about whether or not he would contact me. And then he did. Later, he told me that my comment made him a little nervous. He's really careful about things. Obviously, he's more careful than I am. Basically, if Blue finds out that Martin Addison has screenshots of our emails, I'm pretty sure he'll freak out. But he'll freak out in a totally Blue way.

Meaning, he'll stop emailing me.

I remember exactly how it felt to see that first message from him in my in-box. It was a little bit surreal. He wanted to know about me. For the next few days at school after that, it felt like I was a character in a movie. I could almost imagine a close-up of my face, projected wide-screen.

It's strange, because in reality, I'm not the leading guy. Maybe I'm the best friend.

I guess I didn't really think of myself as interesting until I was interesting to Blue. So I can't tell him. I'd rather not lose him.

I've been avoiding Martin. All week, in class and rehearsal, I see him trying to catch my eye. I know it's kind of cowardly. This whole situation makes me feel like a coward. It's especially stupid, because I've already decided I'll help him. Or I'll cave to his blackmail. Whatever you want to call it. It honestly makes me feel a little sick.

I'm distracted all through dinner. My parents are especially jolly tonight because it's *Bachelorette* night. I'm dead serious. As in the reality show. We all watched the show yesterday, but tonight is the night we Skype with Alice at Wesleyan to discuss it. It's the new Spier family tradition. I could not be more aware that this is perfectly ridiculous.

I don't even know. My family's always been like this.

"And how are Leo and Nicole?" my dad asks, mouth twitching around the edges of his fork. Switching Leah's and Nick's genders is like the pinnacle of Dad-humor.

"They're amazing," I say.

"LOL, Dad," Nora says flatly. My little sister. Recently, she's been using text abbreviations out loud sometimes, even though she never uses them in actual text messages. I think it's supposed to be ironic. She looks at me. "Si, did you see Nick playing guitar outside the atrium?"

"Sounds like Nick's trying to get a girlfriend," says my mom.

That's funny, Mom, because get this. I'm actually trying to prevent Nick from getting the girl he likes, so Martin Addison won't tell the whole school I'm gay. Did I mention I'm gay?

I mean, how do people even begin with this stuff?

Maybe it would be different if we lived in New York, but

I don't know how to be gay in Georgia. We're right outside Atlanta, so I know it could be worse. But Shady Creek isn't exactly a progressive paradise. At school, there are one or two guys who are out, and people definitely give them crap. Not like violent crap. But the word "fag" isn't exactly uncommon. And I guess there are a few lesbian and bisexual girls, but I think it's different for girls. Maybe it's easier. If there's one thing the Tumblr has taught me, it's that a lot of guys consider it hot when a girl is a lesbian.

Though, I guess it happens in reverse. There are girls like Leah, who do these *yaoi* pencil sketches and post them to websites.

Which I guess is cool with me. Leah's drawings are actually kind of awesome.

And Leah's also into slash fanfiction, which got me curious enough to poke around the internet and find some last summer. I couldn't believe how much there was to choose from: Harry Potter and Draco Malfoy hooking up in thousands of ways in every broom closet at Hogwarts. I found the ones with decent grammar and stayed up reading all night. It was a weird couple of weeks. That was the summer I taught myself how to do laundry. There are some socks that shouldn't be washed by your mom.

After dinner, Nora sets up Skype on the desktop computer in the living room. In the camera window, Alice looks a little disheveled, but it's probably the hair—wood-blond and rumpled. All three of us have ridiculous hair. In the background, Alice's bed is unmade and covered with pillows, and someone's purchased a round, shaggy carpet to cover the few feet of floor space. It's still strange to imagine Alice sharing a dorm room with a random girl from Minneapolis. Like, who would have ever guessed I'd see anything sports-related in Alice's room? Minnesota Twins, indeed.

"Okay, you're pixelated. I'm going to—no wait, you're good. Oh my God, Dad, is that a rose?"

Our dad is holding a red rose and cackling into the webcam. I'm not even kidding. My family is all freaking business when it comes to *The Bachelorette*.

"Simon, do your Chris Harrison imitation."

Fact: my Harrison imitation is utter and complete genius. At least, it is under normal circumstances. But I'm not at the top of my game today.

I'm just so preoccupied. And it's not just Martin saving the emails. It's the emails themselves. I've been feeling a little strange about the girlfriend thing ever since Blue asked about it. I wonder if he thinks I'm really fake. I get the impression that once he realized he was gay, he didn't date girls, and it was as simple as that.

"So Michael D. claims to have used the fantasy suite for talking," Alice says. "Do we believe that?"

"Not for a minute, kid," Dad replies.

"They always say that," says Nora. She cocks her head, and

I just now notice that her ear has five piercings, all the way up and around.

"Right?" says Alice. "Bub, are you going to weigh in?"

"Nora, when did you do that?" I touch my earlobe.

She kind of blushes. "Last weekend?"

"Let me see," Alice demands. Nora turns her ear toward the webcam. "Whoa."

"I mean, why?" I ask.

"Because I wanted to."

"But, like, why so many?"

"Can we talk about the fantasy suite now?" she says. Nora gets squirmy when the focus is on her.

"I mean, it's the fantasy suite," I say. "They totally did it. I'm pretty sure the fantasy doesn't involve talking."

"But that doesn't necessarily mean intercourse."

"MOM. Jesus Christ."

I guess it was easy being in relationships where I didn't really have to think about all the tiny humiliations that come with being attracted to someone. It's like, I get along well with girls. Kissing them is fine. Dating them was really manageable.

"How about Daniel F.?" Nora asks, tucking a lock of hair behind her ear. Seriously, the piercings. I don't get her.

"Okay, Daniel F.'s the hottest one," says Alice. My mom and Alice are always using the phrase "eye candy" to talk about these people.

"Are you kidding me?" my dad says. "The gay one?"

"Daniel's not gay," Nora objects.

"Kid, he's a one-man Pride Parade. An eternal flame."

My whole body tenses. Leah once said that she'd rather have people call her fat directly than have to sit there and listen to them talking shit about some other girl's weight. I actually think I agree with that. Nothing is worse than the secret humiliation of being insulted by proxy.

"Dad, stop," says Alice.

And so Dad starts singing that song "Eternal Flame" by the Bangles.

I never know if my dad says that kind of stuff because he means it, or if he's just trying to push Alice's buttons. I mean, if that's the way he feels, I guess it's good to know. Even if I can't un-know it.

So, the other issue is the lunch table. It's been less than a week since the blackmail conversation, but Martin intercepts me on my way back from the lunch line.

"What do you want, Martin?"

He glances at my table. "Room for one more?"

"Um." I look down. "Not really."

There's this weird beat of silence.

"We've got eight people already."

"Didn't realize the seats were assigned."

I don't have a clue what to say to that. People sit where they always sit. I thought that was basically a law of the universe.

You can't just switch around the lunch tables in October.

And my group is weird, but it works. Nick, Leah, and me. Leah's two friends, Morgan and Anna, who read manga and wear black eyeliner, and are basically interchangeable. Anna and I actually dated freshman year, and I still think she and Morgan are interchangeable.

Then you have the holy randomness of Nick's soccer friends: awkward silence Bram and semi-douche Garrett. And Abby. She moved here from DC just before the beginning of the school year, and I guess we were sort of drawn to each other. It was some combination of fate and alphabetical homeroom assignments.

Anyway, that's the eight of us. And it's basically locked down. Already, we're squeezing two extra chairs into a six-person table.

"Yeah, well." Martin tilts backward in his chair and looks up at the ceiling. "I just figured we were on the same page here with the Abby thing, but . . ."

Then he raises his eyebrows at me. Seriously.

So, we haven't exactly laid out the terms of this blackmail arrangement, but clearly it goes something like this: Martin asks for whatever the hell he wants. And then I'm supposed to do it.

It's just so fucking awesome.

"Look, I want to help you."

"Whatever you say, Spier."

"Listen." I lower my voice, almost to a whisper. "I'm gonna talk to her and stuff. Okay? But you've got to let me handle it."

He shrugs.

I feel his stink-eye on me all the way to my table.

I have to act normal. It's not like I can say anything. I mean, now I have to say something about him to Abby, I guess. But it'll be the exact opposite of what I want to say.

It may be a little hard getting Abby to like this kid. Because I kind of can't stand him.

I guess that's beside the point now.

Except the days keep ticking by, and I still haven't handled it. I haven't talked to Abby, or invited Martin along to crap, or locked them into empty classrooms together. I don't even know what he wants, honestly.

I'm kind of hoping to avoid finding out for as long as humanly possible. I guess I've been doing a lot of disappearing. Or glomming onto Nick and Leah, so Martin won't try to talk to me. I pull into the parking lot on Tuesday, and Nora hops out—but when I don't follow, she pokes her head back inside.

"Um, are you coming?"

"Eventually," I say.

"All right." She pauses. "Are you okay?"

"What? Yeah."

She looks at me.

"Nora. I'm fine."

"Okay," she says, stepping back. She shuts the door with a soft click and heads toward the entrance. I don't know. Nora's weirdly observant sometimes, but talking to her about stuff can be kind of awkward. I never really noticed it until Alice left for school.

I end up playing around on my phone, refreshing my email and watching music videos on YouTube. But there's a knock on the passenger side window, and I almost jump. I think I've started expecting to see Martin everywhere. Except it's just Nick. I gesture through the window for him to come in.

He climbs into the seat. "What are you doing?"

Avoiding Martin.

"Watching videos," I say.

"Oh man. Perfect. I've got this song in my head."

"If it's by the Who," I inform him, "or Def Skynyrd or anyone like that, then no freaking way."

"I'm going to pretend you didn't just say 'Def Skynyrd.'"

I love messing with Nick.

We end up watching part of an episode of *Adventure Time* as a compromise, and it's the exact perfect distraction. I keep an eye on the clock, because I don't actually want to miss English class. I just want to cut off that margin of time before class begins, where Martin might try to talk to me.

And it's funny. I know Nick can tell something's up with me, but he doesn't ask questions or try to make me talk. It's just one of those things about us. I know his voice and expressions and his weird little habits. His random existential monologues. The way he taps his fingertips along the pad of his thumb when he's nervous. And I guess he probably knows the same kinds of things about me. I mean, we've known each other since we were four. But really, I don't have a clue what goes on inside his head most of the time.

It actually reminds me a lot of the thing Blue posted on the Tumblr.

Nick takes my phone and starts scrolling through the videos. "If we can find one with Christ imagery, we can totally justify skipping English."

"Um, if we find Christ imagery, I'm using *Adventure Time* for my free-response essay."

He looks at me and laughs.

The thing is, it isn't lonely with Nick. It's just easy. So maybe it's a good thing.

I'm a little early for Thursday's rehearsal, so I slip out the side door of the auditorium and walk around to the back of the school. It's actually pretty chilly for Georgia, and it looks like it rained sometime after lunch. Really, though, there are only two kinds of weather: hoodie weather and weather where you wear a hoodie anyway.

I must have left my earbuds in my backpack in the auditorium. I hate listening to stuff through the speakers of my phone, but music is always better than no music. I lean against the brick wall behind the cafeteria, searching my music library for an EP by Leda. I haven't listened to it yet, but the fact that Leah and Anna are obsessed is a promising sign.

Suddenly, I'm not alone.

"Okay, Spier. What's your deal?" Martin asks, sidling up beside me against the wall.

"My deal?"

"I think you're avoiding me."

We're both wearing Chucks, and I can't decide if my feet look small or if his look huge. Martin probably has six inches on me. Our shadows look ridiculous next to each other.

"Well, I'm not," I say. I step off the wall and start walking back toward the auditorium. I mean, I'm not trying to piss off Ms. Albright.

Martin catches up to me. "Seriously," he says, "I'm not going to show anyone the emails, okay? Stop freaking out about it."

But I think I'll take that with about a million fucking grains of salt. Because he sure as hell didn't say he was deleting them.

He looks at me, and I can't quite read his expression. It's funny. All the years I've been in class with this kid, laughing along with everyone at the random shit he says. All the times I've seen him in plays. We even sat next to each other in choir for a year. But really, I barely know him. I guess I don't know him at all.

Never in my life have I underestimated someone so severely.

"I said I was going to talk to her," I say finally. "Okay?"

My hands are on the auditorium door.

"Wait," he says. I look up at him, and he's holding his phone. "Would it be easier if we exchanged numbers?"

"Do I have a choice?"

"I mean . . ." He shrugs.

"Jesus Christ, Martin." I grab his phone, and my hands are practically vibrating with total fury as I punch my number into his contacts.

"Awesome! And I'll just call you so you have mine."

"Whatever."

Fucking Martin Addison. I'm definitely putting him in my contacts as "Monkey's Asshole."

I push through the door, and Ms. Albright herds us on stage. "All right. I need Fagin, Dodger, Oliver, and boys. Act One, Scene Six. Let's go."

"Simon!" Abby flings her arms around me, and then pokes me in the cheeks. "Never leave me again."

"What did I miss?" I kind of force a smile.

"Nothing," she says under her breath, "but I'm in Taylor hell here."

"The blondest circle of hell."

Taylor Metternich. She's the worst kind of perfect. Like, if perfection had a dark side. I don't know how else to explain it. I always imagine her sitting in front of a mirror at night, counting strokes as she brushes her hair. And she's the kind of person who posts on Facebook asking you how you did on the history quiz. Not to be supportive. She wants to know your grade.

"Okay, boys," says Ms. Albright. Hilarious, because Martin, Cal Price, and I are the only ones onstage who technically qualify. "Bear with me, because we're going to do some blocking." She combs her bangs out of her eyes and tucks them behind her ear. Ms. Albright is really young for a teacher, and she has bright red hair. Like, electric red.

"Act One, Scene Six is the pickpocket scene, right?" asks Taylor, because she's also the kind of person who pretends to ask a question just to show off what she already knows.

"Right," Ms. Albright says. "Take it away, Cal."

Cal is the stage manager. He's a junior like me, and he carries a double-spaced copy of the script clipped into a giant blue binder, exploding with pencil notes. It's funny that his job is basically to order us around and be stressed out, because he's the least authoritative person I've ever met. He's a little bit soft-spoken, and he has an actual southern accent. Which is something you almost never hear in Atlanta, really.

He also has those kind of shaggy brown bangs I like, and dark, ocean-colored eyes. I haven't heard anything about him being gay, but there's this kind of vibe I get, maybe.

"All right," says Ms. Albright, "Dodger has just befriended Oliver, and he's bringing him back to the hideout for the first time to meet Fagin and the boys. So. What's your objective?"

"To show him who's boss," says Emily Goff.

"Maybe to mess with him a little?" says Mila Odom.

"You got it. He's the new guy, and you're not going to make it easy for him. He's a nerd. You want to intimidate him and steal his crap." That makes a couple of people laugh. Ms. Albright is moderately badass for a teacher.

She and Cal put us into position—Ms. Albright calls it "setting the tableau." They want me lying down propped up by my elbows on a platform, tossing a little coin bag. When Dodger and Oliver enter, all of us are supposed to jump up and make a grab for Oliver's satchel. I have the idea to stuff it under my shirt and stagger around the stage with my hand on my lower back like I'm pregnant.

Ms. Albright totally loves it.

Everyone laughs, and honest to God, this is the absolute best kind of moment. The auditorium lights are off except for the ones over the stage, and we're all bright eyed and giggle-drunk. I fall a little bit in love with everyone. Even Taylor.

Even Martin. He smiles at me when he catches my eye, and I really just have to grin back at him. He's such a freaking asswipe, seriously, but he's just so gangly and fidgety and ridiculous. It takes some of the passion out of hating him.

So yeah. I'm not going to write a poem in his honor. And I don't know what he expects me to say to Abby. No clue. But I guess—I'll think of something.

Rehearsal ends, but Abby and I dangle our feet off the edge of one of the platforms, watching Ms. Albright and Cal make notes in the big blue binder. The south county late bus doesn't leave for another fifteen minutes, and then it's another hour until Abby gets home. She and most of the other black kids spend more time commuting to school each day than I do in a week. Atlanta is so weirdly segregated, and no one ever talks about it.

She yawns and leans back flat on the platform with one arm tucked behind her head. She's wearing tights and one of those short patterned dresses, and her left wrist is loaded with woven friendship bracelets.

Martin sits across the stage, a few feet away, zipping his backpack so slowly it must be deliberate. He seems to be making a point of not looking at us.

Abby's eyes are closed. She has the kind of mouth that always rests in a faint smile, and she smells a little like French toast. If I were straight. The Abby thing. I do think I get it.

"Hey, Martin," I say, and my voice sounds strange. He looks up at me. "Are you going to Garrett's tomorrow?"

"I, uh," he says. "Like a party?"

"It's a Halloween party. You should come. I'll send you the address."

Just a quick text to Monkey's Asshole.

"Yeah, maybe," he says. He leans forward and stands, and immediately trips over his shoelace. Then he tries to play it off like some kind of dance move. Abby laughs, and he grins, and I'm not even kidding: he actually takes a bow. I mean, I don't even know what to say to that. I guess there's this hazy middle ground between laughing at someone and laughing with someone.

I'm pretty sure that middle ground is Martin.

Abby turns her head to look at me. "Didn't know you were friends with Marty," she says.

Which is just about the most hilarious fucking statement ever.

4

FROM: hourtohour.notetonote@gmail.com
TO: bluegreen118@gmail.com
DATE: Oct 30 at 9:56 PM
SUBJECT: Re: hollow wieners

Blue,

I guess I never tried to pull off something truly scary. My family is really all about the funny costumes. We used to get competitive about whose costume would make my dad laugh the hardest. My sister was a trash can one year. Not Oscar the Grouch. Just a trash can full of trash. And I was pretty much a one-trick pony. The boy-in-a-dress concept never got old (until it did, I guess—I was in fourth grade and had this amazing flapper costume, but then I looked in the mirror and felt this electric shock of mortification).

Now, I'll say I aim for the sweet spot of simplicity and badassery. I can't believe you're not dressing up. Don't you realize you're throwing away the perfect opportunity to be someone else for an evening?

Disappointedly yours,

—Jacques

FROM: bluegreen118@gmail.com
TO: hourtohour.notetonote@gmail.com
DATE: Oct 31 at 8:11 AM
SUBJECT: Re: hollow wieners

Jacques,

Sorry to disappoint. I'm not opposed to dressing up, and you make a compelling case for it. I completely see the appeal of being someone else for the evening (or in general). Actually, I was a bit of a one-trick pony myself when I was little. I was always a superhero. I guess I liked to imagine myself having this complicated secret identity. Maybe I still do. Maybe that's the whole point of these emails.

Anyway, I'm not dressing up this year, because I'm not going out. My mom has some kind of work party, so I'm stuck at home on chocolate duty. I'm sure you understand that there's nothing sadder than a sixteen-year-old boy home alone on Halloween answering the door in full costume.

Your family sounds interesting. How did you talk your parents into buying you dresses? I bet you were an awesome flapper. Did your parents try to ruin all your costumes by making them weather appropriate? I remember throwing this ridiculous tantrum one year because THE GREEN LANTERN DOES NOT WEAR A TURTLENECK. Though, in retrospect, he actually kind of does. Sorry, Mom!

Anyway, I hope you enjoy your day off from being Jacques. And I hope everyone likes your ninja costume (that has to be it, right? The perfect mix of simple and badass?).

—Blue

FROM: hourtohour.notetonote@gmail.com
TO: bluegreen118@gmail.com
DATE: Oct 31 at 8:25 AM
SUBJECT: Re: hollow wieners

A ninja? Suck a good guess, but no dice.
—Jacques

FROM: hourtohour.notetonote@gmail.com
TO: bluegreen118@gmail.com
DATE: Oct 31 at 8:26 AM
SUBJECT: Re: hollow wieners

Aaaah—autocorrect fail. DICK a good guess.

FROM: hourtohour.notetonote@gmail.com
TO: bluegreen118@gmail.com
DATE: Oct 31 at 8:28 AM
SUBJECT: Re: hollow wieners

GAHHHHH!!!!!
SUCH a good guess. SUCH. Jesus Christ. This is why
I never write you from my phone.

Anyway, I'm going to go die of embarrassment now.
—J

5

HONEST TO GOD, THERE IS nothing better than Halloween on a Friday. All day in school, there's a kind of charged feeling, and it seems to make the work less boring and the teachers funnier. I've got felt cat ears duct taped to my hoodie, and a tail pinned to the butt of my jeans, and kids I don't know are giving me smiles in the hallways. Laughing in a nice way. It's just an awesome day.

Abby comes home with me, and we'll walk over to Nick's later so Leah can pick us all up. Leah's already seventeen, which makes a difference in Georgia with your license. I can drive one other person at a time besides Nora right now, and that's the end of the story. My parents aren't strict about a lot of things, but they're evil mad dictators when it comes to driving.

Abby collapses to the floor to cuddle with Bieber as soon as we walk into the kitchen. She and Leah may not have much in common, but they're both obsessed with my dog. And Bieber is now lying pathetically on his back, belly exposed, staring up at Abby dreamily.

Bieber is a golden retriever, and he has these big, brown, kind of manic eyes. Alice was way too pleased with herself when she came up with his name, but I'm not going to lie. It seriously fits.

"So where is this thing?" Abby asks, looking up at me. She and Bieber are intertwined in an eternity embrace, her headband sliding down over her eyes. A lot of people did the toned-down school version of Halloween today—animal ears and masks and things like that. Abby showed up wearing a full-on, head-to-toe Cleopatra costume.

"Garrett's house? Somewhere off Roswell Road, I think? Nick knows."

"So it's going to be mostly soccer people?"

"Probably. I don't know," I say.

I mean, I did get a text from Monkey's Asshole confirming he'd be there. But I don't feel like bringing him into the conversation.

"Well, whatever. It'll be fun." She tries to extract herself from the dog, and her costume rides almost all the way up her thigh. She does have tights on, but really. I guess it's funny. As far as I know, everyone thinks of me as straight, but already Abby seems to have figured out that she doesn't have to be self-conscious around me. But maybe that's just how she is.

"Hey, are you hungry?" she asks. And I realize I'm supposed to have offered her something.

We end up cooking grilled cheese in the toaster oven and bringing it into the living room to eat in front of the TV. Nora is tucked into her corner of the couch reading *Macbeth*. I guess that's kind of Halloween-ish. Nora never really goes out. I catch her eyeing our sandwiches, and then she slides off the couch to make one for herself. I mean, if she wanted grilled cheese, she really should have just told me. Our mom gives Nora crap about being more assertive. Though I guess I could have asked if she was hungry. I have a hard time getting into other people's heads sometimes. It's probably the worst thing about me.

We watch some random shows on Bravo with Bieber stretched between us on the couch. Nora comes in with her sandwich and goes back to reading. Alice, Nora, and I tend to do our work in front of the TV or with music playing, but we all get good grades, regardless.

"Hey, we better get dressed, right?" Abby says. Abby has an entirely different costume for the party, because by now everyone has seen Cleopatra.

"We don't have to be at Nick's until eight."

"But don't you want to dress up for the trick-or-treaters?" she says. "I always hated it when people weren't in costume."

"Um, if you say so. But I promise you, the kids here are all about the candy, and they seriously don't care where it comes from."

"That's a little concerning," says Abby.

I laugh. "Yeah, it is."

"Okay, well, I'm taking over your bathroom now. Time for the transformation."

"Sounds good," I say. "I'll transform in here."

Nora looks up from her book. "Simon. Eww."

"It's a dementor robe over my clothes. I think you'll survive."

"What's a dementor?"

I mean, I can't even. "Nora, you are no longer my sister."

"So it's some Harry Potter thing," she says.

Garrett bumps fists with Nick when we walk in. "Eisner. What. Is. Up."

And there's this throb of music and random bursts of laughter and people holding cans that aren't Coke. Already, I'm feeling a little out of my depth. So, here's the thing—I'm used to the other kind of party. The kind where you get to someone's house and their mom shows you down to the basement, and there's junk food and Apples to Apples and a bunch of people randomly singing. Maybe some people playing video games.

"So, what can I get you to drink?" Garrett asks. "We have beer and, um, vodka and rum."

"Yeah, thanks, no," says Leah. "I drove."

"Oh, well, we have Cokes and juice and stuff."

"I'll have vodka with orange juice," says Abby. Leah shakes her head.

"A screwdriver for Wonder Woman, coming right up. Eisner, Spier? Anything? Can I get you a beer?"

"Sure," I say. My heart is doing some noticeable thumping.

"Spier, a beer," Garrett says, and then he laughs. I guess because it rhymes. He disappears to get us drinks, which my mom would probably say is really excellent hosting. Not that there's any way in holy hell I'm telling my parents about the alcohol. They would be too goddamn amused.

I pull my dementor hood over my head and lean against the wall. Nick has gone upstairs to get Garrett's dad's guitar, so it's that weird quiet tension of being alone with Abby and Leah. Abby sings along under her breath to the music and kind of shimmies her shoulders.

I feel myself kind of shrinking toward Leah. Sometimes I just know she's feeling the exact way I am.

Leah looks at the couch. "Wow, is that Katniss making out with Yoda?"

"Who making out with who?" says Abby.

There's this pause. "Yeah . . . forget it," says Leah.

I think Leah gets extra sarcastic when she's nervous. But Abby never seems to notice that edge in her voice.

"Where the heck is Nick?" she asks.

Just hearing Abby say Nick's name makes Leah suck in her lips.

"Feeling up a guitar somewhere?" I suggest.

"Yeah," says Leah. "Most awkward way ever to get a splinter." Which sets Abby off giggling. Leah looks kind of flushed and pleased with herself.

It's the weirdest thing. There are these moments with Abby and Leah where it honestly just seems like they're showing off for each other.

But then Garrett walks over with an armload of drinks, and something in Leah's expression slams shut.

"All right—screwdrivers for the ladies . . . ," Garrett says, handing one to each of them.

"This is . . . okay," says Leah, rolling her eyes and leaving the drink on the table behind her.

"And a beer for—whatever the hell you're supposed to be."

"A dementor," I say.

"What in God's holy name is that?"

"A dementor? From Harry Potter?"

"Well, put your hood back, for the love of Jesus. And who are you supposed to be?"

"Kim Kardashian," says Leah, just completely deadpan.

Garrett looks confused.

"Tohru from *Fruits Basket*."

"I . . ."

"It's a manga," she says.

"Ah." There's a crash of dissonant piano notes from across the room, and Garrett's eyes skate past us. A couple of girls are sitting on the piano bench, and I guess one of them knocked her elbow into the keys. There's this burst of wild, drunk laughter.

And I almost wish I were home with Nora, watching Bravo and listening for the door and stuffing my face with fun-size Kit Kats. Which, for the record, are way less fun than full-size Kit Kats. I don't know. It's not that I'm having a bad time, exactly. But being here feels strange.

I take a sip of my beer, and it's—I mean, it's just astonishingly disgusting. I don't think I was expecting it to taste like ice cream, but holy fucking hell. People lie and get fake IDs and sneak into bars, and for this? I honestly think I'd rather make out with Bieber. The dog. Or Justin.

Anyway, it really makes you worry about all the hype surrounding sex.

Garrett leaves Nick's drink with us and joins the girls at the piano. I think they're freshmen. Their costumes are surprisingly clever—one of them is wearing a black silk nightgown with a picture of Freud's face taped to the front. A Freudian slip. Nick will like that. But they're Nora's age. I can't believe they're drinking. Garrett quickly pulls down the lid over the piano keys, and the fact that he's worried about the piano makes me like him better.

"There you are," says Abby. Nick is back, holding on to this acoustic guitar like a lifeline. He settles onto the floor to tune it, his back against the side of the couch. A couple of people glance over at him without breaking their conversations.

It's weird, because pretty much everyone looks familiar, but it's all soccer people and other miscellaneous jocks. Which is fine, obviously. It's just that I don't really know them. It's pretty clear that I won't be seeing Cal Price in this crowd, and I don't know where the heck Martin is.

I sit, and Leah slides down the wall next to me, leaning against it with her legs tucked awkwardly to the side. She's wearing a skirt with her costume, and I can tell she's trying to keep her thighs from showing. Which is so ridiculous and so Leah. I scoot close to her, and she smiles a little bit without looking at me. Abby settles in cross-legged facing us, and it's really kind of nice. We basically have our own corner of the room.

I feel kind of happy and hazy now, and beer doesn't taste so bad after the first few sips. Garrett or someone must have turned the stereo off, and a couple of people have come over to listen to Nick. I don't know if I mentioned this, but Nick has the most raspy-perfect singing voice in the world. Of course, he has this weird, dad-like obsession with classic rock, but I guess that's not always a bad thing. Because right now he's singing Pink Floyd's "Wish You Were Here," and I'm thinking about Blue. And I'm thinking about Cal Price.

Here's the thing. I have this feeling in my gut that Blue is Cal Price. I just do. I think it's the eyes. He has ocean eyes: just waves and waves of blue-green. And sometimes when I look at Cal, I feel like we understand each other, and he gets it, and it's perfect and unspoken.

"Simon, how much did you drink?" asks Leah. I'm twisting the ends of her hair. Leah's hair is so pretty, and it smells exactly like French toast. Except that's Abby. Leah smells like almonds.

"One beer." One most excellent, most delicious beer.

"One beer. I can't even begin to express how ridiculous you are." But she's almost smiling.

"Leah, did you know you have a really Irish face?"

She looks at me. "What?"

"You guys know what I mean. Like an Irish face. Are you Irish?"

"Um, not as far as I know."

Abby laughs.

"My ancestors are Scottish," someone says. I look up, and it's Martin Addison wearing bunny ears.

"Yeah, exactly," I say as Martin sits beside Abby, close but not too close. "Okay, and it's so weird, right, because we have all these ancestors from all over the world, and here we are in Garrett's living room, and Martin's ancestors are from Scotland, and I'm sorry, but Leah's are totally from Ireland."

"If you say so."

"And Nick's are from Israel."

"Israel?" says Nick, fingers still sliding all over the frets of the guitar. "They're from Russia."

So I guess you learn something new every day, because I really thought Jewish people came from Israel.

"Okay, well, I'm English and German, and Abby's, you

47

know . . ." Oh God, I don't know anything about Africa, and I don't know if that makes me racist.

"West African. I think."

"Exactly. I mean, it's just the randomness of it. How did we all end up here?"

"Slavery, in my case," Abby says.

And fucking fuck. I need to shut up. I needed to shut up about five minutes ago.

The stereo kicks back in again.

"Hey, I think I'm going to grab a drink," Martin says, jumping up again in that spastic Martin way. "Can I get you all anything?"

"Thanks, but I'm driving," says Leah. But she wouldn't be drinking even if she wasn't driving. I know that. Because there's this invisible line, and on one side are people like Garrett and Abby and Nick and every musician ever. People who go to parties and drink and don't get wasted off of one beer. People who have had sex and don't think it's a huge deal.

On the other side of the line are people like Leah and me.

But the one thing that makes it weirdly better is knowing that Blue is one of us. I'm reading a little between the lines here, but I actually don't think Blue has ever kissed anyone. It's funny—I don't even know if it counts that I have.

I've never kissed a guy. That's something I think about all the time.

"Spier?" asks Martin.

"Sorry, what?"

"Anything to drink?"

"Oh, thanks. I'm good." Leah makes this little noise like a snort.

"I'm done, too. Thanks, though." Abby kicks her foot against my foot. "At home, I'd just take the Metro and sneak in through our back door, so it didn't matter." When Abby says "home," she's still talking about DC. "But I figure Simon's parents don't need to see me drunk."

"I don't think they would care."

Abby pushes her bangs to the side and looks up at me. "I think you'd be surprised."

"They let my sister pierce her ear a million times."

"Wow. Nora's such a badass," says Leah.

"Okay, Nora's the opposite of a badass." I shake my head. "I am such a badder ass than Nora."

"And don't let anyone tell you otherwise," says Martin, settling back in beside Abby with a beer in hand.

Abby stretches and pulls herself up, resting her hand on my hood. "Come on. People are dancing."

"Good for people," says Nick.

"*We* are dancing." Abby extends both arms toward him.

"Noooooo." But he puts the guitar down, and lets her pull him up.

"Um, but have you even seen my sweet moves?" asks Martin.

"Let's see them."

He does this weird, rhythmic pantomime of swimming, followed by this side-to-side shoulder lurch/butt scoot combo.

"Yeah, you're awesome," Abby says. "Come on." She tugs his hands, and he springs up, beaming. Then she guides her little harem to this carpeted area near the stereo, where people are drinking and grinding to Kanye. Except Abby kind of goes into her own world when she dances, so Nick and Martin end up bobbing self-consciously and pointedly not looking at each other.

"Oh my God," says Leah. "It's happening. We're finally witnessing something more painful than Nick's bar mitzvah."

"Awkwardness achievement unlocked."

"Should we be filming this?"

"Just savor it." I hook my arm around her shoulders, pulling her in closer. And Leah's weird about hugs sometimes, but today she buries her face in my shoulder and murmurs something into the fabric of my robes.

"What?" I nudge her.

But she just shakes her head and sighs.

Leah drops us all off at Nick's at midnight, and from there, it's a seven-minute walk to my house. The indoor lights are off everywhere, but the neighborhood is still lit up orange. There are a few smashed pumpkins and lots of toilet paper tangled through branches. Shady Creek may be a magical fairyland of a suburb most of the time, but when the candy runs out on Halloween, the criminal underbelly emerges. At least in my neighborhood.

It's chilly and unnaturally quiet—if Abby weren't with me,

I would have to drown out the silence with music. It feels like we're the last survivors of a zombie apocalypse. Wonder Woman and a gay dementor. It doesn't bode well for the survival of the species.

We turn at the end of Nick's street. I could do this walk with my eyes closed.

"All right, I have something to ask you," Abby says.

"Oh yeah?"

"So, Martin was talking to me when you were in the bathroom."

I feel something freeze up inside of me.

"Okay," I say.

"Yeah, and this is—maybe I'm reading this wrong, but he was talking about homecoming, and he brought it up like three times."

"Did he ask you to the dance?"

"No. It was like—I guess it seemed like he was maybe trying to?"

Martin freaking Addison. He's like the opposite of suave.

But holy fuck, I'm so relieved he didn't tell her.

"I'm guessing he didn't get anywhere with that."

Abby bites her lip and smiles. "He's a really nice guy."

"Yup."

"But I'm already going with Ty Allen. He asked me two weeks ago."

"Really? How did I not know that?"

"Sorry—was I supposed to announce it on the Tumblr?"

She grins. "Anyway, I don't know if you might be able to mention that to Martin. You're friends with him, right? I'd just rather not deal with him asking me, if I can avoid it."

"Um. I'll see what I can do."

"What about you? Are you still boycotting?" Abby asks.

"Of course." Leah, Nick, and I are of the mind that homecoming is just achingly lame, and we skip it every year.

"You could ask Leah," Abby says. She looks at me sidelong, with a weird, probing expression.

I feel a storm of laughter brewing. "You think I like Leah."

"I don't know," she says, smiling and shrugging. "You looked so sweet together tonight."

"Me and Leah?" I ask. *But I'm gay. GAY. Gaaaaaaaayyyyyy.* God, I should really just tell her. I can kind of picture her reaction. Eyes widening. Mouth falling open.

Yeah. Maybe not tonight.

"Hey," I say, not quite looking at her. "Do you think you would ever be into Martin?"

"Martin Addison? Um. Why do you ask?"

"Nothing. I don't know. He's a decent guy. I guess." My voice sounds thin and high. Like Voldemort. I can't believe I'm doing this.

"Aww. It's cute that you guys are friends."

I don't even know what to say to that.

My mom is waiting for us in the kitchen when we walk in, and it's time to brace myself. The thing about my mom is she's a child psychologist. And it shows.

"So, tell me about the party, guys!"

Here we go. *It was awesome, Mom. Good thing Garrett had so much booze.* I mean, really.

Abby is better at this than I am—she launches into a really detailed description of everyone's costumes, while my mom brings over this epic plate of snacks from the counter. My parents are usually in bed by ten, and I can tell my mom is exhausted. But I knew she'd be awake when we got home. She seriously lives for opportunities to be a *hey guys I'm cool* kind of mom.

"And Nick played guitar," Abby says.

"Nick's very talented," says my mom.

"Oh, I know," Abby replies. "Girls were like swooning over him."

"That's why I keep telling Simon to learn guitar. His sister used to play."

"I'm going to bed," I say. "Abby, are you good?" My mom has Abby staying in Alice's room, which is hilarious, considering Nick has been spending the night on my bedroom floor for about ten years.

It isn't until I'm in my room that I can finally relax. Bieber is already passed out at the foot of my bed in a nest of jeans and hoodies. My dementor robes end up in a heap on the floor. I did aim for the hamper. I'm kind of comically unathletic.

I lie on top of my bed without getting in it. I hate messing up the sheets before I absolutely have to. I know this is weird, but I make my bed every single day, even though the rest of my room is a hellscape of paper and laundry and books and clutter. Sometimes I feel like my bed is a lifeboat.

I put in my earbuds. Nora and I share a wall, so I'm not supposed to listen to anything through the speakers after she goes to bed.

I need something familiar. Elliott Smith.

I'm wide awake and still kind of electrified from the party. I think it was good. I don't have a lot to compare it to. It's a little bit crazy to think that I had a beer. I know it's astonishingly lame to even think that about a single beer. Garrett and all the soccer guys probably think it's crazy to stop at one. But they're not me.

I don't think I'll tell my parents about it. I'm pretty sure I wouldn't get in trouble if I did. I don't know. I need to spend some time in my head with this new Simon. My parents have a way of ruining things like this. They get so curious. It's like they have this idea of me, and whenever I step outside of that, it blows their minds. There's something so embarrassing about that in a way I can't even describe.

I mean, telling my parents was easily the weirdest, most horrible thing about having a girlfriend. All three times. It was honestly worse than any of the breakups. I'll never forget the day I told them about my eighth-grade girlfriend. Rachel Thomas. Oh my God. First, they wanted to see her yearbook picture. My dad actually brought the yearbook into the kitchen where the light is better, and he was perfectly silent for a full minute. And then:

"That girl has some eyebrows."

I mean, I hadn't noticed until he said it, but after that, it was kind of all I could think about.

My mom was the one who got obsessed with the idea that I had a girlfriend even though I had never had one before. I don't know why that came as such a freaking surprise to her, since I'm pretty sure most people start out never having had one. But yeah. And she wanted to know everything: how Rachel and I got together, and what my feelings were, and whether we needed her to drive us anywhere. She was just so bizarrely interested in all of it. It didn't help that my sisters never talk about boys or dating, so it was like a huge spotlight on me.

Honestly, the weirdest part is how they made it feel like this big coming out moment. Which can't be normal. As far as I know, coming out isn't something that straight kids generally worry about.

That's the thing people wouldn't understand. This coming out thing. It's not even about me being gay, because I know deep down that my family would be fine with it. We're not religious. My parents are Democrats. My dad likes to joke around, and it would definitely be awkward, but I guess I'm lucky. I know they're not going to disown me. And I'm sure some people in school would give me hell, but my friends would be fine.

Leah loves gay guys, so she'd probably be freaking thrilled.

But I'm tired of coming out. All I ever do is come out. I try not to change, but I keep changing, in all these tiny ways. I get a girlfriend. I have a beer. And every freaking time, I have to reintroduce myself to the universe all over again.

6

FROM: bluegreen118@gmail.com
TO: hourtohour.notetonote@gmail.com
DATE: Nov 1 at 11:12 AM
SUBJECT: Re: hollow wieners

Jacques,

I hope your Halloween was excellent, and that your simplicity and badassery hit the mark. Things were really quiet around here. We only had about six trick-or-treaters. Of course, that means I am contractually obligated to eat the leftover Reese's cups.

I can't believe it's already almost homecoming. I'm excited about it. Make no mistake, football is still my least favorite sport, but I actually really like going to the homecoming game. I guess it's something about the lights and the drumbeats and the scent of the air. Fall air always smells like possibility. Or maybe I just like ogling the cheerleaders. You know me.

Are you doing anything interesting this weekend? We're supposed to have suck nice weather. Excuse me, dick nice weather. ☺

—Blue

FROM: hourtohour.notetonote@gmail.com
TO: bluegreen118@gmail.com
DATE: Nov 1 at 5:30 PM
SUBJECT: Reese's are better than sex

Very funny, Blue. VERY FUNNY.

Anyway, I'm sorry you got stuck at home last night for only six trick-or-treaters. What a waste. Next year, couldn't you just stick the bowl on the porch with a note telling the kids to take two? Granted, the kids in my neighborhood would have taken candy by the fistful while cackling with villainous laughter, and they probably would have peed on the note for good measure. But maybe the kids in your neighborhood are more civilized.

But seriously, leftover Reese's? Is it possible to send chocolate over email these days? PLEASE SAY IT IS.

My Halloween wasn't bad. I won't say too much about it, but I ended up going to this guy's party. I don't think it was really my scene, but it was definitely interesting. I guess it was nice to step out of my comfort zone (wait—I didn't just ruin my chance of convincing you I'm a hardcore party ninja, right?).

So, I keep thinking about the idea of secret identities. Do you ever feel locked into yourself? I'm not sure if I'm making sense here. I guess what I mean is that sometimes it seems like everyone knows who I am except me.

Okay, I'm glad you mentioned homecoming, because I totally forgot that Spirit Week is this week. Monday is Decades Day, right? I guess I should check online so I can avoid making an ass of myself. Honestly, I can't believe they schedule Spirit Week right after Halloween. Creekwood really blows its load on costume days all at once. How do you think you'll dress up for Monday? I know you're not going to answer that.

And I totally figured you'd be ogling the cheerleaders on Friday, because you're all about the ladies. Me too, Blue. Me too.

—Jacques

FROM: bluegreen118@gmail.com
TO: hourtohour.notetonote@gmail.com
DATE: Nov 2 at 1:43 PM
SUBJECT: Re: Reese's are better than sex

Reese's are better than sex? Admittedly, I wouldn't know, but I have to hope you're wrong about that one. Maybe you should stop having heterosexual sex, Jacques. I'm just saying.

The kids in your neighborhood sound really charming. Urine isn't a huge issue here, so maybe next year, I'll take your advice. It will probably be moot, anyway, because my mom almost never goes out. She just can't keep up with your party ninja ways, Jacques. ☺

I completely understand what you mean about feeling locked into yourself. For me, I don't even think it has anything to do with other people thinking they know me. It's more that I want to leap in and say certain things and do certain things, but I always seem to hold myself back. I think a big part of me is afraid. Even thinking about it makes me nauseated. Did I mention I get nauseated easily?

Of course, that's the exact reason I don't want to say anything about Spirit Week and costumes. I don't want you to put two and two together and figure out who I am. Whatever it is we're doing here, I don't think it works if we know each other's real identities. I have to admit that it makes me nervous to think of you as someone actually connected with my life, rather than a mostly anonymous person on the internet. Obviously, some of the things I've told you about myself are things I've never talked about with anyone. I don't know, Jacques—there's something about you that makes me want to open up, and that's slightly terrifying for me.

I hope this isn't too awkward. I know you were kidding when you asked what costume I was going to wear, but I wanted to put this out there—just in case it wasn't entirely a joke? I have to admit I'm curious about you sometimes, too.

—Blue

P.S. I'm attaching a Reese's cup to this email. I hope this is what you had in mind.

FROM: hourtohour.notetonote@gmail.com
TO: bluegreen118@gmail.com
DATE: Nov 3 at 6:37 PM
SUBJECT: Re: Reese's are better than sex

Blue,

I think I made you uncomfortable, and I'm really, really sorry. I'm kind of a nosy person. It's always been a problem. I'm so sorry, Blue. I know I sound like a broken record. I don't know if I've mentioned this outright, but our emails are really important to me. I would never forgive myself if I fucked this up. Effed this up. Sorry, I don't even know if you cuss.

So, I might have given you the wrong idea with this subject line. I have to admit that I don't TECHNICALLY know whether Reese's are better than sex. Reese's are really freaking incredible, don't get me wrong. And I'm guessing they're better than hetero sex, a.k.a. "intercourse" (per my mom).

Non-hetero sex, though? I imagine it may be a little better than Reese's. Is it weird that I can't talk about this without blushing?

Anyway, speaking of Reese's, thank you so much for the photo. That was exactly what I had in mind. Instead of actually eating one, I just wanted to IMAGINE how salty and chocolaty and awesome it would be to eat one. It's great, because I really wanted to torture myself, but I didn't feel like making the effort to Google Reese's cups myself.

I would raid our own supply of leftover chocolate, but it didn't even come close to surviving the weekend.

—Jacques

Partying harder than Blue's mom since 2014.

7

WEDNESDAY IS GENDER BENDER DAY, which basically amounts to southern straight people cross-dressing. It's definitely not my favorite.

We're watching *Twelfth Night* in first period, because every English teacher is a comedian. Mr. Wise has this warped, ratty couch in his classroom that smells a little like beer, and I'm pretty sure people sneak in here to have sex and rub their fluids all over it after school. It's that kind of couch. But we all fight to the death to sit on it during class, I guess because everything's just a million times more bearable when you're not in a desk.

Today, it's been taken over by soccer boys in Creekwood cheerleading uniforms—specifically, Nick, Garrett, and Bram. That's generally what the jocks do for Gender Bender. There are only about twenty cheerleaders in all, so I have no idea how they meet the demand. Maybe they all have ten uniforms each. Who the hell knows what this school spends its money on.

But I have to admit that there's something kind of awesome about soccer calves and scuffed tennis shoes coming out of pleated cheerleading skirts. I can't believe Bram Greenfeld dressed up. Bram from my lunch table. He's this quiet black kid who's supposed to be really smart, but I've never heard him speak unless he's forced to. He leans way back into the corner of the couch, shuffling the toe of one foot against the other, and I never noticed it before, but he's actually kind of adorable.

Mr. Wise has already started the movie when Abby charges into the room. Between cheerleading, the play, and all of her committees, there's always a reason for Abby to be late to first period, but she never gets called out. It really pisses Leah off, especially because the people on the couch always seem to be willing to scoot over to make room for Abby.

She takes one look at the lineup on the couch and bursts out laughing. And Nick looks so ridiculously pleased with himself. The expression on his face is exactly the same as the day he found a dinosaur bone buried beneath the elementary school playground.

I mean, it turned out to be a chicken bone, but still.

"What the heck?" Abby says, sliding into the desk behind me. She's wearing a full suit and tie and this long, Dumbledorian fake beard. "You guys didn't dress up!"

"I'm wearing hair clips," I point out.

"Okay, well, they're invisible." She turns to Leah. "And you're in a dress?"

Leah looks at her and shrugs without explaining. Dressing extra feminine for Gender Bender is just something Leah does. It's her way of being subversive.

So, here's the thing. I would have left the godforsaken industrial-strength hair clips in Alice's drawer where I found them if I thought I could get away with it. But everyone knows I participate in this kind of crap. Ironically, of course. But still. It would be weirdly conspicuous if I didn't cross-dress at least a little bit today. It's funny how it ends up being the straightest, preppiest, most athletic guys who go all out for Gender Bender. I guess they feel secure enough in their masculinity that they don't care.

I actually hate when people say that. I mean, I feel secure in my masculinity, too. Being secure in your masculinity isn't the same as being straight.

I guess the one thing that's weird for me is dressing like a girl. What no one knows, even Blue, is that dressing up used to mean something to me. I don't know how to explain it or reconcile it, but I haven't forgotten the feeling of silk and air against my legs. I always knew I was a boy, and I've never wanted to be anything but a boy. But when I was younger, I used to wake up at night in April dreaming of Halloween. I would try my costume on a dozen times each October, and all through November, I obsessively fantasized about pulling it out of my closet one more time. But I never crossed that line.

I don't know. There's just something kind of mortifying to me about the intensity of those feelings. I remember them so clearly. I can't even stomach the idea of cross-dressing now. I don't even like to think about it too much. A lot of the time, I can't believe that was me.

The classroom door opens, and there stands Martin Addison, framed by the bright light of the hallway. He managed to find a cheerleading uniform, and he even went to the trouble of stuffing his chest with weirdly realistic boobs. Martin's really tall, so the amount of his skin on display is actually pretty obscene.

Someone in the back row whistles. "Looking hot, Adderall."

"Late pass, Mr. Addison," says Mr. Wise. And maybe it's just Leah getting into my head, but I can't help but think it's unfair that Abby didn't have to get one.

Martin stretches his arms up against the frame of the doorway like he's hanging from monkey bars, and the top of his uniform rides up even higher. Some of the girls giggle a little bit, and Martin grins and blushes. I swear to God, that kid will whore himself out completely for a cheap laugh. But I guess he's kind of a genius for that, because I've never met a nerd so beloved by the popular kids. I mean, I'm not going to lie. They kind of live to tease him. But there's no bite to it. It's like he's their mascot.

"Any day, Mr. Addison," says Mr. Wise.

He tugs his top down, pushes his boobs back into position, and walks out of the room.

On Friday, the math and science hallway is covered in hay. It's probably three inches thick under my feet, and a few strands of it jut out stiffly from the slats of my locker. Dust seems to rise off the ground, and even the light looks different.

The theme this year is music, and out of every genre in the world, the junior class picked country. Only in Georgia. Which is why I'm wearing a bandana and a cowboy hat. School freaking spirit.

Okay. So, homecoming sucks and country music is just embarrassing, but I'm in love with the hay. Even though it means Anna and Taylor Metternich and all the other asthmatics will have to skip science and math today. It just transforms everything. The hallway looks like another universe.

When I get to lunch, I seriously almost lose my shit. It's the freshmen. They're adorable and ridiculous, and oh my God. I can't stop laughing at them. Their genre is emo, and it's basically a sea of bangs and wristbands and tears. I begged Nora last night to show up in a black wig, eyeliner, and for the love of God, at least a My Chemical Romance shirt. She basically looked at me like I had suggested she show up naked.

I catch a glimpse of her now across the cafeteria, and her curly blond hair is really the opposite of emo. But it looks like she talked herself into the raccoon eyeliner, probably once she saw everyone else doing it. She's a perfect chameleon.

It's hard to believe this is the same person who once insisted on dressing up as a trash can.

Martin's at the table right next to ours, and he's wearing overalls. Seriously, he owns overalls. He tries to catch my eye, but I look away abruptly. Avoiding Martin is like a reflex for me at this point.

I take a seat between Leah and Garrett, who carry on arguing right over me.

"Who the hell is that?" asks Leah.

"You seriously haven't heard of Jason Aldean?" says Garrett.

"I seriously haven't."

Garrett slaps his hands down on the table. So I slap my hands down to imitate him, and he shoots me a self-conscious smile.

"Hey," says Nick, settling into the seat across from me and opening his lunch bag. "So, I have a thought," he says. "I think we should go to the game tonight."

"You're kidding me," says Leah.

Nick looks at her.

"What about WaHo?" she says. We always hang out at Waffle House during football games.

"What about it?" asks Nick.

Leah's head is tilted down, so her eyes look kind of scary, and her lips are sucked into a straight line. Everyone is quiet for a moment.

And maybe my timing sucks here, but I guess I'm not really thinking about Leah.

"I'll go to the game," I say. Because I'm pretty sure Blue will be at the game. I like the idea of sitting in the same bleachers as Blue.

"Seriously?" Leah says. I feel her eyes on me, though I make a point to look straight ahead. "Et tu, Brute?"

"Holy overreaction, Batman—" Nick starts to say.

"You shut up." Leah cuts him off.

Garrett laughs nervously.

"Did I miss something?" Abby arrives to find us caught in this thick, weird silence. She sits down next to Nick. "Is everything okay?"

"Yeah, everything's fine." Nick glances at her, and his cheeks look sort of pink.

"Okay," she says, and grins. Abby isn't wearing a cowboy hat. She's wearing a full-on stack of cowboy hats. "So, are you guys psyched for the game tonight?"

Leah stands abruptly, pushes her chair in, and leaves without a word.

The game starts at seven, but there's a parade at six. I walk over to Nick's house after school, and we drive back to school together.

"So, we're on Leah's shit list," I say as we turn onto the road leading to Creekwood. Already, cars are parallel parked on the

69

street, which has to mean the parking lot is full. I guess a lot of people like football.

"She'll get over it," he says. "Is that a space?"

"No, it's a hydrant."

"Crap, okay. Geez, it's crowded."

I think it's the first time Nick has been here for a football game. It's definitely the first time for me. It takes us another ten minutes to find a spot that Nick can pull up into from behind, because he hates parallel parking. In the end, we have to walk about a million miles through the rain to get to the school, but I guess those cowboy hats are good for something after all.

It's really the first time I've ever noticed the stadium lights. I mean, they've always been there, and I've probably seen them turned on before. I never realized how incredibly bright they are. Blue loves them. I wonder if he's already a part of the mass of people milling around the field. We pay a couple of dollars and they give us tickets, and then we're in. The marching band plays a weirdly awesome medley of Beyoncé songs and does this stiff little dance in the stands. And really, despite the rain and the fact that it's homecoming, I think I understand why Blue loves this. It feels like anything could happen.

"There you are!" says Abby, jogging toward us. She gives us each a giant hug. "I just texted both of you. Do you guys want to walk in the parade?"

Nick and I look at each other.

"Okay," I say. Nick shrugs.

We end up following Abby to the teacher parking lot, where a bunch of student council people have assembled around the junior class float. It's built onto a flatbed trailer with a frame constructed up the back, and it definitely looks like country music. There are bales of hay lining the entire surface of the trailer, stacked up higher along the back, and red bandanas knotted together like streamers all around the border of the frame. Everything is lined with Christmas lights. Twangy pop-country music blasts through someone's iPod speakers.

Abby's in the thick of it, of course. She'll be riding the float with some of the other cheerleaders, wearing short denim skirts and flannel shirts knotted up to show their midriffs. There are a couple of guys in overalls, including one dude sitting against the hay bales pretending to play an acoustic guitar. I have to grin at Nick, because nothing pisses him off more than someone faking on the guitar. Especially someone who can't even be bothered to move his fingers along the frets.

This girl Maddie from student council lines us up behind the float in rows, and then someone passes down pieces of straw for us to hold in our teeth.

"And y'all have to chant," Maddie says, looking deadly serious. "They're judging us on spirit."

"Gah jernyrs," I mutter to Nick, who snorts. There's only so much you can do with a piece of straw clamped between your teeth.

Maddie looks panicked. "Oh my God, everyone, okay.

Change of plans. No straw. Everyone take out the straw. Okay, good. Be loud, y'all. Remember to smile."

The float starts moving around the parking lot, where it falls into place behind some kind of rock 'n' roll monstrosity the sophomores have put together. We follow behind it, taking our cue from Maddie, who calls out cheers and randomly yells, "Woo hoo," when things get too quiet. The parade actually leaves the school grounds, where it loops around for a block before coming onto the track circling the football field. The lights shine down on us, and people cheer, and I can't believe Nick and I ended up in the middle of this. It's so Johnny high school. I feel like I'm supposed to make some comment to underscore the ridiculousness of it all, but honestly? It's sort of nice not to have to be cynical for a change.

I guess it feels like I'm a part of something.

Abby and the other cheerleaders rush off to the bathroom as soon as the parade ends to get into their uniforms, and Nick and I look up at the bleachers. The faces blur together, and it's hard to find anyone we recognize. It's a little overwhelming.

"Soccer team's up there," Nick says finally, pointing up to the left and a few rows down from the top. I follow him up the concrete stairs, and then we end up having to squeeze past people to get over to them. God. Just when you think you've discovered every kind of awkwardness there is. And then comes the issue of finding a place to actually sit. Garrett pushes in closer to Bram to make room, but I'm still basically sitting on Nick's lap, and that sure as hell isn't going to work. I stand up again immediately, feeling twitchy and self-conscious.

"Okay," I say, "I'm going to go sit with drama club people." I spot Taylor's bright blond, super-brushed hair a couple rows ahead of us next to the stairs, and she's sitting with Emily Goff and a couple of the others. A couple of the others including Cal Price. My heart beats faster. I knew Cal would be here.

I squeeze through my row and back down the stairs, feeling like every eye in the stadium is on me. Then I reach under the banister to tap Cal on the shoulder.

"What's up, Simon?" he says. I like that he calls me Simon. A lot of the guys call me Spier, and I don't mind that, but I don't know. Honestly, I think I would like whatever Cal Price called me.

"Hey," I say. "Can I join you guys?"

"Definitely." He scoots over a few feet. "Plenty of room." And there is—I won't have to sit on his lap, anyway. It's actually kind of unfortunate.

I spend a full minute trying to think of something to say. My brain feels foggy.

"I don't think I've ever seen you at a game," Cal says, pushing his bangs out of his eyes.

And seriously, I can't even. Because Cal's bangs. Cal's eyes. The fact that he apparently notices me enough to know I'm not at football games.

"This is my first time," I say. Because I just have to say the most virginy thing ever.

"That's cool." And he's so calm. He's not even facing me, because he can talk and watch the game at the same time. "I like coming when I can. I try to make it to homecoming at least."

I try to think of a way to ask the thing I can't ask him. Maybe if I mentioned something about the smell of the air, just to see how he would react. But if I said that and Cal really is Blue, he'd know immediately that Jacques is me. And I don't think I'm ready for that.

I'm so freaking, ridiculously, absurdly curious, though.

"Hey." Suddenly, someone slides in next to me on the bleacher. It's Martin. I scoot down automatically to make room.

"Adderall," some guy behind us grunts, messing up Martin's hair. Martin grins up at him. Then he smooths his hair back down, or tries to, and chews his lip for a minute.

"What's up, Spier?"

"Nothing," I say, and my heart sinks. He turns his body toward mine, and he's clearly in the mood for a conversation. So much for talking to Cal. So much for the air smelling like possibility.

"Hey, so, this Abby thing."

"Yeah?"

"I asked her to the dance," he says, super quietly, "and she shot me down."

"Okay, um. Sorry. That sucks."

"Did you know she already had a date?"

"Um, yeah, I think I did know that. Sorry," I say again. I probably should have gotten around to speaking to Martin about that.

"Could you give me a heads-up next time," he asks, "so I don't embarrass myself?" He looks so miserable. I feel weirdly guilty. Even though he's blackmailing me, I feel guilty. So that's a little fucked up.

"I don't think they're like boyfriend-girlfriend," I say.

"Whatever," he says. I look at him. I don't know if he's giving up on Abby, or what. And if he does give up on her—what happens to the emails? Maybe he gets to hold them over my head forever.

I actually can't think of anything worse than that.

8

FROM: hourtohour.notetonote@gmail.com
TO: bluegreen118@gmail.com
DATE: Nov 11 at 11:45 PM
SUBJECT: Re: all of the above

Blue,

Okay, first of all, Oreos absolutely qualify as a food group. Second of all, they're the ONLY food group that matters. My sisters and I actually made up this place called the Shoreo a few years ago one night when we were staying at our aunt's house. It's like this place where everything is made of some kind of Oreo, and the river is an Oreo milk shake, and you sit on top of this massive

Oreo and float down it. You get to scoop up cups of milk shake whenever you want. It's kind of like that scene in *Willy Wonka*, I guess. Who the hell knows what we were thinking. We were probably just hungry that night. My aunt is a really shitty cook.

Anyway, I forgive you for your ignorance. I know you didn't realize you were talking to an expert.

—Jacques

FROM: bluegreen118@gmail.com
TO: hourtohour.notetonote@gmail.com
DATE: Nov 12 at 5:37 PM
SUBJECT: Re: all of the above

Jacques,

It's true, I had no idea I was talking to such an Oreo connoisseur. The Shoreo sounds like a magical place. So, Doctor, how many servings of Oreo products are necessary for a balanced diet?

I'm getting the impression that you have a bit of a sweet tooth.

—Blue

FROM: hourtohour.notetonote@gmail.com
TO: bluegreen118@gmail.com
DATE: Nov 13 at 7:55 PM
SUBJECT: Sweet tooth?

I can't imagine why you'd think that.

All right—I have a sneaking suspicion that you're not 100% committed to your Oreo diet. The guidelines are really pretty basic. No excuses. Breakfast is obviously an Oreo granola bar or Oreo Pop-Tart. No, they're not gross. Shut up. They're amazing. Lunch should be Oreo pizza with an Oreo milk shake and a couple of those Oreo truffles my mom makes (a.k.a. the most delicious freaking things in the universe). Dinner is deep-fried Oreos served on top of Oreo ice cream, and for a drink, it's Oreos dissolved in milk. No water. Only Oreo milk. Dessert can be Oreos straight up. Sound reasonable? It's for your health, Blue.

I swear to God, typing this is actually making me hungry. This totally used to happen to me when I was younger. Isn't it funny the way you fantasize about junk food when you're a kid? It's really all-consuming. I guess you have to obsess about something before you know about sex.

—Dr. Jacques

FROM: bluegreen118@gmail.com
TO: hourtohour.notetonote@gmail.com
DATE: Nov 14 at 10:57 PM
SUBJECT: Re: Sweet tooth?

Jacques,

I really appreciate you looking out for my health. It will be hard, but I know my body will thank me. Seriously, I can't argue with the fact that Oreos are extremely delicious, and the menu you described actually sounds amazing. Although, for me, I'll have to leave out the deep-fried Oreo dinner. I made the mistake of eating one once at a carnival right before going on the Tilt-A-Whirl. I'll spare you the details, but let it be said that people who get nauseated easily have no business riding the Tilt-A-Whirl. I haven't been able to look at deep-fried Oreos the same way since. Sorry to even have to tell you that. I know Oreos are really important to you.

I have to admit I like to imagine you as a kid fanta-sizing about junk food. I also like to imagine you now fantasizing about sex. I can't believe I just wrote that. I can't believe I'm hitting send.

—Blue

9

HE LIKES TO IMAGINE ME fantasizing about sex.

That's something I probably shouldn't have read right before bed. I lie here in the pitch-darkness, reading that particular line on my phone again and again. I'm jittery and awake and completely in knots, all from an email. And I'm hard. So, that's kind of strange.

It's really confusing. A good kind of confusing. Blue is normally so careful about what he writes.

He likes to imagine me fantasizing about sex!

I thought I was the only one who had those kinds of thoughts about us.

I wonder what it would be like to meet him in person, after all this time. Would we even have to speak? Would we go straight into making out? I think I can picture it. He's in my bedroom, and we're totally alone. He sits beside me on the bed and turns to look at me with his blue-green eyes. Cal Price's eyes. And then his hands cup my face, and all of a sudden, he's kissing me.

My hands cup my face. Well. My left hand cups my face. My right hand is occupied.

I picture it. He kisses me, and it's nothing like Rachel or Anna or Carys. I can't even. It's not even in the same stratosphere. There's this electric tingly feeling radiating through my whole body and my brain has gone fuzzy and I actually think I can hear my heartbeat.

I have to be so, so quiet. Nora's on the other side of the wall.

His tongue is in my mouth. His hands slide up under my shirt, and he trails his fingers across my chest. I'm so close. It's almost unbearable. *God*. Blue.

My whole body turns to jelly.

On Monday, Leah intercepts me as I walk into school.

"Hey," she says. "Nora, I'm stealing him."

"What's up?" I ask. The ground slopes, and there's this concrete ledge that curves around the courtyard. Parts of it are just low enough to the ground that it makes a kind of shelf for your butt.

Leah avoids my eyes. "I made you a mix," she says, handing me a CD in a clear plastic case. "You can load it onto your iPod when you get home. Whatever."

I turn the case over in my hands. Instead of a track list, Leah has composed what appears to be a haiku:

> *Wrinkled neck, gray hair*
> *Sorry to say this, Simon*
> *But you're fucking old.*

"Leah. It's so beautiful."

"Yeah, okay." She scoots backward on the ledge and leans back on her hands, looking at me. "All right. Are we cool?"

I nod. "You mean about . . ."

"About you guys ditching me on homecoming."

"I'm really sorry, Leah."

The edges of her mouth tug up. "You're so freaking lucky it's your birthday."

And then she pulls a cone-shaped party hat out of her bag and straps it onto my head.

"Sorry if I overreacted," she adds.

There's a massive sheet cake at lunch, and when I get to the table, everyone is wearing party hats. That's the tradition. No one gets cake without the hat. Garrett seems to be gunning for two pieces, actually. He's got a pair of cones strapped onto his head like horns.

"Siiimon," Abby says, except she actually sings it in this low, husky opera voice. "Hands out, eyes closed." I feel something nearly weightless drop onto my palm. I open my eyes, and it's a piece of paper folded into a bow tie and colored in with a gold crayon.

A couple of people from other tables look at us, and I feel myself grinning and blushing. "Should I wear it?"

"Uh, yeah," she says. "You have to. Golden bow tie for your golden birthday."

"My what?"

"Your golden birthday. Seventeen on the seventeenth," Abby says. Then she tilts her chin up dramatically and extends her hand. "Nicholas, the tape."

Nick has been holding three pieces of Scotch tape on the ends of his fingertips for who knows how long. Honest to God. He's like her little pet monkey.

Abby tapes on my bow tie and pokes my cheeks, which is something she does weirdly often because apparently my cheeks are adorable. Whatever the heck that means.

"So, whenever you're ready," Leah says. She's holding a plastic knife and a stack of plates, and she seems to be making a point of not looking at Nick or Abby.

"So ready."

Leah slices it into perfect little squares, and seriously, it's like waves of magical deliciousness have shot into the atmosphere. Guess which table of A.P. nerds have somehow become the most popular kids in school.

"No hat, no cake." Morgan and Anna lay down the law

from the other end of the table. A couple of kids tape pieces of loose-leaf paper into cone hats, and one dude manages to wedge a brown paper lunch bag on his head like a chef's hat. People are shameless when it comes to cake. It's a beautiful thing to see.

The cake itself is so perfect that I know Leah picked it out: half chocolate and half vanilla, because I can never commit to a favorite, and covered in that weirdly delicious Publix icing. And no red icing. Leah knows I think it tastes too red.

Leah's really amazing at birthdays.

I bring the leftovers to rehearsal, and Ms. Albright lets us have a cake picnic on the stage. And by cake picnic, I mean drama kids hunched over the box like vultures shoveling cake by the fistful.

"Ohmigod, I think I just gained five pounds," says Amy Everett.

"Aww," says Taylor, "I guess I'm lucky I have a really fast metabolism."

Seriously, that's Taylor. I mean, even I know people can justifiably kill you for saying stuff like that.

And speaking of cake-related casualties: Martin Addison is sprawled out on the stage with his face in the empty cake box.

Ms. Albright steps over him. "All right, guys. Hop to it. Pencils out. I want you writing this stuff down in your scripts."

I don't mind the writing. The scene we're blocking takes place in a tavern, and I'm basically just making notes reminding myself to act drunk. It's kind of too bad these aren't the notes we'll be tested on for our finals. That would really improve some people's grades.

We push through without a break today, but I'm not in every scene, so I actually have quite a bit of downtime. There are risers pushed to the side of the stage left over from a choir concert. I sit near the bottom and rest my elbows on top of my knees. Sometimes I forget how nice it is to just sit back and watch things.

Martin is standing downstage left, telling a story to Abby and using lots of twitchy gestures. She's shaking her head and laughing. So maybe Martin hasn't given up after all.

And suddenly Cal Price is standing in front of me, nudging my foot with the toe of his sneaker. "Hey," he says. "Happy birthday."

This is a happy birthday.

He sits beside me on the riser, a foot or so away. "Doing anything to celebrate?"

Oh.

Okay. I don't want to lie. But I don't exactly want him to know that my plans consist of hanging out with my family and reading birthday messages on Facebook. It's a Monday, right? I'm not actually expected to do anything cool on a Monday.

"Yeah, I guess so," I say finally. "I think we're having ice cream cake. Oreo," I add.

I just have to put the Oreo thing out there.

"That's cool," he says. "Hope you saved room for it."

No discernible reaction to the Oreos. But I guess that doesn't have to mean anything.

"Okay, well," Cal says, scooting forward. I will him not to stand up. He stands up. "Enjoy it."

But then he puts his hand on my shoulder for the briefest fraction of a second. I almost don't believe it happened.

I mean, I'm dead serious. Birthdays are fucking amazing.

10

FROM: hourtohour.notetonote@gmail.com
TO: bluegreen118@gmail.com
DATE: Nov 18 at 4:15 AM
SUBJECT: Why why why?

Oh my God, Blue, I'm so tired my face hurts. Do you ever have those random nights where your brain won't shut off, even though your body feels like five hundred pounds of exhausted? I'm just going to email you and I hope that's okay and I know this is probably going to be totally incoherent so you can't judge me, okay? Even if I fuck up my grammar. You're like the best writer, Blue, and normally I try to check everything like three times because I don't want to disappoint you. So sorry in advance for all the wreckage with your you're there their they're and everything else.

Today has been pretty freaking great actually. I'm trying not to think about what a zombie I'll be tomorrow. Of course I have five quizzes in the next two days including one in une autre langue that I suck at completement. LE FUCK.

So didn't there used to be a reality show where people had to date each other in pitch-darkness? We should do that. We should find a room somewhere that's totally dark and then we could hang out and it would be totally anonymous. That way we wouldn't ruin anything. What do you think?

—Jacques

FROM: bluegreen118@gmail.com
TO: hourtohour.notetonote@gmail.com
DATE: Nov 18 at 7:15 AM
SUBJECT: Re: Why why why?

Zombie Jacques,

I don't know what to say. On one hand, I'm sorry you're pretty much guaranteed a shitty day today, and I really hope you were able to squeeze in at least an hour or two of sleep. On the other hand, you're pretty cute when you're exhausted. And, by the way, you were very coherent and grammatical for four in the morning.

Hang in there today with the quizzes, though, and just power through. Bonne chance, Jacques. I'm rooting for you.

I have absolutely never heard of that show. I guess I don't know all that much about reality TV. It's an interesting concept, but how would we keep from recognizing each other's voices?

—Blue

FROM: hourtohour.notetonote@gmail.com
TO: bluegreen118@gmail.com
DATE: Nov 18 at 7:32 PM
SUBJECT: Re: Why why why?

So, I'm a little scared to read what I wrote to you last night. I'm glad I was cute and grammatical. I think you're cute and grammatical, too. Anyway, I don't know what the hell that was all about. Too much sugar yesterday, I guess. Sorry sorry sorry.

Yeah. I'm still so totally brain-dead. I don't even want to think about how I did on my quizzes.

Don't know much about reality TV? You mean your

parents don't make you watch it? Because mine do. And I bet you think I'm kidding.

You bring up a good point about our voices. I guess we would have to use some kind of robotic megaphone to warp them so they sound like Darth Vader. Or we could just do other things instead of talking. I mean. I'm just saying.

—Your Zombie Jacques

11

IT'S THE DAY AFTER THANKSGIVING, and Alice is home, and we're on the back porch after dinner. It's actually warm enough for hoodies and pajama pants and leftover ice cream cake and Scattergories.

"All right. Famous duos and trios?"

"Abbott and Costello," says my mom.

Nora and I both say "Adam and Eve." It's a little surprising, considering we're probably the only family in the South without a Bible.

"The Axis powers," says my dad, and you can tell he's so proud of that one.

"Alice and the Chipmunks," says Alice, casually, and all of us just lose it. I don't know. The Chipmunks are kind of our thing. We had the voices perfected and the theme song choreographed, and we used to do these performances on the ledge in front of the fireplace. It seriously went on for years. Our lucky parents. Though, they're the ones who named us Alice, Simon, and Eleanor, which means they were basically asking for it.

Alice rubs Bieber's back with her feet, and her socks don't match, and it's almost impossible to believe that this is the first time she's been home in three months. I don't think I realized until this moment how weird it's been without her.

Nora must be thinking the same thing I am, because she says, "I can't believe you have to go back in two days."

Alice purses her lips for a minute, but doesn't speak. The air feels chilly, and I slide my hands into the sleeves of my hoodie. But then my phone buzzes.

Text from Monkey's Asshole: *hey is there anything going on this weekend*

A moment later: *like with Abby I mean*

It seems Martin doesn't give a shit about punctuation, which is totally not surprising.

I write back: *Sorry, family stuff. Sister's in town.*

His instantaneous reply: *its cool spier, my brother's in town too. He says hi ;)*

And I don't even know if it's supposed to be a joke or a threat or what, but I hate him. I seriously fucking hate him right now.

"Hey," Alice says, eventually, tucking her legs up onto her

chair. Our parents have gone to bed, and it's definitely getting colder out here. "I don't know if anyone's still hungry, but I have like three-quarters of a box of Chips Ahoy! still sitting in my carry-on bag. Just putting that out there."

Thank God for Alice.

Thank God for Chips Ahoy!

I'm going to have an awesome night with my sisters, and I'm going to stuff my face with cookies, and I'm definitely going to forget about Monkey's Asshole and his shady little winky emoticon. We relocate to the living room couch, and Bieber passes out cold with the whole front end of his body in Alice's lap.

"Anyone want a Nick Eisner?" Nora asks.

"Are you serious? Yes. Go get the peanut butter," says Alice in her bossy voice.

A Nick Eisner is a cookie with a random glop of peanut butter on top, because when we were five, Nick thought that's what people meant by peanut butter cookies. Admittedly, they're delicious. But in my family, you never live something like that down.

"How is little Nick Eisner?"

"He's the same. Still glued to his guitar." And he'd be totally butthurt if he knew Alice still calls him little. Nick has had a minor-level crush on Alice since we were in middle school.

"I was about to ask. So cute."

"I'll tell him you said that."

"Yeah, don't do that." Alice sinks her head back into the

couch cushion, rubbing her eyes behind her glasses. "Sorry." She yawns. "Early flight. And catching up from this week."

"Midterms?" asks Nora.

"Yup," says Alice. And it's so obvious that there's something else, but she doesn't elaborate.

Bieber does this sudden loud-ass yawn and rolls onto his side, so his ear flips inside out. And then his lips twitch. He's a weirdo.

"Nick Eisner," Alice says again. And then she grins. "Remember his bar mitzvah?"

Nora giggles.

"Oh God," I say. It's really the perfect time to bury my head in a pillow.

"Boom boom boom."

No wait. It's the perfect time to smack Alice with a pillow.

She blocks it with her feet. "Really, Simon. We can clear a spot on the floor right now if you want," Alice says.

"Simon Spier dance break," says Nora.

"Yup. Okay." Nick's mistake was inviting my whole family to his bar mitzvah. Mine was attempting to pop and lock to "Boom Boom Pow" in front of them. There's no such thing as a good idea when you're in seventh grade.

"Don't you wish you could go back in time and just shut it down? Like, hey. Middle school Alice: stop it. Stop everything you're doing."

"OMG." Nora shakes her head. "I can't even think about middle school."

Seriously?

I mean, Alice was the one who once spent a month wearing elbow-length silk gloves. And I'm pretty sure it was me who ate five cookie cones at the Ren Faire in sixth grade, and then vomited into a wax mold of my own hand. (Worth it.)

But Nora? I don't even know what she has to be embarrassed about. It doesn't seem like this would be genetically or developmentally possible, but she was kind of cool in middle school. Under-the-radar cool. The kind of cool that comes from teaching yourself guitar and wearing normal clothes and not running a Tumblr called "Passion Pit OBSESSION."

I guess even Nora is haunted by the ghosts of middle school.

"Yeah, I wish someone would have told middle school Simon to please try to be awesome. Just try."

"You're always awesome, bub," says Alice, stretching over Bieber to tug the end of my foot.

I'm bub and Nora is boop. But only to Alice.

"And your dance moves are super awesome," she adds.

"Shut up," I say.

Everything is a little more perfect when she's here.

And then Alice leaves and school starts again in all its suckery. When I get to English class, Mr. Wise gives us a villainous smile that can only mean he's finished grading our short essay quizzes on Thoreau.

And I'm right. He starts handing them back to people, and I can see that most of them are wrecked with red ink. Leah barely glances at hers before folding and tearing off the bottom and creasing it into an origami crane. She looks extra pissed today. I'm 100 percent certain it's because Abby came in late and squeezed in between her and Nick on the couch.

Mr. Wise flips through the stack and licks his finger before touching my paper. I'm sorry, but some teachers are seriously gross. He probably rubs those fingers all over his eyeballs, too. I can just picture it.

When I see the perfect score circled at the top of my paper, I'm a little bit amazed. It's not that I'm bad at English, and I actually did like *Walden*. But I think I got about two hours of sleep, max, the night before that quiz. There's just no freaking way.

Oh wait. I'm right. There is no freaking way, because this isn't my freaking test. Way to remember my name, Mr. Wise.

"Hey," I say. I lean across the aisle to tap Bram on the shoulder. He turns sideways in his chair to face me. "Looks like this is yours."

"Oh. Thanks," he says, reaching out to take it. He has long, kind of knobbly fingers. Cute hands. He looks down at the paper, glances back up at me, and blushes slightly. I can tell he feels weird about me seeing his grade.

"No problem. I mean, I'd keep the grade if I could."

He smiles a little bit and looks back down at his desk. You never really know what he's thinking. But I have this theory that Bram's probably really funny inside his own head. I don't even know why I think that.

But seriously: whatever inside jokes he has with himself, I think I'd like to be in on them.

When I walk into rehearsal that afternoon, Abby is sitting in the front row of the auditorium with her eyes closed and her lips moving. Her script is open on her lap, and she's got one hand covering some of the lines.

"Hey," I say.

Her eyes snap open. "How long have you been standing here?"

"Just a second. Are you working on your lines?"

"Yup." She turns the script upside down, using her leg to hold her place. There's something odd about her clipped tone.

"You okay?"

"Yeah, fine." She nods. "A little stressed," she adds finally. "Did you know we have to be off book by the end of break?"

"By the end of Christmas break," I say.

"I know."

"That's like over a month away. You'll be fine."

"Easy for you to say," she says. "You don't have any lines."

And then she looks up at me with raised eyebrows and a perfectly round mouth, and I can't help but laugh.

"That was so bitchy of me. I can't believe I said that."

"It was super bitchy," I say. "You're like a stealth bitch."

"What did you call her?" asks Martin.

I swear to God, that kid pops up out of nowhere and burrows into every conversation.

"It's okay, Marty. We're just messing around," says Abby.

"Yeah, well, he called you a bitch. I really don't think that's okay."

Oh my God. He's seriously going to bust in here, totally miss the joke, and then turn around and lecture me about my fucking language. That's great, Martin. Just knock me down so you can look good in front of Abby. And, I mean, the whole idea of Martin Addison taking the moral high ground when he's in the middle of blackmailing me—that's just so fucking awesome.

"Martin, really. We were kidding. I called myself a bitch." She laughs, but it comes out strained. I stare down at my shoes.

"If you say so." Martin's face is extra pink, and he's playing with the skin on his elbow. I mean, seriously, if he's so dead set on impressing Abby, maybe he should stop being so twitchy and awkward and annoying all the time. Maybe he should stop pulling the goddamn skin around his elbow. Because it's completely disgusting. I don't even know if he realizes he's doing it.

The worst part of it is, I know perfectly well that if Alice heard me using that word, she would call me out, too. Alice is pretty hardcore about when it's appropriate to use the word "bitch."

Appropriate: "The bitch gave birth to a litter of adorable puppies."

Inappropriate: "Abby is a bitch."

Even if I said she was a stealth bitch. Even if I was joking.

It may be crazy Alice logic, but I feel a little weird and awful about it anyway.

I choke out an apology, and my face is burning. Martin's still standing there. I seriously can't get away fast enough. I walk up the steps to the stage.

Ms. Albright is sitting next to Taylor on one of the platforms, pointing at something in Taylor's script. Downstage, the girl who plays Nancy is giving a piggyback ride to the guy who plays Bill Sikes. And offstage left, this sophomore girl named Laura sits on top of a stack of chairs, crying into her sleeve, and I guess Mila Odom is comforting her.

"You don't even know that," Mila says. "Seriously, look at me. Look at me."

Laura looks up at her.

"It's the freaking Tumblr, okay. Half that shit is made up."

Laura's voice is broken and sniffly. "But there's . . . a little . . . bit of . . . truth . . . to . . . every—"

"That's seriously bullshit," says Mila. "You need to just talk to him." And then she sees me standing there listening and shoots me the stink-eye.

So here's the thing: Simon means "the one who hears" and Spier means "the one who watches." Which means I was basically destined to be nosy.

Cal and two of the senior girls are sitting outside the dressing room with their backs to the wall and their legs stretched out in front of them. He looks up at me and smiles. He has a really nice, easy smile. You can tell it's the kind that looks cute in pictures. I still feel a little unpleasant about the whole Abby and Martin conversation, but I think I may be on my way to feeling better.

"Hey," I say. The girls sort of smile at me. Sasha and Brianna are both Fagin's boys like me. It's funny. I'm literally the only one of Fagin's boys played by an actual guy. I guess it's because girls are smaller or look younger or something. I don't even know. But it's slightly awesome, because it means I'm the tallest person onstage during those scenes. Which doesn't happen all that often, to be honest.

"What's up, Simon?" Cal says.

"Oh, well. Nothing. Hey, are we supposed to be doing anything right now?" And as soon as I ask it, I start blushing, because the way I phrased it totally makes it sound like I'm propositioning him. *Hey, Cal. Are we supposed to be making out right now? Are we supposed to be having mind-blowing sex in the dressing room right now?*

But maybe I'm just paranoid, because Cal doesn't seem to read anything into it. "Nah, I think Ms. Albright is just finishing some stuff up, and then she'll tell us what to do."

"Works for me," I say. And then I notice their legs. Sasha's leg overlaps with Cal's just the tiniest bit, almost at the ankle. So, who the hell knows what that means.

I think I'm ready for this shitty day to be over.

Of course, it's pouring down rain when Ms. Albright lets us out, and I soak a big butt-shaped wet spot into the upholstery of my car. I can barely dry off my glasses because my clothes are so wet. And I don't remember to put my headlights on until I'm already halfway home, which means I'm honestly lucky I didn't get arrested by now.

As I make the right into my neighborhood, I see Leah's car stopped at the light, waiting to make a left. So, I guess she's leaving Nick's house. I wave to her, but it's raining so hard that it's pointless. The wipers arc back and forth, and there's this kind of tightness in my chest. It shouldn't bother me when Nick and Leah hang out without me. It just feels like I'm on the outside somehow.

Not all the time. Just sometimes.

But yeah. I feel irrelevant. I hate that.

12

FROM: bluegreen118@gmail.com
TO: hourtohour.notetonote@gmail.com
DATE: Dec 2 at 5:02 PM
SUBJECT: I should be . . .

. . . writing an essay for English class. I'd rather write
to you. I'm in my room, and I have a window right next to
my desk. It's so sunny out, and it looks like it should be
really warm outside. I feel like I'm dreaming.

So, Jacques, I have to confess that I've been curious
about your email address for a long time. I finally broke
down and consulted the Mighty Googler, and now I see
that it's a lyric from an Elliott Smith song. I've actually

heard of him, but I had never heard his music, so I downloaded "Waltz #2." I hope that doesn't freak you out. I really like it. It surprised me, because it's a really sad song, and that's not what I would expect coming from you. But I've listened to it a few times now, and the funny thing is, it really does remind me of you somehow. It's not the lyrics or even the overall mood of the song. It's something intangible. I think I can imagine you lying on a carpet somewhere listening to it, eating Oreos, and maybe writing in a journal.

I also have to confess that I've been looking extra carefully at people's T-shirts at school to see if someone might be wearing an Elliott Smith shirt. I know it's a long shot. I also know it's really unfair, because I shouldn't be trying to figure out your identity when I don't give you any good clues about my own.

Here's something. My dad's driving in from Savannah this weekend, and we're doing the traditional Hotel Hanukkah. It will be just him and me, and I'm sure we'll hit all the awkward highlights. We'll do the non-lighting of the menorah (because we won't want to set off the smoke detectors). And then I'll give him something underwhelming like Aurora coffee and a bunch of my English essays (he's an English teacher, so he likes getting those). And then he'll have me open eight presents in a row, which just drives home the fact that I won't see him again until New Year's.

And the thing is, I'm actually considering doubling down on the awkward factor and turning this mess into a coming out thing. Maybe I should capitalize that: Coming Out Thing. Am I crazy?

—Blue

FROM: hourtohour.notetonote@gmail.com
TO: bluegreen118@gmail.com
DATE: Dec 2 at 9:13 PM
SUBJECT: Re: I should be . . .

Blue,

Okay, first things first—how did I not know you were Jewish? I guess this is you giving me a clue, right? Should I be looking in the halls for guys in yarmulkes? Yes, I looked up how to spell that. And your people are very creative, phonetically speaking. Anyway, I hope the HH goes well, and by the way, Aurora coffee is totally not underwhelming. In fact, I'll probably steal your idea, because dads freaking love coffee. And my dad will especially go for it, because of the Little Five Points factor. My dad has this hilarious idea that he's a hipster.

So, most importantly, Blue: the Coming Out Thing. Wow. I mean, you're not crazy. I think you're awesome.

Are you worried about how he'll react? And are you going to tell your mom, too?

Okay, I am also very impressed that you Googled your way to Elliott Smith, who was quite possibly the greatest songwriter since Lennon and McCartney. And then everything you said about the song reminding you of me is just so flattering and amazing that I don't even know what to say. I'm speechless, Blue.

I'll say this: you are dead right about the Oreos and the carpet, but wrong about the journal. The closest thing I've ever had to a journal is probably you.

Now you should go download "Oh Well, Okay" and "Between the Bars." I'm just saying.

So, I hate to say it, but it's probably a waste of your time to try to figure out who I am by looking at the bands on people's T-shirts. I almost never wear band T-shirts, even though I kind of wish I did. I think, for me, listening to music is a very solitary thing. Or maybe that's just something people say when they're too lame to go to live shows. Either way, I am basically glued to my iPod, but I haven't really seen anyone live, and then I end up feeling like wearing a band's shirt without going to their show would be kind of like cheating. Does that make sense? For some reason, the whole thought of ordering some band's shirt online makes me feel weirdly embarrassed. Like maybe the musician wouldn't respect it. I don't know.

Anyway, all things considered, I agree that this was a far more satisfying use of my time than writing English essays. You are very distracting.

—Jacques

FROM: bluegreen118@gmail.com
TO: hourtohour.notetonote@gmail.com
DATE: Dec 3 at 5:20 PM
SUBJECT: Re: I should be . . .

Jacques,

About you not knowing I was Jewish—I know I've never mentioned it. I'm not even Jewish, technically, because Judaism is matrilineal, and my mom's Episcopalian. Anyway, I still haven't decided if I'm really going to go through with it. It wasn't something I thought I'd be ready to do anytime soon. I don't know why, but lately, I've just felt this urge to put it out there. Maybe I just want to get it over with. What about you? Have you thought about the Coming Out Thing?

It gets complicated when you bring religion into the equation. Technically, Jews and Episcopalians are supposed to be gay-friendly, but it's hard to really know how that applies to your own parents. Like, you read about these gay kids with really churchy Catholic parents, and the parents end up doing PFLAG and Pride Parades and everything. And then you hear about parents who are totally fine with homosexuality, but can't handle it when their own kid comes out. You just never know.

I think instead of downloading the Elliott Smith songs you mentioned, I'll just drop a hint to my dad that I want a couple of his albums for Hotel Hanukkah. I guarantee you that he has about six of my presents picked out, and is desperate for some kind of hint about what else he should be getting me.

So, I know you and I can't really buy each other gifts in real life, but just know that if I could, I would order you all kinds of band T-shirts online. Even if it meant losing the respect of musicians everywhere (because I'm sure that's how it works, Jacques). Or we could just go to a live show. I mean, I don't actually know anything about music, but I'm guessing it would be fun if it was with you. Maybe one day.

I'm glad that you find me distracting. It wouldn't be fair, otherwise.

—Blue

13

IT'S THURSDAY, AND I'M IN history class, and apparently Ms. Dillinger just asked me a question, because everyone is looking at me like I owe them something. So now I'm blushing and trying to bullshit my way through it, and judging by her twisty, teacherly frown, I don't think it's going very well.

I mean, when you think about it, it's a little fucked up that teachers think they get to dictate what you think about. It's not enough if you just sit there quietly and let them teach. It's like they think they have a right to control your mind.

I don't want to think about the War of 1812. I don't want to know what the hell was so impressive to a bunch of freaking sailors.

What I want is to sit here and think about Blue. I think I'm starting to get a little obsessed with him. On one hand, he's so careful all the time about not giving me details about himself—and then he turns around and tells me all kinds of personal stuff, and it's the kind of stuff that I could totally use to figure out his identity if I really wanted to. And I do want to. But I also don't. It's just so totally confusing. He's confusing.

"Simon!" Abby taps me frantically from behind. "I need a pen."

I hand one back to her, and she thanks me under her breath. I look around and realize that everyone is writing. Ms. Dillinger has written a website address down on the board. I don't know what the heck it's for, but I guess I'll find out when I get around to looking it up. I copy the address into the margin of my notes, and then outline it in zigzags like a comic book *POW!*

I'm a little hung up on Blue's parents being religious. I feel like a freaking moron, honestly, because I'm basically the most blasphemous person in the world. Like, I don't even know how not to use the Lord's name in vain. But maybe it's not a big deal to him. Him being Blue, not the Lord. I mean, Blue's still emailing me, so I guess he couldn't have been too offended.

Ms. Dillinger gives us a break, but it's not the kind of break where you can go anywhere, so I just sit and stare into space. Abby comes over and kneels and rests her chin on my desk. "Hey. Where are you today?"

"What are you talking about?"

"You're like a million miles away."

Out of the corner of my eye, I see Martin climbing over someone's chair to join us. Every time. I swear to God.

"What's up, guys?"

"Haha," says Abby. "Your shirt is hilarious." Martin is wearing a T-shirt that says "Talk nerdy to me."

"Are you guys going to rehearsal today?"

"Oh, it's optional now?" I ask. And then I do this thing I picked up from Leah, where you kind of cut your eyes to the side and narrow them. It's more subtle than rolling your eyes. Much more effective.

Martin just looks at me.

"Yeah, we're going," Abby says, after a moment.

"Yeah. Spier," Martin says suddenly, "I've been meaning to talk to you." His cheeks have gone pink, and a red blotch unfurls around the collar of his T-shirt. "I've been thinking. I really want to introduce you to my brother. I think you guys have a lot in common."

Blood rushes to my face, and I feel that familiar fucking prickle behind my eyes. He's threatening me again.

"That's so cute," Abby says. She looks back and forth from Martin to me.

"Oh, it's adorable," I say. I stare Martin down, but he turns away quickly, looking miserable. Seriously? That asshole deserves to feel miserable.

"Yeah, well." Martin shuffles his feet, still staring at this random point over my shoulder. "I'm just going to . . ."

I'm just going to talk about your sexual orientation now like it's my business, Simon. I'm just going to tell the whole goddamned school right here, right now, because I'm an asshole, and that's just how it's going to go down.

"Hey, wait," I say. "This is random, but I was just thinking. Do you guys want to go to Waffle House tomorrow, after school? I could quiz you on your lines."

I hate myself. I hate myself.

"I mean, if you can't—"

"Oh my gosh. Seriously, Simon? That would be awesome. Tomorrow after school, right? I actually think I can get my mom's car." Abby smiles and pokes me in the cheek.

"Yeah, thanks, Simon," Martin says quietly. "That would be great."

"Great," I say.

I'm officially doing it. I'm letting Martin Addison blackmail me. I don't even know how I feel. Disgusted with myself. Relieved.

"You're seriously amazing, Simon," says Abby.

I'm not. At all.

And now it's Friday night, and I'm on my second plate of hash browns, and Martin won't stop asking Abby questions. I think it's his way of flirting.

"Do you like waffles?"

"I do like waffles," she says. "That's why I got them."

"Oh," he says, and there's a lot of wild, unnecessary nodding. He's basically a Muppet.

They're sitting next to each other, and I'm across from them, and we've managed to get the booth back near the bathrooms where no one really bothers you. It's not all that crowded for a Friday night. There's a pissed-off-looking middle-aged couple in the booth behind us, two hipster guys at the counter, and a couple of girls in private school uniforms eating toast.

"Aren't you from DC?"

"Yes."

"That's cool. What part?"

"Takoma Park," she says. "You know DC?"

"I mean, not really. My brother's a sophomore at Georgetown," Martin says.

Martin and his freaking brother.

"Are you okay, Simon?" asks Abby. "Drink some water!"

Can't stop coughing. And now Martin's offering me his water. Pushing it toward me. Martin can freaking bite me. Seriously. Like he's so calm and collected.

He turns back to Abby. "So, you live with your mom?"

She nods.

"What about your dad?" he says.

"He's still in DC."

"Oh. I'm sorry."

"Don't be," Abby says, with a short laugh. "If my dad lived in Atlanta, I wouldn't be hanging out with you guys right now."

"Oh, is he really strict?" asks Martin.

"Yup," she says. Her eyes cut toward me. "So, do you think we should start Act Two?"

Martin stretches and yawns in this weird vertical maneuver, and I watch as he attempts to position his arm next to Abby's on the table. Abby pulls her arm away immediately and scratches her shoulder.

I mean, it's pretty terrible to watch. Terrible and fascinating.

We run through the scene. Speaking of disasters. I don't have a speaking part, so I shouldn't judge. And I know they're trying. But we're having to stop at every freaking line, and it's getting a little ridiculous.

"He got took away," Abby says, covering her script with one hand.

I nod at her. "Got took away in a . . ."

She squeezes her eyes shut. "In a . . . coach?"

"You got it." She opens her eyes, and I see her lips moving silently. *Coach. Coach. Coach.*

Martin stares into space, grinding his knuckle into his cheek. He has extremely prominent knuckles. Martin has prominent everything: huge eyes, long nose, full lips. Looking at him is exhausting.

"Martin."

"Sorry. My line?"

"Dodger just said he got took away in a coach."

"A coach? What coach? Where coach?"

Almost. Never perfect. Always almost. We start the scene over again. And I think: it's Friday night. In theory, I could be

113

out getting drunk. I could be at a concert.

I could be at a concert with Blue.

But instead, it's Oliver getting taken away in a coach. Again and again and again.

"I'm never going to learn this," Abby says.

"Don't we have until the end of Christmas break?" Martin asks.

"Yeah, well. Taylor has everything memorized already."

Abby and Martin both have huge parts in the play, but Taylor is the lead. As in, the play is *Oliver!* and Taylor plays Oliver.

"But Taylor has a photographic memory," Martin says, "allegedly."

Abby smiles a little bit.

"And a very fast metabolism," I add.

"And a natural tan," says Martin. "She never goes out in the sun. She was just born tan."

"Yeah, Taylor and her tan," says Abby. "I'm so jealous." Martin and I both burst out laughing, because Abby definitely wins for melanin.

"So would it be weird if I ordered another waffle?" asks Martin.

"It would be weird if you didn't," I say.

I don't really understand it. I almost think he's growing on me.

14

FROM: hourtohour.notetonote@gmail.com
TO: bluegreen118@gmail.com
DATE: Dec 6 at 6:19 PM
SUBJECT: Coming Out Thing

Did you do it, did you do it, did you do it?
—Jacques

FROM: bluegreen118@gmail.com
TO: hourtohour.notetonote@gmail.com
DATE: Dec 6 at 10:21 PM
SUBJECT: Re: Coming Out Thing

Okay. I didn't exactly do it.

I got there, and my dad had everything set up for Hotel Hanukkah: the menorah, presents wrapped and lined up on the nightstand, and a plate of latkes and two glasses of chocolate milk (my dad has to have chocolate milk with all fried stuff). Anyway, it looked like he put a lot of effort into it, so that was kind of nice. My stomach was churning, because I was really planning on telling him. But I didn't want to do it straight out of the gate, so I figured I'd wait until we finished opening presents.

So, you know how you hear stories about people coming out to their parents, and the parents say they already knew somehow? Yeah, my dad isn't going to say that. I'm officially certain that he has no idea I'm gay, because you will not believe what book he picked out to give me. *History of My Life* by Casanova (or, as you would say, by "freaking" Casanova).

Looking back, there was probably a perfect opportunity hiding in there somewhere. Maybe I should have asked him to exchange it for Oscar Wilde. I don't know, Jacques. I guess it kind of stopped me in my tracks. But now I'm thinking it might be a blessing in disguise, because in a weird way, I think it would have hurt my mom's feelings if I told my dad first. It can be a little complicated with divorced parents. This whole thing is really overwhelming.

Anyway, my new plan is I'm going to tell my mom first. Not tomorrow, because tomorrow is Sunday, and I just think it would be better if I don't do it right after church.

Why is it so much easier talking about this stuff with you?

—Blue

FROM: hourtohour.notetonote@gmail.com
TO: bluegreen118@gmail.com
DATE: Dec 7 at 4:46 PM
SUBJECT: Re: Coming Out Thing

Blue,

I can't believe your dad got you a book by freaking Casanova. Just when you think your parents couldn't be more clueless, right? No wonder you couldn't tell him then. I'm sorry, Blue. I know you were kind of excited to do it. Or maybe you were just nauseated, in which case I'm sorry you got nauseated over nothing. I can't even wrap my mind around the politics of coming out to divorced parents. I was basically planning to sit my parents down on the couch at some point and get it over with in one go. But you really can't do that, can you? It makes my heart hurt for you, Blue. I just wish you didn't have to deal with that extra layer of awfulness.

As for why it's easier to talk to me about this stuff— maybe it's because I'm so cute and grammatical? And do you really think I'm grammatical? Because Mr. Wise says I have a thing about sentence fragments.

—Jacques

FROM: bluegreen118@gmail.com
TO: hourtohour.notetonote@gmail.com
DATE: Dec 9 at 4:52 PM
SUBJECT: Re: Coming Out Thing

Jacques,

Just so you know, your being cute isn't the reason you're easy to talk to, because it really should be the opposite. In real life, I go totally silent around cute guys. I just freeze up. I can't help it. But I know the real reason you were asking was because you wanted to hear me call you cute again, so I will. You're cute, Jacques. And I guess you do have a thing about sentence fragments, but I sort of love it.

So, I'm not sure whether you meant to tell me your English teacher's name. You're dropping a lot of clues, Jacques. Sometimes I wonder if you drop more clues than you mean to.

Anyway, thanks for listening. Thanks for everything. It was such a strange, surreal weekend, but talking to you about it made it so much better.

—Blue

FROM: hourtohour.notetonote@gmail.com
TO: bluegreen118@gmail.com
DATE: Dec 10 at 7:11 PM
SUBJECT: Re: Coming Out Thing

Blue,

Arg—yeah. Mentioning Mr. Wise was not intentional. I guess you can really narrow things down in a major way, if you choose to. I feel kind of strange about that. Sorry I'm such a huge freaking idiot.

So, who are all these cute guys who make you so nervous? They can't be that cute. You better not love THEIR sentence fragments.

Keep me posted about all forthcoming conversations with your mom, okay?

—Jacques

15

I GUESS WE'RE MAKING THIS our thing. Reading Dickens at the WaHo. Abby doesn't have a car tonight, so she comes home with me after school on Friday and brings her overnight bag. I know it must suck for Abby living so far away, but I kind of love our sleepovers.

Predictably, we arrive before Martin. It's more crowded tonight. We get a table, but it's near the entrance, so it already feels like we're under a spotlight. Abby sits down across from me and immediately gets to work building this fussy little house out of jam and sugar pouches.

Martin bursts in, and within sixty seconds, he changes his drink order twice, burps, and manages to level Abby's sugar house with an overly enthusiastic finger poke. "Arg. Sorry. Sorry," he says.

Abby shoots me a quick smile.

"And I forgot my script. Crap."

He's on a freaking roll tonight.

"You can look on with me," says Abby, scooting closer to him. The look on Martin's face. I almost start laughing.

We dive straight into Act Two, and it's a little bit less of a disaster than it was a week ago. At least I don't have to prompt every single line this time. My mind starts to wander.

I'm thinking about Blue—always Blue—because really, my mind only wanders in one direction. I got another email from him this morning. Lately, we've been emailing almost every day, and it's a little crazy how much he's been on my mind. I almost fucked up a chem lab today because I was emailing Blue in my head and I kind of forgot I was pouring nitric acid.

It's weird, because Blue's emails used to be this extra thing that was separate from my actual life. But now I think maybe the emails are my life. Everything else sort of feels like I'm slogging through a dream.

"Oh my gosh, Marty. No," says Abby, "just no."

Because, suddenly, Martin is kneeling in the booth, head flung back, clutching his chest, and singing. He's just launched into this big awesome number from the second act of the play. I mean, it's his full-on Fagin voice—low and trembly and vaguely British. And he's completely swept away in the moment.

People are gaping at us. And I'm speechless. Abby and I just stare at each other in the most stunned holy awkward silence that's ever unfolded.

He sings the entire song. I guess he's been practicing. And then—I'm not even kidding. He slides back down into his seat like nothing happened and starts pouring syrup on his waffle.

"I don't even know what to say to you," says Abby. And then she sighs. And then she hugs him.

Honest to God, he's like a freaking anime character. I can almost see hearts popping out of his eyes. He catches my eye, and his big banana mouth is just beaming. I can't help but grin back at him.

Maybe he's my blackmailer. Maybe he's also becoming my friend. Who the hell knows if that's even allowed.

Or maybe it's just that I'm feeling weirdly amped up and excited. I don't know how to explain it. Everything is funny. Martin is funny. Martin singing at Waffle House is entirely, incomprehensibly hilarious.

Two hours later, we wave good-bye to him in the parking lot, and Abby tucks into my passenger seat. The sky is dark and clear, and we shiver for a minute while we wait for the heat to kick in. I back out of the spot and pull onto Roswell Road.

"Who's this?" Abby asks.

"Rilo Kiley."

"I don't know them." She yawns.

We're listening to the birthday mix Leah made me, which

includes three Rilo Kiley songs from their first two albums. Leah has a girlcrush on Jenny Lewis. You can't not have a crush on Jenny Lewis. I'm twenty years younger than her and unquestionably gay, but yeah. I'd make out with her.

"Martin tonight," Abby says, shaking her head.

"What a weirdo."

"Kind of a cute weirdo," she says.

I make the left onto Shady Creek Circle. The car has warmed up, and the streets are almost empty, and everything feels quiet and cozy and safe.

"Definitely cute," she decides, "though, sadly, not my type."

"Not my type either," I say, and Abby laughs. I feel this tug in my chest.

I should really just tell her.

Blue is coming out to his mom tonight—at least that's the plan. They're having dinner at home, and he's going to try to make sure she has a little wine. And then he's just going to suck it up and do it. I'm nervous for him. Maybe a little jealous of him.

And I guess him telling her feels like a strange sort of loss. I think I liked being the only one who knew.

"Abby. Can I tell you something?"

"Sure, what's up?"

The music seems to fall away. We're stopped at a red, and I'm waiting to turn left, and all I can hear is the frantic clicking of my turn signal.

I think my heart is beating to its rhythm.

"You can't tell anyone," I say. "No one else knows this."

She doesn't speak, but I perceive her angling her body toward me. Her knees are folded up onto the passenger seat. She waits.

I didn't plan to do this tonight.

"So. The thing is, I'm gay."

It's the first time I've said those words out loud. I pause with my hands on the steering wheel, waiting to feel something extraordinary. The light turns green.

"Oh," says Abby. And there's this thick, hanging pause.

I turn left.

"Simon, pull over."

There's a little bakery ahead on my right, and I pull into its driveway. It's closed for the night. I put the car in park.

"Your hands are shaking," Abby says quietly. Then she tugs my arm closer, pushes my sleeve up, and cups my hand between her own. She sits cross-legged on the seat and turns completely sideways, facing me. I barely look at her.

"This is the first time you've told anyone?" she says, after a moment.

I nod.

"Wow." I hear her take a breath. "Simon, I'm really honored."

I lean back and sigh and twist my body toward her. My seat belt feels tight. I tug my hand away from Abby's to unlatch it. Then I give it back to her, and she laces her fingers through mine.

"Are you surprised?" I say.

"No." She looks at me directly. Lit only by streetlights, Abby's eyes are almost all pupil, edged thinly with brown.

"You knew?"

"No, not at all."

"But you're not surprised."

"Do you want me to be surprised?" She looks nervous.

"I don't know," I say.

She squeezes my hand.

I wonder how it's going for Blue. I wonder if Blue is feeling the same flutter in his stomach that I feel right now. Actually, he's probably feeling more than a flutter. He's probably so nauseated he can hardly choke the words out.

My Blue.

It's weird. I almost think I did this for him.

"What are you going to do?" Abby asks. "Are you going to tell people?"

I pause. "I don't know," I say. I haven't really thought about it. "I mean, eventually, yeah."

"Okay, well, I love you," she says.

She pokes me in the cheek. And then we go home.

16

FROM: bluegreen118@gmail.com
TO: hourtohour.notetonote@gmail.com
DATE: Dec 13 at 12:09 AM
SUBJECT: out and about

Jacques, I did it. I told her. I almost can't believe it.
I'm still feeling so wild and jittery and not myself. I don't
think I'll be able to sleep tonight.

I think she took it well. She didn't bring Jesus into
it at all. She was pretty calm about the whole thing.
Sometimes I forget that my mom can be very rational
and analytical (she's actually an epidemiologist). She
seemed mostly concerned that I understand the impor-
tance of Practicing Safe Sex Every Time, Including Oral.

No, I'm not kidding. She didn't seem to believe me when I told her I'm not sexually active. So, I guess that's flattering.

Anyway, I want to thank you. I didn't tell you this before, Jacques, but you should really know that you're the reason I was able to do this. I wasn't sure I'd ever find the courage. It's really kind of incredible. I feel like there's a wall coming down, and I don't know why, and I don't know what's going to happen. I just know you're the reason for it. So, thanks for that.

—Blue

FROM: hourtohour.notetonote@gmail.com
TO: bluegreen118@gmail.com
DATE: Dec 13 at 11:54 AM
SUBJECT: Re: out and about

Blue,

Shut up. I'm so freaking proud of you. I would hug you right now if I could.

Wow, so between Ms. Every Time Including Oral and Mr. Let's Read About Freaking Casanova, your parents are seriously invested in your sex life. Parents need to stop being so freaking awkward. I will say, though, you shouldn't even be thinking about sex unless it's with someone really, really awesome. Someone who is such a badass that the insane kids in his neighborhood don't even THINK about peeing on his porch. Someone who has a little bit of a problem with fragmented sentences and accidental self-disclosures. Yup.

So, you inspired me, Blue. I had my own Coming Out Thing last night. Not to my parents. But I told one of my best friends, even though I wasn't planning to, and it was awkward and weird and really kind of nice. I feel mostly relieved and a little embarrassed, because I feel like I made it into a bigger deal than it needed to be. It's funny, though. A part of me feels like I jumped over some kind of border, and now I'm on the other side realizing I can't cross back. I think it's a good feeling, or at least an exciting feeling. But I'm not sure. Am I making any sense at all?

But all of this about the walls coming down? I think you're giving me way too much credit. You're the hero tonight, Blue. You brought your own wall down. Maybe mine, too.

—Jacques

FROM: bluegreen118@gmail.com
TO: hourtohour.notetonote@gmail.com
DATE: Dec 14 at 12:12 PM
SUBJECT: Re: out and about

Jacques,

I don't even know what to say. I'm so proud of you, too. This is really momentous, isn't it? I'm guessing this is the kind of thing we remember for the rest of our lives.

I know exactly what you mean about crossing the border. I think this is the kind of process that moves in one direction. Once you come out, you can't really go back in. It's a little bit terrifying, isn't it? I know we're so lucky we're coming out now and not twenty years ago, but it's still really a leap of faith. It's easier than I thought it would be, but at the same time, it's so much harder.

Don't worry, Jacques. I only ever think about sex with people who hide from their eighth-grade girlfriends in bathrooms on Valentine's Day, and eat tons of Oreos, and listen to weirdly depressing and wonderful music, but never wear band T-shirts.

I guess I have a very specific type.

(I'm not kidding.)

—Blue

17

I HAVE TO MEET HIM.

I don't think I can keep this up. I don't care if it ruins everything. I'm this close to making out with my laptop screen.

Blue Blue Blue Blue Blue Blue Blue.

Seriously, I feel like I'm about to combust.

I spend the entire school day with my stomach in knots, and it's completely pointless, because it's not attached to anything real. Because, really, it's just words on a screen. I don't even know his freaking name.

I think I'm a little bit in love with him.

All through rehearsal, I stare at Cal Price, hoping he'll fuck it up somehow and give me some sort of clue. Something. Anything. He pulls out a book, and my eyes go straight to the author's name on the cover. Because maybe the book is by freaking Casanova, and I only know one person who owns a book by freaking Casanova.

But it's *Fahrenheit 451*. Probably something for English class.

I mean, how does a person look when his walls are coming down?

Really, a lot of people are having trouble focusing today, because everyone's obsessed with this sophomore who snuck into the chem lab and got his junk stuck in a beaker. I don't even know. Apparently it was on the Tumblr. But I guess Ms. Albright is sick of hearing about it, so she lets us out early.

Which means it's actually still light out when I pull into the driveway. Bieber pretty much explodes with joy when he sees me. It looks like I'm the first one home. I sort of want to know where Nora is. The fact that she's out is highly freaking unusual, to be honest.

I'm feeling so restless. I don't even want a snack. Not even Oreos. I can't just sit around. I text Nick to see what he's up to, even though I know he's playing video games in the basement, because that's what he always does in the afternoons until soccer season starts. He says Leah is on her way over. So I hook Bieber onto his leash and lock the door behind us.

Leah is pulling into the driveway when we get there. She slides her window down and calls to Bieber, who naturally breaks away from me to jump up against her car. "Hello, sweet one," she says. His paws rest on the frame of her car door, and he gives her a single polite lick.

"Are you just getting off rehearsal?" she asks as we walk around the path to Nick's basement door.

"Yeah." I turn the doorknob and push the door open. "Bieber. NO. Come on."

Like he's never seen a squirrel before. Good freaking lord.

"Geez. So, what, it's two hours a day, three days a week?"

"Four days a week now," I say. "Every day but Friday. And we have an all-day rehearsal this Saturday."

"Wow," she says.

Nick shuts off the TV when we enter.

"*Assassin's Creed*?" asks Leah, nodding toward the blank screen.

"Yup," says Nick.

"Awesome," she says. And I just kind of shrug. I give precisely zero shits about video games.

I lie on the carpet next to Bieber, who is on his back looking absurd with his lips flapped up over his gums. Nick and Leah end up talking about *Doctor Who*, and Leah tucks into the video game chair, tugging the frayed hem of her jeans. Her cheeks are sort of pink behind her freckles, and she's making some point and getting really animated about it. They're both totally absorbed in the philosophy of time travel. So I let my eyes slide closed. And I think about Blue.

Okay. I have a crush. But it's not like having a crush on some random musician or actor or Harry freaking Potter. This is the real deal. It has to be. It's almost debilitating.

I mean, I'm lying here on Nick's basement carpet, the site of so many Power Rangers transformations and lightsaber battles and spilled cups of juice—and all I want in the entire world is for Blue's next email to arrive. And Nick and Leah are still talking about the freaking TARDIS. They don't have a clue. They don't even know I'm gay.

And I don't know how to do this. Ever since I told Abby on Friday, I kind of thought it would be easy to tell Leah and Nick. Easier, anyway, now that my mouth is used to saying the words.

It's not easier. It's impossible. Because even though it feels like I've known Abby forever, I really only met her four months ago. And I guess there hasn't been time for her to have any set ideas about me yet. But I've known Leah since sixth grade, and Nick since we were four. And this gay thing. It feels so big. It's almost insurmountable. I don't know how to tell them something like this and still come out of it feeling like Simon. Because if Leah and Nick don't recognize me, I don't even recognize myself anymore.

My phone buzzes. Text from Monkey's Asshole: *hey maybe another Waffle House thing soon?*

I ignore it.

I hate feeling so distant from Nick and Leah. It's not like keeping a normal crush a secret, because we never talk about our crushes anyway, and it works out fine. Even Leah's crush on Nick. I see it, and I'm sure Nick sees it, but there's this unspoken agreement that we never talk about it.

I don't know why the gay thing isn't like that. I don't know why keeping it from them makes me feel like I'm living a secret life.

My phone starts vibrating, and it's my dad calling. Which probably means dinner is on the table.

I hate that I feel so relieved.

I really am going to tell Nick and Leah eventually.

I spend the first Saturday of Christmas break at school. Everyone sits in a circle on the stage in pajamas, eating donut holes and drinking coffee out of Styrofoam cups. Except I'm next to Abby at the edge of the stage. My feet dangle over the orchestra pit, and her legs are in my lap.

My fingers are sticky with powdered sugar. I feel so far away. I stare at the bricks. Some of the bricks on the back wall of the auditorium are a darker shade, almost brown, and they form this double helix design. It's just so random. But so weirdly deliberate.

Double helixes are interesting. Deoxyribonucleic acid. I'll think about that.

Trying not to think about something is like playing freaking Whac-a-Mole. Every time you push one thought down, another one nudges its way to the surface.

I guess there are two moles. One is the fact that I've hung out with Nick and Leah after rehearsal three days this week, which means three chances to tell them about the gay thing, and three times wussing out. And then there's Blue, with his perfect grammar, who has no freaking clue how many times I proofread every email I send to him. Blue, who is so guarded and yet so surprisingly flirtatious sometimes. Who thinks about sex, and thinks about it with me.

But, you know: double helixes. Twisty, loopy, double helixes.

Martin walks in through the doors in the back of the auditorium. He's wearing a long, old-fashioned nightgown and curlers.

"Oh. Wow. He really—okay." Abby nods, grinning up at Martin, who does a pirouette and immediately gets tangled in his nightgown. But he catches himself on the armrest of a chair, and gives this triumphant smile. That's Martin. Everything's part of the show with him.

Ms. Albright joins the circle onstage and calls us to order. Abby and I scoot in closer to the group. I end up next to Martin, and flash him a smile. He punches my arm lightly but keeps his eyes locked forward, like a T-ball dad. A T-ball dad who dresses like my grandma.

"So, here's the plan, pajama gang," says Ms. Albright. "We're going to fine-tune the musical numbers this morning. Big ensemble numbers first, and then we'll split into smaller groups. We break for pizza at noon, and after that, we run through the whole caboodle."

Over her shoulder, I see Cal sitting on a platform, writing

something in the margin of his script.

"Any questions?" she asks.

"For those of us who are already off book, should we still carry our scripts to take notes?" asks Taylor. Just making sure we know she's memorized her lines.

"This morning, yes. This afternoon, no. We'll go through the notes after we're done. I'd like to run both acts once without stopping. Obviously, it will be messy, and that's okay." She yawns. "All right, so. Let's take five, and then we'll jump into 'Food, Glorious Food.'"

I pull myself up, and before I can talk myself out of it, I walk over and sit beside Cal on his platform. I nudge him in the knee.

"Nice polka dots," I say.

He smiles. "Nice Labradors."

I mean, he's cute, so I'll let it slide, but the dogs on my pants are clearly golden retrievers.

I sneak a look at his script. "What are you drawing?"

"Oh, this? I don't know," he says. He pushes his bangs back and blushes, and good God, he's adorable.

"I didn't know you could draw."

"Sort of." He shrugs and tilts the binder toward me.

He has this style of drawing that's all movement and sharp angles and bold pencil lines. It's not bad. Leah's drawings are better. But it hardly matters at all, because the important thing is that Cal's drawing is of a superhero.

I mean, *a superhero*. My heart almost squeezes to a stop. Blue loves superheroes.

Blue.

I slide an inch closer, so our legs are touching, just barely.

I'm not sure if he notices.

I don't know why I'm so brave today.

I'm 99.9 percent sure that Cal is Blue. But there's that fraction of a percent chance that he's not. For some reason, I can't seem to come out and ask him.

So, instead, I ask, "How's the coffee?"

"Pretty good, Simon. Pretty good."

I look up and realize that Abby is watching me with great interest. I flash her the stink-eye, and she looks away, but she has this tiny knowing smile that just kills me.

Ms. Albright sends a bunch of us to the music room and puts Cal in charge. All things considered, it's a perfect situation.

To get there, we have to walk all the way past the math and science classrooms and down the back stairway. Everything is dark and spooky and awesome on a Saturday. The school is totally empty. The music room is tucked into its own alcove at the end of the hall downstairs. I used to do choir, so I've spent some time here. It hasn't changed. I get the impression that it hasn't changed in about twenty years.

There are three rows of chairs on built-in platforms that edge around the sides of the classroom in a split hexagon shape.

In the center of the room is a big wooden upright piano. There's a laminated sign taped to the front reminding us to have outstanding posture. Cal sits on the edge of the piano bench, stretching his arm back behind his head.

"So. Um, maybe we could start with 'Consider Yourself' or 'Pick a Pocket or Two,'" he says, shuffling his foot against the leg of the piano bench. He looks so lost. Martin attempts to transfer one of his curlers onto Abby's ponytail, and Abby stabs him in the gut with a wooden drumstick, and a couple of people have taken out the guitars and started plucking out random pop songs.

No one is really listening to Cal except me. Well, and Taylor.

"Do you want us to clear away these music stands?" I ask.

"Uh, yeah. That would be awesome," he says. "Thanks, y'all."

There's a piece of paper on one of the stands that catches my eye—neon orange, with the words "SET LIST" written in black Sharpie. Underneath that is a list of songs—classic, awesome songs, like "Somebody to Love" and "Billie Jean."

"What's that?" asks Taylor. I shrug, handing it to her.

"I don't think this is supposed to be here," she says, throwing it away. Of course she doesn't. Taylor is the enemy of everything awesome.

Cal has Ms. Albright's laptop, which has piano recordings of the accompaniment to all the songs. Everyone's a pretty good sport about running through everything once, and it's not a total disaster. As much as I hate to admit it, Taylor probably has the best voice out of anyone in the school other than Nick, and Abby is such a good dancer that she can seriously carry the whole ensemble. And anything Martin touches is strange and absurd and hilarious. Especially when he's wearing a nightie.

There's still almost an hour before we're supposed to reconvene in the auditorium, and we're probably supposed to run through everything again, but I mean, really. It's Saturday, we're in an empty, dark school, and we're a bunch of theater kids wearing pajamas and jacked up on donuts.

We end up singing Disney songs in the stairwell. Abby weirdly knows every word to every song in *Pocahontas*, and everyone knows *The Lion King* and *Aladdin* and *Beauty and the Beast*. Taylor can improvise harmonies, and I guess we're all warmed up from singing the *Oliver!* songs, because it just sounds really amazing. And the acoustics in the stairwell are freaking awesome.

And then we go back upstairs, and Mila Odom and Eve Miller pull a bunch of rolling chairs out of the computer lab. It's pretty convenient that Creekwood has such long, straight hallways.

Perfect happiness is: gripping the bottom of a rolling chair with both hands, while Cal Price pushes me down the hall in a full-on run. We race against two of the sophomore girls from the ensemble. Cal is kind of a slow-moving person, so they totally dominate, but I don't even care. His hands grip my shoulders, and we're both laughing, and the rows of lockers are a toothpaste-blue blur. I let down my legs, and we skid to a stop. And I guess I have to get up. I raise my hand to give Cal a high five, but instead, he threads his fingers through mine for just a second. Then he looks down and smiles, and his eyes are hidden by his bangs. We untangle our hands, and my heart is thudding. I have to look away from him.

Then Taylor, of all people, mounts one of the chairs. Her blond hair flies backward as Abby pushes her, and they're the indisputable champions. Abby and her leg muscles, I guess. I had no idea she was so freaking fast.

Abby collapses into me, laughing and panting, and we slide to the floor against the lockers. She leans her head on my shoulder, and I slide my arm around her back. Leah can get weird about touching, and it's this unspoken thing that I don't really touch Nick. But Abby's a huggy person, and I sort of am, too, so that's been nice. And everything has just felt really natural and comfortable between us since that night in the car after the Waffle House. It's pretty cozy sitting next to Abby and smelling her magical French toast scent, while we watch the freshmen take turns racing in the chairs.

Abby and I sit like that for so long my arm starts to prickle. But it isn't until we're finally about to head back to the auditorium that I realize two people have been watching us.

The first is Cal.

The second is Martin, and he looks pretty goddamn furious.

"Spier. We need to talk." Martin pulls me into a stairwell.

"Um, now? Because Ms. Albright wants us to—"

"Yeah, Ms. Albright can fucking wait a second."

"Okay. What's up?" I lean against the railing and look up at him. The stairwell is dark, but my eyes are pretty well-adjusted, and I can see the tension in Martin's jaw. He stops and waits until the others are too far down the hall to overhear.

"So, I guess you think this is all hilarious," he says under his breath.

"What?"

He doesn't elaborate.

"I have no freaking clue what you're talking about," I say finally.

"Right, of course not." Martin crosses his arms in front of his chest and tugs on his elbow, and he just radiates the stink-eye.

"Marty, seriously. I don't know why you're upset. If you want to fill me in, great. Otherwise, I don't know what to tell you."

He exhales loudly and leans into the railing. "You're trying to humiliate me. And believe me, I get it. I get that you weren't a hundred percent on board with our arrangement—"

"Our arrangement? You mean you blackmailing me? Yeah, I'm not on board with being blackmailed, if that's what you're wondering."

"You think I'm fucking blackmailing you?"

"What the hell else would you call it?" I say. But it's funny—I'm not really pissed off at him. A little bewildered at the moment, but not angry.

"Look. It's over. The Abby thing is done, okay? So you can forget about the whole goddamn thing."

I pause. "Did something happen with Abby?"

"Yes, something fucking happened with Abby. She fucking rejected me."

"What? When?"

Martin stands abruptly, his face flushed. "Roughly five minutes before she draped herself all over you," he says.

"*What?* Yeah, that's not what—"

"You know what? Save it, Spier. Actually, you know what you can do? You can tell Ms. Albright I'll see her in fucking January."

"You're leaving?" I ask.

I seriously don't know what the hell is happening. He flips me the bird as he walks away. He doesn't even turn around to look at me.

"Martin, are you—"

"Merry goddamned Christmas, Simon," he says. "Hope you're happy."

18

FROM: bluegreen118@gmail.com
TO: hourtohour.notetonote@gmail.com
DATE: Dec 20 at 1:45 PM
SUBJECT: Oh baby

Jacques,

You're not going to believe this.

I got home from school yesterday, and both of my parents were there. I know that doesn't sound crazy, but you have to realize that my mom almost never leaves work early, and my dad has literally never driven up here with no advance notice before. And he was just up here two weeks ago. They were sitting on the couch in the living room, and they had been laughing about something, but they stopped abruptly when I walked in.

I felt so queasy, Jacques. I was positive my mom had told my dad I was gay, which would just be—I don't know. Anyway, there was this excruciating half hour of small talk, and then my mom finally stood up and said she was going to leave my dad and me alone for a minute. And then she went into her bedroom. The whole thing was just so weird.

Anyway, my dad seemed really nervous, and I was really nervous. We were talking, and I forgot what he said, but I realized my mom hadn't told him anything. And suddenly I wanted him to know. I felt like it had to be that very second. So, I was listening to him talk and waiting for an opportunity to tell him—but he just kept talking and talking, and it was strange and tangential and boring.

Then, all of a sudden, pretty much out of nowhere, he tells me that my stepmother is pregnant. She's due in June.

I was really, really not expecting that. I've been an only child my whole life.

So, yeah. If anyone can find the humor in this, it's you. Please. Or just distract me. You're good at that, too.

Love,

Blue

FROM: hourtohour.notetonote@gmail.com
TO: bluegreen118@gmail.com
DATE: Dec 20 at 6:16 PM
SUBJECT: Re: Oh baby

Blue,

Wow. I'm just—wow. Congratulations? I don't know. I can't tell a hundred percent how you feel about it, but it seems like you're not thrilled. I guess I wouldn't be. Especially if I was used to being an only child. And then there's the dad having sex factor, which is always horrifying (and he bought YOU a book by freaking Casanova?). Ugh.

Also, I'm sorry you got all prepared again to come out, and didn't get a chance to do it. That really sucks.

I'm trying to find the humor here for you. Poop? Poop is funny, right? I guess there will be a lot of it. I don't know why it doesn't seem funny to me right now. POOP!!!!! I mean, I'm trying.

That's so weird the way your parents told you, like they were both in on it. I guess he wanted to give your mom a heads-up first or something? And then he was nervous to tell you. It's like he's our age telling his parents he knocked someone up. Which is totally the straight person equivalent of coming out.

As a side note, don't you think everyone should have to come out? Why is straight the default? Everyone should have to declare one way or another, and it should be this big awkward thing whether you're straight, gay, bi, or whatever. I'm just saying.

Anyway, I don't know if any of this is helping. I guess I'm a little off my game (kind of a weird day for me, too). But just know I'm sorry this is hitting you out of nowhere. And I'm thinking about you.

Love,

Jacques

FROM: bluegreen118@gmail.com
TO: hourtohour.notetonote@gmail.com
DATE: Dec 21 at 9:37 AM
SUBJECT: POOP

Jacques,

First of all, your email helped a lot. I don't know— something about poop and Casanova and the phrase "knocked up" in reference to my dad. It's all such a train wreck. I think I do see the humor. I guess it's not neces- sarily a bad thing to have a little fetus sibling. I'm pretty curious to find out if it's a boy or a girl. Anyway, I feel a lot better now that I've gotten some sleep. And I think just talking it over with you makes everything better.

Sorry you had a weird day, too. Want to talk about it?

It is definitely annoying that straight (and white, for that matter) is the default, and that the only people who have to think about their identity are the ones who don't fit that mold. Straight people really should have to come out, and the more awkward it is, the better. Awkwardness should be a requirement. I guess this is sort of our version of the Homosexual Agenda?

Love,

Blue

P.S. By the way, guess what I'm eating at this very moment.

FROM: hourtohour.notetonote@gmail.com
TO: bluegreen118@gmail.com
DATE: Dec 21 at 10:11 AM
SUBJECT: Re: POOP

Blue,

I hope for your sake that Little Fetus is a boy, because sisters are a freaking handful. I'm glad you're feeling a little better about things. I don't know how I did it, but I'm glad I was able to help somehow.

Eh, don't worry about my weird day. Someone got

angry at me, and it's kind of hard to explain, but it's a stupid misunderstanding. Whatever.

The Homosexual Agenda? I don't know. I think it's more like the Homo Sapiens Agenda. That's really the point, right?

Love,

Jacques

P.S. You have me curious. A banana? Hot dog? Cucumber? ☺

FROM: bluegreen118@gmail.com
TO: hourtohour.notetonote@gmail.com
DATE: Dec 21 at 10:24 AM
SUBJECT: The Homo Sapiens Agenda

Jacques,

I love it.

Love,

Blue

P.S. Mind out of the gutter, Jacques.

P.P.S. More like a giant baguette.

P.P.P.S. No, really. It's Oreos. In your honor.

FROM: hourtohour.notetonote@gmail.com
TO: bluegreen118@gmail.com
DATE: Dec 21 at 10:30 AM
SUBJECT: Re: The Homo Sapiens Agenda

Blue,

I love that you're having Oreos for breakfast. And I love your giant baguette.

So, here's the thing. I've been typing this and deleting this and trying to think of a better way to phrase this. I don't know. I'm just going to come out and say it: I want to know who you are.

I think we should meet in person.

Love,

Jacques

19

IT'S CHRISTMAS EVE DAY, AND something feels a little bit off.

Not bad. Just off. I don't know how to explain it. We're hitting every one of the Spier traditions. My mom made reindeer turds, a.k.a. Oreo truffles. The tree is lit up and fully decorated. We've done the Chipmunks song.

It's noon, and we're all still in our pajamas, and everyone is sitting in the living room on separate laptops. I guess it's a little awful that we have five computers—Shady Creek is that kind of suburb, but still. We're scavenger hunting on Facebook.

"Call it, Dad," says Alice.

"Okay," he says. "Someone visiting somewhere tropical."

"Got it," says my mom, turning her laptop around to show us someone's pictures. "Done and done. All right. A breakup."

We're all quiet for several minutes, scrolling through our

newsfeeds. Finally, Nora's got one. "Amber Wasserman," she reads. *"Thought I knew u. Looks like I was wrong. One day ur gonna turn around and realize what u thru away."*

"I'd call that an implied breakup," I say.

"It's legit."

"But you could interpret it literally," I say. "Like she's calling him out for throwing away her iPhone."

"That's Simon logic," says Alice, "and I won't allow it. Go, boop. Your turn."

My dad invented the concept of Simon logic, and I can't seem to outgrow it. It means wishful thinking supported by flimsy evidence.

"Okay," says Nora. "The opposite. A mushy, disgusting couple."

An interesting choice, coming from Nora, who basically never talks about anything related to dating.

"Okay, got one," I say. "Carys Seward. *Feeling so grateful to have Jaxon Wildstein in my life. Last nite was perfect. I love you so much baby.* Winky face."

"Gross," says Nora.

"Is that your Carys, bub?"

"I don't have a Carys," I say. But I know what Alice is asking. I dated Carys for almost four months last spring. Though none of our "nites" together were that sort of perfect.

But here's the crazy thing: for the first time ever, I almost get it. It's weird, it's gross, and that creepy little winky face pushes it into the realm of TMI. But yeah. Maybe I'm losing my edge, but all I can think about is how Blue has been signing emails lately using the word "love."

I guess I can imagine us having perfect nights sometimes. And I'll probably feel like shouting it from the rooftops, too.

I refresh my browser. "My turn. Okay. Someone Jewish," I say, "posting about Christmas."

My Jewish-Episcopalian email boyfriend. I wonder what he's doing right now.

"Why doesn't Nick ever post anything?" asks Nora.

Because he thinks Facebook is the lowest common denominator of social discourse. Though he does like to talk about social media as a vehicle for constructing and performing identity. Whatever the hell that means.

"Got one. Jana Goldstein. *Movie theater listings in one hand; takeout menus in the other. Ready for tomorrow. Merry Christmas to Jew!*"

"Who's Jana Goldstein?" my mom asks.

"Someone from Wesleyan," says Alice. "Okay. Something about lawyers." She's distracted, and I realize her phone is buzzing. "Sorry. Be right back."

"Lawyers? What the heck, Alice?" says Nora. "That blatantly favors Dad."

"I know. I feel bad for him," Alice calls over her shoulder, before disappearing up the stairs. "Hey," she says, answering her phone. A moment later, we hear her bedroom door shut.

"Got one!" My dad beams. He generally sucks at this game, because he has about twelve Facebook friends total. "Bob Lepinski. *Happy holidays to you and yours, from Lepinski and Willis, P.C.*"

"Good one, Dad," says Nora. She looks at me. "Who's she talking to?"

"Hell if I know," I say.

Alice is on the phone for two hours. It's unprecedented.

The scavenger hunt fizzles. Nora curls up with her laptop on the couch, and our parents disappear to their room. And I don't even want to think about what they're up to in there. Not after what Blue's dad and stepmom went and did. Bieber whines in the entryway.

My phone buzzes with a text from Leah: *We're outside your door.* Leah's weird about knocking. I think she gets shy around parents.

I walk over to let her in, and find Bieber on his hind legs basically trying to make out with her through the window.

"Down," I say. "Come on, Bieb." I grab him by the collar and swing the door open. It's cold but sunny out, and Leah wears a black woolen hat with cat ears. Nick stands sort of awkwardly behind her.

"Hi," I say, pulling Bieber to the side so they can step past him.

"We were actually thinking about taking a walk," says Leah.

I look at her. Something in her tone is a little strange. "Okay," I say. "Let me get dressed." I'm still wearing my golden retriever pajama pants.

Five minutes later, I'm in jeans and a hoodie. I throw a leash on Bieber, and we're out the door.

"So you guys just wanted to take a walk, or what?" I ask finally.

They look at each other. "Yeah," says Nick.

I raise my eyebrows at him, waiting to see if he'll say more, but he looks away.

"How are things going, Simon?" Leah asks, in this strange, gentle voice.

I stop short. We're barely out of my driveway. "What's going on?"

"Nothing." She fiddles with the pom-poms that string down from her hat. Nick stares at the road. "Just seeing if you wanted to talk."

"About what?" I ask. Bieber crosses over to Leah and sits on his haunches, staring up at her with pleading eyes.

"Why are you looking at me like that, sweet one?" she asks, ruffling his ears. "I don't have any cookies."

"What do you want to talk about?" I ask again. We're not walking. We stand by the curb, and I shift my weight from one foot to the other.

Leah and Nick exchange another look, and it hits me.

"Oh my gosh. You guys hooked up."

"What?" Leah says, turning bright red. "No!"

I look from Leah to Nick and back to Leah. "You didn't . . ."

"Simon. No. Just stop." Leah isn't looking at Nick. In fact, she's bent all the way over with her face pressed against Bieber's snout.

"Okay, then what are we talking about here?" I ask. "What's going on?"

"Um," says Nick.

Leah stands. "Okay, yeah. I'm gonna go. Merry Christmas, guys. Happy Hanukkah. Whatever." She gives me this curt little nod. Then she bends down again and lets my dog kiss her on the lips. And then she's gone.

Nick and I stand there in silence. He touches his thumb briefly to the tip of each finger.

"Hanukkah is over," he says finally.

"What's going on, Nick?"

"Look—don't worry about it." He sighs, staring up the street at Leah's retreating form. "She's parked at my house. I guess I have to give her a minute, so it's not like I'm following her."

"You can come in," I say. "My parents won't care. Alice is home."

"Yeah?" he says, glancing back at my house. "I don't know. I'm just going to . . ." He turns to me, and there's this look on his face. I've known Nick since we were four years old. I've never seen this expression before.

"Look." He puts his hand on my arm. I look down at his

hand. I can't help it. Nick never touches me. "Have a good Christmas, Simon. Really."

And then he takes back his hand, and waves, and trudges up the road after Leah.

Spier family tradition dictates that Christmas Eve dinner is French toast, per my grandma's technique: thick slices of challah aged one day for maximum egg absorption, cooked in tons of butter in pans partially covered by pot lids. When my grandma makes them, she constantly moves the lids around and flips the bread over and fusses with all of it (she's kind of a hardcore grandma). It never comes out quite as custardy when my dad makes it, but it's pretty freaking good anyway.

We eat it at the actual dining table on our parents' wedding china, and my mom brings out the manger scene centerpiece that rotates like a fan when you light a candle beneath it. It's really hypnotic. Alice dims the lights, and my mom puts out cloth napkins, and everything feels really fancy.

But it's weird. It doesn't really feel like Christmas Eve. There's this spark missing, and I don't know what it is.

I've felt like this all week, and I don't understand it. I don't know why everything feels so different this year. Maybe it's because Alice has been gone. Or maybe it's because I'm spending every minute pining for some boy who doesn't want to meet me in person. Or who's "not ready" to meet me in person. But he's also a boy who signs his emails with "love." I don't know. I don't know.

In this moment, all I want is for things to feel like Christmas again. I want it to feel how it used to feel.

After dinner, my parents put on *Love Actually* and settle in on the love seat with Bieber wedged between them. Alice disappears again to talk on the phone. Nora and I sit for a while on our opposite ends of the couch, and I stare into the lights of the tree. If I squint my eyes, everything looks sort of bright and hazy, and I can almost catch the feeling I remember. But it's pointless. So I go into my own room and fling myself back on the bed and listen to my music on shuffle.

Three songs later, there's a knock on my door.

"Simon?" It's Nora.

"What?" Ugh.

"I'm coming in."

I prop myself halfway up against the pillows and give her a mild stink-eye. But she walks in anyway, and pushes my backpack off my desk chair. And then she sits, with her legs tucked up and her arms around her knees. "Hey," she says.

"What do you want?" I say.

She looks at me through her glasses—she's already taken her contact lenses out. Her hair is pulled back messily, and she's changed into a Wesleyan T-shirt, and it's really remarkable how much she's starting to look like Alice.

"I need to show you something," she says. She swivels the chair back toward my desk and starts opening my laptop.

"Are you kidding me?" I jump up. Seriously. She seriously thinks I'm about to give her open access to my laptop.

"Fine. Whatever. You do it." She unplugs it and rolls the chair closer to the bed, handing the laptop over to me.

"So, what am I looking at?"

She sucks her lips in and looks at me again. "Pull up the Tumblr."

"Like . . . creeksecrets?"

She nods.

I have it bookmarked. "It's loading," I say. "Okay. I've got it. What's up?"

"Can I sit with you?" she asks.

I look up at her. "On the bed?"

"Yeah."

"Um, okay."

She climbs up next to me, and looks at the screen. "Scroll down."

I scroll. And then I stop.

Nora turns to face me.

Oh my fucking God.

"You okay?" she asks softly. "I'm sorry, Si. I just thought you'd want to know about it. I'm assuming you didn't write it."

I shake my head slowly. "No, I didn't," I say.

December 24, 10:15 A.M.
SIMON SPIER'S OPEN INVITATION TO ALL DUDES
Dear all dudes of Creekwood,
With this missive, I hereby declare that I am supremely gay and

open for business. Interested parties may contact me directly to
discuss arrangements for anal buttsex. Or blue-jobs. But don't
give me blue balls. Ladies need not apply. That is all.

"I already reported it," said Nora. "They'll take it down."

"People have already seen it, though."

"I don't know." She's quiet for a moment. "Who would post something like that?"

"Someone who doesn't know that 'anal buttsex' is redundant."

"That's so effed up," she says.

I mean, I know who posted it. And I guess I should be grateful he didn't post one of his freaking screenshots. But honest to God: that sly fucking reference to Blue makes him the biggest, most cavernous gaping asshole who ever lived.

God, what if Blue sees it?

I slam the laptop closed and shove it onto the chair. Then I lean my head back, and Nora scoots back against the headboard. The minutes tick past.

"I mean, it's true," I say finally. I don't look at her. We both stare at the ceiling. "I am gay."

"I figured," she says.

Now I look at her. "Really?"

"From your reaction. I don't know." She blinks. "So what are you going to do about it?"

"Wait for them to take it down. What can I do?"

"But are you going to tell people?"

"I think Nick and Leah already read it," I say slowly.

Nora shrugs. "You could deny it."

"Okay, I'm not going to deny it. I'm not ashamed of it."

"All right, well, I didn't know. You haven't said anything up until now."

Oh my God. Seriously?

I sit up. "Yeah, you don't have a fucking clue what you're talking about."

"I'm sorry! Geez, Simon. I'm just trying to . . ." She looks at me. "I mean, it's obviously not something to be ashamed of. You know that, right? And I think most people are going to be cool about it."

"I don't know what people think about it."

She pauses. "Are you going to tell Mom and Dad? And Alice?"

"I don't know." I sigh. "I don't know."

"Your phone keeps buzzing," Nora says. She hands it to me.

I've got five texts from Abby.

Simon, are u ok?

Call me when you can, ok?

Ok. I don't know how to say this, but u should check the tumblr. I love u.

Please know I didn't tell anyone. I would never tell anyone. I love u, ok?

Call me?

● ● ●

And then it's Christmas. I used to wake up at four every year in a total frenzy of greed. It didn't matter how thorough I had been about poking for clues—and make no mistake, I was thorough. But Santa was a ninja. He always managed to surprise me.

So, it looks like I got one hell of a Christmas surprise this year. And good fucking tidings to you, too, Martin.

At seven thirty, I walk downstairs, and everything inside me twists and clenches. The lights are still off, but the morning sun is bright through the living room windows, and the tree is fully lit. Five overstuffed stockings lean up against the couch cushions, too heavy for the mantel. The only one awake is Bieber. I bring him out for a quick pee and give him his breakfast, and then we lie together on the couch and wait.

I know Blue is at church right now with his mom and uncle and cousins, and they all went last night, too. He's basically putting in more church time over these past two days than I have in my entire life.

It's funny. I didn't think this was going to be a big deal. But I think I'd actually rather be at church than here, doing what I'm about to do.

By nine, everyone's awake and the coffee's on, and we're having cookies for breakfast. Alice and Nora are reading stuff on their phones. I pour myself a mug of coffee and add an avalanche of sugar. My mom watches me stir.

"I didn't know you drink coffee."

Okay, this. She does this every freaking time. Both of them. They put me in a box, and every time I try to nudge the lid open, they slam it back down. It's like nothing about me is allowed to change.

"Well, I do."

"Okay," she says, putting her hands up like *whoa there, buck.* "That's fine, Si. It's just different. I'm just trying to keep up with you."

If she thinks me drinking coffee is big news, it's going to be quite a fucking morning.

We turn to the pile of presents. Blue told me that in his family, presents are opened one at a time, and all the cousins and everyone else just sit and watch each other do it. And then after a few rounds of that, they stop for a while and have lunch or something. It's just so civilized. It takes them all afternoon to clear out the Christmas tree.

Not so with the Spiers. Alice works her way underneath the tree in crouch position and starts passing bags and boxes down the line, and everyone talks at once.

"A Kindle case? I don't have a—"

"Open the other one, honey."

"Hey, Aurora coffee!"

"No, put it on the other way, boop. Everyone wears these at Wesleyan."

In twenty minutes, it's like a freaking Paper Source exploded all over the living room. I'm on the floor, leaning into the front of the couch, winding the cords of my new earbuds around my fingers. Bieber tucks a bow between his paws, and he nips and tugs on it, and everyone's just kind of draped over various pieces of furniture.

It's clearly my moment.

Though, if this moment really belonged to me, it wouldn't be happening. Not now, I mean. Not yet.

"Hey. I want to talk to you guys about something." I try to sound casual, but my voice is froggy. Nora looks at me and gives me a tiny, quick smile, and my stomach sort of flips.

"What's up?" says my mom, sitting up straight.

I don't know how people do this. How Blue did this. Two words. Two freaking words, and I'm not the same Simon anymore. My hand is over my mouth, and I stare straight ahead.

I don't know why I thought this would be easy.

"I know what this is," says my dad. "Let me guess. You're gay. You got someone pregnant. *You're* pregnant."

"Dad, stop it," says Alice.

I close my eyes.

"I'm pregnant," I say.

"I thought so, kid," says my dad. "You're glowing."

I look him in the eye. "Really, though. I'm gay."

Two words.

Everyone is quiet for a moment.

And then my mom says, "Honey. That's . . . God, that's . . . thank you for telling us."

163

And then Alice says, "Wow, bub. Good for you."

And my dad says, "Gay, huh?"

And my mom says, "So, talk me through this." It's one of her favorite psychologist lines. I look at her and shrug.

"We're proud of you," she adds.

And then my dad grins and says, "So, which one of them did it?"

"Did what?"

"Turned you off women. Was it the one with the eyebrows, the eye makeup, or the overbite?"

"Dad, that's so offensive," says Alice.

"What? I'm just lightening the mood. Simon knows we love him."

"Your heterosexist comments aren't lightening the mood."

I mean, I guess it's about what I expected. My mom's asking me about my feelings, Dad's turning it into a joke, Alice is getting political, and Nora is keeping her mouth shut. You could say there's a kind of comfort in predictability, and my family is pretty goddamn predictable.

But I'm so exhausted and unhappy right now. I thought it would feel like a weight had been lifted. But it's just like everything else this week. Strange and off-kilter and surreal.

"So, that's pretty big news, bub," Alice says, following me into my room. She shuts the door behind her, and settles in cross-legged on the end of my bed.

"Ugh," I say. I collapse facedown into the pillows.

"Hey." She leans her body sideways, until it's level with mine. "Everything's cool. It's nothing to mope about."

I ignore her.

"I'm not leaving, bub. Because you're going to wallow. You're going to put on that playlist. What's it called?"

"The Great Depression," I mutter. It's like all Elliott Smith and Nick Drake and the Smiths. I already have it cued up.

"Right," she says. "The Great Depression. That romp. No way."

"Why are you here?"

"Because I'm your big sister and you need me."

"I need to be left alone."

"No way. Talk to me, bub!" she says. She slides toward me, squeezing in between my body and the wall. "This is exciting. We can talk about guys."

"Okay," I say, pushing up off the bed and maneuvering into a sitting position. "Then tell me about your boyfriend."

"Whoa there," she says. "What?"

I look at her. "The phone calls. Disappearing into your room for hours. Come on."

"I thought we were discussing your love life." She blushes.

"So I get to make a scene and *come out* and have everyone awkwardly debate the whole thing right in front of me. On freaking Christmas," I say, "and you won't even tell me you have a boyfriend?"

She's silent for a moment, and I know I have her. She sighs. "How do you know I don't have a girlfriend?"

"Is it a girlfriend?"

"No," she says finally, leaning back against the wall. "Boyfriend."

"What's his name?"

"Theo."

"Is he on Facebook?"

"Yes."

I pull up the app on my phone and start scrolling through her friends list.

"Oh God. Just stop," she says. "Simon, seriously. Stop."

"Why?" I ask.

"Because this is exactly why I didn't want to tell you guys. I knew you were going to do this."

"Do what?"

"Ask a lot of questions. Stalk him online. Call him out for not liking pie or having facial hair or something."

"He has facial hair?"

"Simon."

"Sorry," I say, leaving the phone on my nightstand. I do get it. Actually, I *really* get it.

We're quiet for a moment.

"I am going to tell them," she says finally.

"Whatever you want to do."

"No, you're right. I'm not trying to be—I don't know." She

sighs again. "I mean, if you have the guts to tell them you're gay, I should . . ."

"You should have the guts to come out as straight."

She cracks a smile. "Something like that. You're funny, bub."

"I try."

FROM: hourtohour.notetonote@gmail.com
TO: bluegreen118@gmail.com
DATE: Dec 25 at 5:12 PM
SUBJECT: Oh holy nightmare

Blue,

I officially had the most epically weird and awful Christmas ever, and most of it I can't even tell you about. Which really sucks. So, yeah. Basically, due to certain mysterious circumstances, I'm now out to my whole family and will soon be out to the whole freaking universe. And I guess that's all I can say about it.

So, it's your turn to distract me, okay? Give me

updates about Little Fetus or the horrifying sexcapades of your parents, or talk about how you think I'm cute. And talk about how you ate too much turkey and now you feel nauseated. Did you know you're the only person I've ever met who uses the word "nauseated" instead of "nauseous"? I finally Googled it, and of course you're right. Of course.

Anyway, I know you're off to Savannah tomorrow, but I hope to God your dad has internet, because I don't think my heart can handle waiting a full week for an email from you. You should give me your number so I can text you. I promise I'm still relatively grammatical over text.

Well, Merry Christmas, Blue. I mean it. And I hope everyone leaves you alone tonight, because that sounds like WAY too much family time. Maybe next year we can sneak away and spend Christmas together somewhere far away, where our families can't find us.

Love,

Jacques

FROM: bluegreen118@gmail.com
TO: hourtohour.notetonote@gmail.com
DATE: Dec 25 at 8:41 PM
SUBJECT: Re: Oh holy nightmare

Oh, Jacques, I'm so sorry. I can't even begin to imagine what mysterious circumstances led to your being outed to the universe, but it doesn't sound pleasant, and I know it's not what you wanted. I wish I could fix it somehow.

No updates on Little Fetus, but suffice it to say that I'm more than a little nauseated now that I've had the pleasure of reading the word "sexcapades" in reference to my parents. And I do think you're cute. You're absurdly cute. I think I spend a little too much time thinking how adorable you are in emails and trying to translate that into a viable mental image for daydreams and the like.

But the texting thing. Ooooh—I don't know. Really, though, you don't have to worry about me going out of town. Internet in Savannah is abundant. You won't even know I'm gone.

Love,

Blue

FROM: hourtohour.notetonote@gmail.com
TO: bluegreen118@gmail.com
DATE: Dec 26 at 1:12 PM
SUBJECT: Daydreams . . . and the like

Specifically, "and the like." Please elaborate.

Love,

Jacques

P.S. Seriously. AND THE LIKE?

FROM: bluegreen118@gmail.com
TO: hourtohour.notetonote@gmail.com
DATE: Dec 26 at 10:42 PM
SUBJECT: Re: Daydreams . . . and the like

And . . . I think I'll shut up now. ☺

Love,

Blue

21

IT'S THE SATURDAY AFTER CHRISTMAS, and Waffle House is packed with old people and kids and random guys sitting at the counter reading actual printed newspapers. People really like to come here for breakfast. I mean, I guess it's technically a breakfast restaurant. Our parents are sleeping in, so it's just my sisters and me, and we're wedged against the wall waiting for a table.

We've been here waiting for twenty minutes, and we're all really just reading our phones. But then Alice says, "Oh, hey." She's looking at this guy sitting in a booth across the room. He looks up and smiles and waves at her. He looks strangely familiar, lanky with curly brown hair.

"Is that . . . ?"

"Simon, no. It's Carter Addison. He graduated a year ahead

of me. He's the nicest guy. Actually, bub, maybe you should talk to him, because—"

"Yeah. I'm leaving," I say. Because I've just figured out why Carter Addison looks familiar.

"What? Why?"

"Because I am." I put my hand out so she can give me the car keys. And then I walk out the door.

I'm sitting in the driver's seat with my iPod plugged in and the heat blasting, trying to pick between Tegan and Sara and the Fleet Foxes. And then the passenger door opens, and Nora slides in.

"So, what's up with you?" she asks.

"Nothing."

"Do you know that guy?"

"What guy?" I ask.

"The one Alice is talking to."

"No."

Nora looks at me. "Then why'd you run away as soon as you saw him?"

I lean back against the headrest and shut my eyes. "I know his brother."

"Who's his brother?"

"You know that creeksecrets post?" I ask.

Nora's eyes get huge. "The one about . . ."

"Yeah."

"Why the heck would he write that?"

I shrug. "Because he likes Abby, and he's a fucking idiot, and he thinks she likes me. I don't even know. It's kind of a long story."

"What an asshole," she says.

"Yeah," I say, looking at her. Nora never cusses.

I'm startled by a loud tap, and I turn around to find Alice's pissed-off face pressed against my window.

"Out," she says. "I'm driving."

I move to the backseat. Whatever.

"So, what the hell was that about?" she asks, eyes flashing in the rearview mirror as she backs out of the parking spot.

"I don't want to talk about it."

"Okay, well, it was a little weird trying to explain to Carter why my brother and sister hauled ass out of the restaurant as soon as they saw him." She pulls onto Roswell Road. "His brother was there, bub. He's in your grade. Marty. Seems like a nice kid."

I don't say anything.

"And I really wanted waffles today," she says grumpily.

"Let it go, Allie," Nora says.

It hangs in the air. Another thing Nora never does is stand up to Alice.

We drive in silence the rest of the way home.

"Simon, the basement fridge. Not later. Not in a minute. Now," my mom says, "or the party is off."

"Mom. Just stop. I'm doing it." I mean, seriously. I have no freaking idea where she got the idea that this is a party. "You do realize that Nick, Leah, and Abby have all been here roughly five zillion times."

"That's fine," she says, "but this time, you're going to make the basement presentable, or else you'll be ringing in the New Year on the couch, smack dab in between your dad and me."

"Or we'll go to Nick's," I mutter.

My mom is halfway up the stairs, but she turns around to catch my eye. "No you won't. And speaking of Nick. Your father and I discussed this, and we want to sit down with you and brainstorm about how we're going to handle him spending the night. I'm not worried about tonight, since the girls will be there, but thinking ahead—"

"Oh my God, Mom, stop. I'm not talking about this right now." Jesus Christ. As if Nick and I can't be in a room together without it turning into frenzied wild sex.

Everyone gets here around six, and we end up packed onto the scraggly basement couch eating pizza and watching reruns of *The Soup*. Our basement is kind of a time capsule, with shaggy, camel-colored carpet and shelves of Barbies and Power Rangers and Pokémon. And there's a bathroom and a little laundry room with a fridge. It's really very cozy and awesome down here.

Leah sits on one end of the couch, and then me, and then Abby—and Nick is on the other end, plucking the strings of

Nora's old guitar. Bieber whimpers from the top of the stairs, and there are footsteps above us, and Abby's telling a story about Taylor. Apparently Taylor said something annoying. I'm trying to laugh in the right places. I think I'm a little overstimulated. Leah is intently focused on the television.

When we finish eating, I run up to open the door for Bieber, who almost trips down the stairs and then flings himself into the room like a cannonball.

Nick mutes the TV and plays a slow, acoustic version of "Brown Eyed Girl." The footsteps above us stop, and I can hear someone say, "Whoa. That's beautiful." One of Nora's friends. Nick's singing voice has this supernatural effect on freshman girls.

Nick sits very, very close to Abby on the couch, and I honestly think I can feel the waves of panic radiating off of Leah. She and I are on the floor now, rubbing Bieber's belly. She hasn't said a word.

"Look at this dog," I say. "No shame. He's like, 'Grope me.'"

I'm feeling this weird pressure to be extra jolly and talkative.

Leah trails her fingers through the curls on Bieber's belly and doesn't respond.

"He has Coke-bottle mouth," I point out.

She looks at me. "I don't think that's a thing."

"No?" I say. Sometimes I forget what's a Spier family invention and what's real.

And then, out of nowhere and without any change in into-nation, she says, "So, they took that post down."

"I know," I say, and there's a nervous flutter in my gut. I haven't talked about the Tumblr post yet with Nick or Leah, though I know they've seen it.

"We don't have to talk about it, though," says Leah.

"It's fine." I glance up at the couch. Abby is leaning back against the cushions with her eyes closed and a smile on her lips. Her head is tilted toward Nick.

"Do you know who wrote it?" Leah says.

"Yes."

She looks at me expectantly.

"It doesn't matter," I say.

We're both quiet for a moment. Nick stops playing, but he hums and taps out a rhythm on the body of the guitar. Leah twists her hair up for a minute and then lets it fall back down, where it hangs past her boobs. I look at her without meeting her eye.

"I know what you're not asking me," I say finally.

She shrugs, smiling slightly.

"I am gay. That part's true."

"Okay," she says.

I realize that Nick has stopped humming.

"But I'm not turning this into a big thing tonight, okay? I don't know. Do you guys want ice cream?" I pull myself up.

"Did you just tell us you're gay?" asks Nick.

"Yes."

"Okay," he says. Abby swats him. "What?"

"That's all you're going to say? 'Okay'?"

"He said not to make a big deal out of it," Nick says. "What am I supposed to say?"

"Say something supportive. I don't know. Or awkwardly hold his hand like I did. Anything."

Nick and I look at each other.

"I'm not holding your hand," I tell him, smiling a little.

"All right"—he nods—"but know that I would."

"Aww, that's better," says Abby.

Leah has been quiet, but she turns to Abby suddenly. "Simon already told you?"

"He, um, yes," says Abby, cutting her eyes to me quickly.

"Oh," says Leah.

And there's this silence.

"Well, I'm getting ice cream," I say, moving toward the stairs, and Bieber collides with my legs in his eagerness to follow.

Hours later, the ice cream's been eaten and the Peach has dropped and my neighbors have finally used up their fireworks. I stare at the ceiling. We have a popcorn ceiling in our basement, and in the darkness, its texture makes shadowy pictures and faces. Everyone brought sleeping bags, but instead of using them, we set up a nest of blankets and sheets and pillows on top of the carpet.

Abby, next to me, is asleep, and I can hear Nick snoring a few feet away. Leah's eyes are closed, but she's breathing like she's awake. I guess it would be wrong of me to nudge her to find out. But then, all of a sudden, she rolls onto her side and sighs, and her eyes snap open.

"Hey," I whisper, rolling my body toward her.

"Hey."

"Are you mad?"

"About what?" she asks.

"About me telling Abby first."

She's quiet for several seconds, and then: "I don't have a right to be mad."

"What are you talking about?"

"This is your thing, Simon."

"But you're entitled to your emotions," I say. I mean, if there's one thing I've learned from having a psychologist for a mother . . .

"This isn't about me, though." She rolls onto her back, folding one arm behind her head.

I don't know what to say to that. We're both quiet for a minute.

"Don't be mad," I say finally.

"Did you think I would have some kind of shitty reaction, or that I wouldn't be okay with it?"

"Of course not. God, Leah, no. Not at all. You're like the most—I mean, you're the one who introduced me to Harry and

Draco. Yeah, that wasn't even a concern."

"Okay, well." Her other hand rests on her stomach over the blankets, and I watch it rise and fall with each breath. "So, who else did you tell?"

"My family," I say. "I mean, Nora saw the Tumblr, so then I had to."

"Right, but I mean, who else other than Abby?"

"No one," I say. But then I close my eyes and think about Blue.

"Then how did it end up on the Tumblr?" she asks.

"Oh, right." I grimace. "Long story," I say, opening my eyes again.

She angles her head toward me, but doesn't reply. I can feel her watching me.

"I think I'm about to fall asleep," I say.

But I'm not. And I don't. Not for hours and hours.

22

FROM: bluegreen118@gmail.com
TO: hourtohour.notetonote@gmail.com
DATE: Jan 1 at 1:19 PM
SUBJECT: Re: auld lang syne

Jacques,

Poor zombie. Hope you're already sleeping again as I type this. The good news is that there are still four days left of vacation, which should clearly be devoted exclusively to sleeping and writing to me.

I missed you last night. The party thing was fine. It was at my stepmother's grandmother's house, and she's about ninety years old, so we were back home in front of the TV by nine. Oh, and Mr. Sexual Awakening was there. His wife is extremely pregnant. She and my stepmom were comparing ultrasound photos of their fetuses at dinner. Our Little Fetus looks like your basic cute little alien with a big head and tiny limbs. You can actually see his or her nose, so that was kind of cool. But, unfortunately, Mr. Sexual Awakening's wife had a 3D ultrasound picture. All I can say, Jacques, is that there are some things you can't un-see.

Any plans until school starts again?

Love,

Blue

FROM: hourtohour.notetonote@gmail.com
TO: bluegreen118@gmail.com
DATE: Jan 1 at 5:31 PM
SUBJECT: Re: auld lang syne

Zombie is right. I'm a freaking mess. We just got back from Target, and I actually fell asleep in the car on the way home. Which, thankfully, my mom was the one driving. But you have to understand that Target is like five minutes away from my house. How weird is that? So now I feel kind of strange and groggy and disoriented, and I think my parents are going to want to do dinner tonight As a Family.

Ugh.

Sorry to hear about the trauma of the 3D ultrasound,

from which you so kindly tried to spare me the details. Unfortunately, I'm a freaking idiot with very little self-control when it comes to Google Images. So now it's forever seared into my memory as well. Oh, the miracle of life. You may also want to look up "reborn dolls." Seriously, go do it.

Nothing much going on here this weekend, other than the fact that every freaking thing in the universe reminds me of you. Target is full of you. Did you know they make these big massive Sharpies called Super Sharpies? And then there's superglue, obviously. It's like an office supply Justice League. I seriously came this close to buying them, just so I could text you pictures of their crime-fighting selves. I would have made capes for them and everything. Except SOMEONE still doesn't want to exchange numbers.

Love,

Jacques

FROM: bluegreen118@gmail.com
TO: hourtohour.notetonote@gmail.com
DATE: Jan 2 at 10:13 AM
SUBJECT: Reborn

I think you've rendered me speechless. I just read the Wikipedia article, and I'm looking through pictures now. I kind of can't stop looking at them. You might have found the creepiest thing on the entire internet, Jacques.

And I seriously laughed out loud at your crime-fighting office supply Justice League. I wish I could have seen them. But about the texting thing—all I can say is that I'm really sorry. The idea of exchanging phone numbers just terrifies me. It does. It's just the idea that you could call me and hear my voice mail message and KNOW. I don't know what to say, Jacques. I'm just not ready for you to know who I am. I know it's stupid, and honestly, at this point, I spend about half my waking hours imagining us meeting in person for the first time. But I can't think of a way for that to happen without everything changing. I think I'm scared to lose you.

Does that make sense? Don't hate me.

Love,

Blue

FROM: hourtohour.notetonote@gmail.com
TO: bluegreen118@gmail.com
DATE: Jan 2 at 12:25 PM
SUBJECT: Re: Reborn

I guess I'm trying to understand where you're coming from with the texting thing. You have to trust me! Yes, I'm nosy, but I'm not going to call you if you're not comfortable with it. I don't mean for this to be a big deal. And I don't want to stop emailing. I just also want to be able to text you like a normal person.

And YES, I want to meet in person. And obviously that would change things—but I think I'm kind of ready for them to change. So maybe this is a big deal. I don't know. I want to know your friends' names and what you do after school and all the things you haven't been telling me. I want to know what your voice sounds like.

Not until you're ready, though. And I could never hate you. You're not going to lose me. Just think about it. Okay?

Love,

Jacques

23

IT'S THE FIRST DAY BACK at school, and I honestly consider spending the entire day in the parking lot. I can't explain it. I thought I would be fine. But now that I'm here, I can't seem to get out of the car. I feel a little sick just thinking about it.

Nora says, "I really don't think anyone is going to remember."

I shrug.

"It was on there for, what, three days? And that was over a week ago."

"Four days," I say.

"I don't even think people really read the Tumblr."

We walk in through the atrium together just as the first bell is ringing. People are stampeding and pushing down the stairs. No one seems to pay any particular attention to me—and for all of Nora's reassurances, I can see that she's as relieved as I am.

I move with the crowd, working my way toward my locker, and I think I'm finally starting to relax. A couple of people wave at me like normal. Garrett from my lunch table nods and says, "What's up, Spier?"

I toss my backpack into my locker and pull out my books for English and French. No one has slid any homophobic notes into the slats of my locker, which is good. No one's etched the word "fag" into my locker yet either, which is even better. I'm almost ready to believe that things have gotten a little better at Creekwood. Or that no one saw Martin's Tumblr post after all.

Martin. God, I don't even want to think about having to see his stupid evil face. And of course he's in my first fucking period.

I guess there's still this quiet pulse of dread when I think about seeing Martin again.

I'm trying to just breathe.

As I'm walking into the language arts wing, this football guy I hardly recognize almost runs directly into me coming down the stairs. I step back to steady myself, but he puts his hand on my shoulder and looks me right in the eye.

"Why, hello there," he says.

"Hi . . ."

Then he grabs me by the cheeks and pulls my face in like he's going to kiss me. "Mwah!" He grins, and his face is so close I can feel the heat of his breath. And all around me, people laugh like fucking Elmo.

I yank my body away from him, cheeks burning. "Where are you going, Spier?" someone says. "McGregor wants a turn." And everyone starts laughing again. I mean, I don't even know these people. I don't know why in God's name this is funny to them.

In English class, Martin won't look at me.

But all through the day, Leah and Abby are like freaking pit bulls, throwing down the stink-eye in all directions whenever anyone even looks at me funny. I mean, it's really pretty sweet. And it isn't a total disaster. Some people sort of whisper and laugh. And a couple of people randomly give me these huge smiles in the hallway, whatever that means. These two lesbian girls I don't even know come up to me at my locker and hug me and give me their phone numbers. And at least a dozen straight kids make a point of telling me that they support me. One girl even confirms that Jesus still loves me.

It's a ton of attention. It kind of makes my head spin.

At lunch, the girls take it upon themselves to discuss and evaluate the fifty million guys they apparently think are boyfriend prospects for me. And it's all perfectly fucking hilarious until Anna makes some joke about Nick being gay. Which causes Nick to drape himself all over Abby. So then Leah's irreparably pissed off.

"We should find Leah a boyfriend, too!" says Abby, which honestly makes me cringe. I love Abby, and I know she's just trying to lighten the mood, but Jesus Christ. There are times when she manages to say the exact opposite of the right thing.

"No fucking thank you, Abby," Leah says, in this sickeningly pleasant tone. Except her eyes are like crackling fireballs of rage. She stands up abruptly, pushing her chair in without a word.

As soon as she leaves, Garrett looks at Bram, and Bram bites his lip. Which I'm pretty sure is straight-dude code for Bram likes Leah.

And I don't know why, but it pisses me the fuck off.

"If you like her, just ask her out," I say to Bram, and he immediately starts blushing.

I don't even know. I'm just so sick of straight people who can't get their shit together.

Somehow, I manage to survive until rehearsal. It's the first day without scripts, and we jump right into running some of the big group scenes. There's an accompanist at rehearsal now, and people are really focused and energized. I guess it's just dawned on everyone that opening night is in less than a month.

But partway through the pickpocket song, Martin suddenly stops singing.

And then Abby says, "You're fucking kidding me."

And everyone is quiet for a minute, looking at each other. Looking everywhere but at me. For a minute, I'm confused, but then I follow Abby's gaze to the back of the auditorium. And there's this pair of random dudes in front of the double helixes who look a little familiar. I think they were in my health class last year. One of them is wearing a hoodie and fake glasses and a skirt over his khakis, and they're both holding giant poster board signs.

The first guy's sign says, "How u doin' Simon?"

And the guy in the skirt's sign says, "WHAT WHAT—IN THA BUTT!"

The guys are grinding and some other people peek through the doorway laughing. This one girl laughs so hard she's clutching her stomach, and someone says, "Stop, y'all! Oh my God, y'all are so bad." But she's laughing, too.

It's strange—I'm not even blushing. I feel like I'm watching this happen from a million miles away.

Then, suddenly, Taylor freaking Metternich, of all people, runs down the steps at the side of the stage and down the aisle of the auditorium. And Abby is right behind her.

"Aww shit," says the guy in the skirt, and the other guy giggles. And then they haul ass out of the auditorium, letting the door slam shut.

Taylor and Abby burst through behind them, and there's this huge commotion of yelling and footsteps. Ms. Albright runs after them and the rest of us just kind of stand there. Except somehow I end up sitting on one of the platforms, smushed in between two senior girls who have their arms around my shoulders.

I catch a glimpse of Martin, and it looks like he's been crumpled. His hands are covering his face.

A few minutes later, Abby bursts back through the door, followed by Ms. Albright, who has her arm around Taylor. And Taylor is splotchy and flushed, like she's been crying. I watch as Ms. Albright guides Taylor to the front row, lets her sit next to Cal, and then kneels down in front of them for a minute to talk to them.

Abby walks straight back up the stairs to me, shaking her head.

"People suck," she says.

I nod slowly.

"I honestly thought Taylor was going to hit one of those guys."

Taylor Metternich. Seriously. Almost hitting some guy. "You're kidding me."

"No, really," Abby says. "I almost did, too."

"Good," says one of the senior girls, Brianna.

I look briefly at Taylor. She's leaning back in her chair with her eyes closed, just breathing. "But she didn't hit him, right? I don't want her to get in trouble because of me."

"Oh my gosh. Don't even say that. None of this is your fault, Simon," Abby says. "Those guys are douchebags."

"They can't get away with that," says Brianna. "Don't we have a zero tolerance policy?"

But Creekwood's zero tolerance bullying policy is enforced about as strictly as the freaking dress code.

"Don't worry," says Abby. "They're sitting in Ms. Knight's

office right now. I think their mommies are getting called."

And sure enough, moments later, Ms. Albright gathers everyone in a circle on the stage. "So, I'm sorry you guys had to see that." She's looking at me especially. "It was beyond disrespectful and inappropriate, and I want you to know that I take this extremely seriously." She pauses for a moment, and I look at her. And I realize that Ms. Albright is absolutely livid. "So, unfortunately, we're going to have to end here for the day so I can deal with this. I know this is unexpected, and I apologize to all of you. We'll pick back up tomorrow."

Then she walks over to me and squats down in front of my platform. "You okay, Simon?"

I feel myself blush a little bit. "I'm fine."

"Okay, well," she says quietly. "Just know that those assholes are getting suspended. I'm not even kidding. I will make it my hill to die on."

Abby, Brianna, and I just stare at her.

It's the first time I've ever heard a teacher cuss.

So, Abby's stuck at school until the late bus leaves, and I feel really terrible about that. I don't know. It just feels like all of this is a little bit my fault. But Abby tells me not to be ridiculous, and that she can kill the time by watching the soccer tryouts.

"I'll come with you," I say.

"Simon, seriously. Go home and relax."

"But what if I want to heckle Nick?"

She can't argue with that. We cut through the science hallway and down the back stairs, toward the music room, where there appears to be some pretty badass drum and guitar business going on behind closed doors. They almost sound professional, except the vocals are strange and random, like the lower part of a harmony. Abby dances to the drumbeat for a minute as we pass, and then we bust out the side door near the soccer fields.

It's really freaking chilly out, and I have no idea how these soccer kids are surviving with their shorts and bare legs. The girls are on the close field, and it's dozens of ponytails in motion. We walk past them to get to the boys, who are running around orange cones and kicking soccer balls back and forth to each other. Abby lets her arms hang over the side of the fence, leaning in to watch. A lot of the guys are wearing these long-sleeved spandex shirts under their soccer shirts, and a few of them are wearing shin guards. And they all have those soccer calves. So it's kind of a nice view.

The coach blows his whistle and all the guys gather around him for a minute while he talks. And then they disperse, passing around bottles of water and dribbling balls and stretching their legs. Nick jogs over to us right away, pink-faced and grinning, and then Garrett and Bram come, too.

"It's weird that they're making you try out again," says Abby.

"I know," says Garrett, panting. He's sweaty and red, and

his eyes look electric blue. "It's like a formality. Kind of. Just to see"—he pauses to catch his breath—"like, where he wants to put us."

"Oh, okay," she says.

"So, what, you're just blowing off rehearsal?" Nick says, smiling at Abby.

"Pretty much," she says. "I was like—*yeah*. I'm gonna go ogle soccer boys now." She leans in closer to Nick, grinning up at him.

"Oh, really?" says Nick.

It's starting to feel like I shouldn't be listening in on this.

"So, it's going well?" I ask, turning to Garrett and Bram.

"Pretty well," says Garrett, and Bram nods.

It's funny that I eat lunch with these guys five days a week, but we never really hang out apart from the group. I kind of wish I knew them better. Even if Bram doesn't have his shit together about Leah. I don't know. For one thing, both Garrett and Bram have been totally cool about the gay thing all day, which I guess I didn't expect from a bunch of athletes.

Also, Bram is cute. Like, really, really cute. He stands a foot or so back from the fence, totally sweaty, with a white turtleneck under his soccer shirt. And he's not really talking, but he has very expressive brown eyes. And light brown skin and soft dark curls and cute, knobbly hands.

"What happens if you really screw up the audition?" I ask. "Can they kick you off the team?"

"Audition?" asks Bram, smiling so quietly. And when he looks at me, I feel this happy sort of ache.

"Tryouts." I blush. And I smile back at him. And then I feel a little guilty.

Because of Blue. Even though he's still not ready. Even though he's just words on a laptop screen.

It's just that I also kind of feel like he's my boyfriend.

I don't even know.

So, maybe it's the winter air or maybe it's soccer boy calves, but after everything that's happened today, I'm actually in a pretty decent mood.

Until I get to the parking lot. Because Martin Addison is leaning against my car.

"Where have you been?" he says.

I wait for him to move. I mean, I don't even want to look at him.

"Can we talk for a second?" he asks.

"I don't have anything to say to you," I say.

"Okay, well." He sighs, and I can actually see his breath. "Simon, just—I seriously owe you an apology."

I just kind of stand there.

He stretches his arms forward, cracking his knuckles under his gloves. "God, I'm just. I'm just so sorry. What happened in there. I didn't know that would—I mean, I didn't think people still did shit like that."

195

"Right, who'd have guessed? Because Shady Creek is just so progressive."

Martin shakes his head. "I just seriously didn't think it would be such a big thing."

I don't even know what to say to that.

"Look, I'm sorry, all right? I was pissed off. The whole Abby thing. I wasn't thinking. And then my brother basically ripped me a new one, and I was just . . . I just feel like shit, okay. And I deleted those screenshots ages ago. I swear to God. So can you please just say something?"

I mean, I almost start laughing. "What the fuck do you want me to say?"

"I don't know," he says. "I'm just trying—"

"Okay, how about this? I think you're an asshole. I think you're a huge fucking asshole. I mean, don't even fucking pretend you didn't know this would happen. You blackmailed me. This was—I mean, wasn't that the whole goddamn point? Humiliating me?"

He shakes his head and opens his mouth to reply, but I cut him off.

"And you know what? You don't get to say it's not a big thing. This is a big fucking thing, okay? This was supposed to be—this is mine. I'm supposed to decide when and where and who knows and how I want to say it." Suddenly, my throat gets thick. "So, yeah, you took that from me. And then you brought Blue into it? Seriously? You fucking suck, Martin. I mean, I don't even want to look at you."

He's crying. He's trying not to, but he's seriously, full-on crying. And my heart sort of twists.

"So can you just step away from my car," I say, "and leave me the fuck alone?"

He nods, puts his head down, and walks away quickly.

I get in my car. And turn it on. And then I just start sobbing.

24

FROM: hourtohour.notetonote@gmail.com
TO: bluegreen118@gmail.com
DATE: Jan 5 at 7:19 PM
SUBJECT: Snow!

Blue,

Look outside! I can't believe it. Actual flurries on the first day back at school. Any chance this will turn into another Snowpocalypse? Because I'd be really, really cool with having the rest of the week off. God, it's been a weird fucking day. I don't even know what to tell you other than the fact that being out to the universe is completely exhausting.

Seriously, I'm just totally spent.

Do you ever get so angry you start crying? And do you ever feel guilty for getting angry? Tell me I'm not weird.

Love,

Jacques

FROM: bluegreen118@gmail.com
TO: hourtohour.notetonote@gmail.com
DATE: Jan 5 at 10:01 PM
SUBJECT: Re: Snow!

I don't think you're weird. It sounds like you've had a shitty day, and I wish there was a way for me to make it better. Have you tried eating your feelings? I hear Oreos can be therapeutic. Also, I'm not really one to talk here, but you really shouldn't feel guilty for getting angry—especially if I'm right about what's making you angry.

Okay. I have to tell you something, and I think it may be something upsetting. I actually don't think my timing could be worse, but I can't think of any way around it, so here goes:

Jacques, I'm almost positive I know who you are.

Love,

Blue

FROM: hourtohour.notetonote@gmail.com
TO: bluegreen118@gmail.com
DATE: Jan 6 at 7:12 PM
SUBJECT: Really?

Wow. Okay. Not upsetting. But this is kind of a big moment, right?

Actually, I think I know who you are, too. So, just for fun, I'm guessing:

1. You share a first name with a former US president.

2. And a comic book character.

3. You like to draw.

4. You have blue eyes.

5. And you once pushed me down a dark hallway in a rolling chair.

Love,

Jacques

FROM: bluegreen118@gmail.com
TO: hourtohour.notetonote@gmail.com
DATE: Jan 6 at 9:43 PM
SUBJECT: Re: Really?

1. Actually, yes.

2. Kind of an obscure character, but yes.

3. Not really.

4. No.

5. Definitely not.

I'm sorry, but I don't think I'm the person you think I am.

—Blue

FROM: hourtohour.notetonote@gmail.com

TO: bluegreen118@gmail.com

DATE: Jan 6 at 11:18 PM

SUBJECT: Re: Really?

Well, I was doing great there until the end.

So yeah. Wow. I guess I was dead wrong. I'm sorry, Blue. I hope that doesn't make things weird between us.

Anyway, maybe you'll guess wrong about me, too? And then we would be even? Though I'm guessing you saw the thing on the Tumblr. God, I feel like such an idiot.

Love,

Jacques

FROM: bluegreen118@gmail.com

TO: hourtohour.notetonote@gmail.com

DATE: Jan 7 at 7:23 AM

SUBJECT: Re: Really?

On the Tumblr—you mean creeksecrets? I honestly don't think I've looked at it since August. What was on there? Anyway, you don't have to feel like an idiot. It's fine. But I really don't think I'm wrong.

Jacques a dit. Right?

—Blue

25

SO, YEAH. I'VE BEEN CARELESS. I guess I left a trail of clues, and I shouldn't be surprised that Blue put them together. Maybe I kind of wanted him to.

Jacques a dit is "Simon Says" in French, by the way. And it's obviously not as clever as I thought it was.

But I really fucked it all up with the Cal thing. I mean, honest to God, I'm a freaking moron. I seriously don't know what I was thinking. Blue-green eyes and a gut feeling that Blue was Cal? It's classic Simon logic. No surprise that I was horribly, epically wrong.

I spend about twenty minutes staring at Blue's email on my laptop that morning before writing back. And then I sit there refreshing the browser over and over again until Nora bangs on my door. We get to school five minutes early anyway. So I spend five more minutes sitting in my parked car staring at my email again on my phone.

I mean, he didn't see the Tumblr post. So that's something. That's a huge something, actually.

I walk in just as the bell is ringing, and I'm in a serious daze. It's lucky that my hands seem to know my locker combination, because my brain has checked out. People talk to me, and I nod along, but absolutely nothing penetrates. I think a couple of pickup truck guys change my name to Semen Queer. I don't know. I don't even think I care.

All I can think about is Blue. I guess a part of me is hoping for something today. Some kind of reveal. I can't believe Blue wouldn't tell me, now that he knows who I am. Which means I'm looking for it everywhere. Leah passes me a note in French class, and my heart starts pounding, thinking it could be a message from him. *Meet me by your locker. I'm ready.* Something like that. But it turns out to be an impressively realistic, manga-style drawing of our French teacher performing fellatio on a baguette. Speaking of things that remind me of Blue.

And when someone taps me on the shoulder in history class, my heart is a pinball. But it's just Abby. "Shh, listen to this."

I listen, and it's Taylor explaining to Martin that she wasn't necessarily *trying* to get a gap between her thighs, but it's just her *metabolism*, and she didn't even *realize* that some girls try to get the gap on purpose. Martin nods and scratches his head and looks bored.

"She can't help her metabolism, Simon," Abby says.

"Apparently not." Taylor may be an undercover, bully-fighting ninja, but she's still kind of awful.

And then Abby nudges me again later to pick up a pen she dropped, and it's pinballs all over again. I can't even help it. There's just this thread of anticipation that I can't seem to quell.

So when the school day ends and nothing extraordinary has happened, it's a tiny heartbreak. It's like eleven o'clock on the night of your birthday, when you realize no one's throwing you a surprise party after all.

On Thursday after rehearsal, Cal very casually mentions that he's bisexual. And that maybe we should hang out sometime. It catches me off guard. All I can do is sort of gape at him. Sweet, slow-moving Cal, with his hipster bangs and his ocean eyes.

But the thing is, he's not Blue.

Blue, who's barely been returning my emails.

Amazingly, I forget all about Cal until the next day in English class. Mr. Wise is out of the room when I walk in, and the nerds are restless. A couple of people are arguing about Shakespeare, and then someone stands on a chair and basically bellows Hamlet's soliloquy into this other dude's ear. The couch is especially crowded for some reason. Nick is perched on Abby's lap.

She leans her head out from behind Nick's torso and calls me over. She's beaming. "Simon, I was just telling Nick about what happened in rehearsal yesterday."

"Yes," says Nick. "Who, pray tell, is this Calvin fellow?"

I shake my head, blushing. "No one. He's from drama club."

"He's no one?" Nick tilts his head. "Are you sure? Because this one tells me—"

"Shut up!" says Abby, clamping a hand over his mouth. "I'm sorry, Simon. I'm just so excited for you. It wasn't a secret, right?"

"No, but it's not—it wasn't anything."

"Well, we'll see," Abby says, with this smug little smile.

I don't know how to explain to her that, for all intents and purposes, I'm already taken. By someone who evidently shares a first name with a president and an obscure cartoon character, and doesn't like to draw, and doesn't have blue eyes, and has not yet pushed me in a rolling chair.

Someone who seemed to like me better before he knew who I was.

26

FROM: hourtohour.notetonote@gmail.com
TO: bluegreen118@gmail.com
DATE: Jan 9 at 8:23 PM
SUBJECT: Re: Really?

I mean, I get it. Just because I was careless doesn't mean it's fair to push you into revealing yourself before you're ready. And believe me, I'm the freaking expert on that. But now you know my superhero identity and I don't know yours—and that's weird, right?

I don't know what else to say. Anonymity served a purpose for us, and I get that. But now I want to know you for real.

Love,

Simon

FROM: bluegreen118@gmail.com

TO: hourtohour.notetonote@gmail.com

DATE: Jan 10 at 2:12 PM

SUBJECT: Re: Really?

Well, Blue is kind of my superhero identity, so you're really talking about my civilian identity. But that's obviously miles away from the point. It's just that I don't know what else to say. I'm truly sorry, Simon.

Anyway, it looks like things are working out the way you wanted them to. So, good for you.

—Blue

FROM: hourtohour.notetonote@gmail.com

TO: bluegreen118@gmail.com

DATE: Jan 10 at 3:45 PM

SUBJECT: Re: Really?

Working out the way I wanted them to? What the heck are you talking about?

???

—Simon

FROM: hourtohour.notetonote@gmail.com
TO: bluegreen118@gmail.com
DATE: Jan 12 at 12:18 AM
SUBJECT: Re: Really?

Seriously, I don't know what in God's holy name you're talking about, because pretty much nothing seems to be working out the way I want it to.

Okay—I get that you don't want to text. And you don't want to meet in person. Fine. But I hate that everything's different now, even in our emails. I mean, yes, it's an awkward situation. I guess what I'm trying to say is that I really do understand if you don't find me attractive or whatever. I'll get over it. But you're kind of my best friend in a lot of ways, and I really want to keep you.

Can we just pretend none of this ever happened and go back to normal?

—Simon

27

WHICH ISN'T TO SAY I'M going to stop thinking about it.

I spend all of Sunday in my room switching between the Smiths and Kid Cudi at top volume, and I don't even care if that's too random for my parents. Their minds can stay blown for all I care. I try to get Bieber to sit with me on my bed, but he keeps pacing, so I put him out in the hallway. But then he whines to come back in.

"Nora, get Bieber," I yell over the music, but she doesn't answer. So I text it to her.

She texts back: *Do it yourself. I'm not home.*

Where are you? I really hate this new thing where Nora's never home.

But she doesn't text back. And I'm feeling too heavy and listless to get up and ask my mom.

I stare up at the ceiling fan. So Blue isn't going to tell me, which means I have to figure it out myself. I've been running through the same list of clues in my head for a few hours now.

Same first name as a president and an obscure comic book character. Half-Jewish. Excellent grammar. Easily nauseated. Virgin. Doesn't really go to parties. Likes superheroes. Likes Reese's and Oreos (i.e., not an idiot). Divorced parents. Big brother to a fetus. Dad lives in Savannah. Dad's an English teacher. Mom's an epidemiologist.

The problem is, I'm beginning to realize I hardly know anything about anyone. I mean I generally know who's a virgin. But I don't have a clue whether most people's parents are divorced, or what their parents do for a living. I mean, Nick's parents are doctors. But I don't know what Leah's mom does, and I don't even know what the deal is with her dad, because Leah never talks about him. I have no idea why Abby's dad and brother still live in DC. And these are my best friends. I've always thought of myself as nosy, but I guess I'm just nosy about stupid stuff.

It's actually really terrible, now that I think about it.

But it's pointless. Because even if I crack the code somehow, it doesn't change the fact that Blue isn't interested. He found out who I am. And now it's broken, and I don't know what to do. I told him I understand if he's not attracted to me. I tried to make it sound like I don't mind.

But I don't understand. And I totally mind.

This fucking sucks, actually.

On Monday, there's a plastic grocery bag looped through the handle of my locker, and my first thought is that it's a jockstrap. I guess I'm picturing some stupid athlete giving me a sweaty jockstrap as a grand gesture of humiliation and douchery. I don't know. Maybe I'm paranoid.

Anyway, it's not a jockstrap. It's a jersey cotton T-shirt with the logo from Elliott Smith's *Figure 8*. Resting on top is a note that says this: *"I'm assuming Elliott understands that you would have made it to his shows if you could have."*

The note is written on blue-green construction paper in perfectly straight print—not a hint of slant. And of course he remembered the second "t" in Elliott. Because he's Blue. He would.

The shirt is a medium, and it's vintage soft, and everything about it is entirely, amazingly perfect. For one wild moment, I think I'll find a bathroom and change into it right now.

But I stop myself. Because it's still weird. Because I still don't know who he is. And the idea of him seeing me in the shirt makes me really self-conscious for some reason. So, I keep it neatly folded in the bag, and then I put the bag in my locker. And then I float through the day in a jittery, happy daze.

But then I get to rehearsal, and there's this sudden seismic shift. I don't even know. It has something to do with Cal. He's leaving the auditorium to go to the bathroom just as I arrive, and he stops for a minute in the doorway. And then we sort of smile at each other and both keep walking.

It's nothing. It's not even a moment. But there's this sunburst of anger that starts in my chest. I mean, I can actually physically feel it. And it's all because Blue is a goddamn coward. He'll hang a fucking T-shirt from the door of my locker, but he doesn't have the guts to approach me in person.

He's ruined everything. Now there's this adorable guy with awesome bangs who maybe even likes me, and it's completely pointless. I'm not ever going to hang out with Cal. I'll probably never have a boyfriend. I'm too busy trying not to be in love with someone who isn't real.

The rest of the week is this exhausting blur. Rehearsals are an extra hour every night now, which means I'm having vertical dinners over the kitchen counter and trying not to drop crumbs in my textbooks. My dad says he misses me this week, which really just means he's sad about having to TiVo *The Bachelor.* I haven't heard from Blue at all, and I haven't emailed him either.

Friday's a big day, I guess. It's a week before opening night, and we're performing *Oliver!* twice in full costume during the school day: freshmen and seniors in the morning, and juniors and sophomores in the afternoon. We have to be at school an hour early to get ready, which means Nora gets stuck hanging out in the auditorium. But Cal puts her to work, and she seems content taping up cast photos on the wall of the atrium, next to some screenshots from the Mark Lester movie version and a super-enlarged list of the cast and crew.

Backstage is the best kind of chaos. Props are missing and people wander around partially in costume, and the various Creekwood music prodigies are in the orchestra pit running through the overture. It's actually our first time doing the play with the orchestra, and just hearing them practice makes it seem that much more real. Taylor is already dressed and in makeup, and she stands in the wings doing some awkward vocal warm-up that she invented herself. Martin can't find his beard.

I wear my first of three costumes, which is this scraggly, oversized oatmeal-colored shirt and baggy drawstring pants and no shoes. A couple of the girls put some junk in my hair to make it messy, which is basically like putting high heels on a giraffe. And then they tell me I have to wear eyeliner, which I absolutely detest. It's bad enough that they want me to wear my contacts.

The only person I trust to do it is Abby, who puts me in a chair by the window in the girls' dressing room. None of the girls care that I'm in there, and it's not even about me being gay. The dressing rooms are just generally a total free-for-all, and anyone who cares about privacy at all changes in the bathroom.

"Close them," she says.

I shut my eyes, and Abby's fingertips tug softly next to my eyelid. Then there's this scritch scritch feeling like I'm being drawn on, because I'm not even kidding—eyeliner actually comes in a freaking pencil.

"Do I look ridiculous?"

"Not at all," she says. She's quiet for a minute.

"I have a question for you."

"Yep?"

"Why is your dad in DC?"

"Well, he's still looking for a job here."

"Oh," I say. And then, "Are he and your brother moving down here?"

She swipes her fingertip over the edge of my eyelid.

"My dad is, eventually," she says. "My brother's a freshman at Howard."

And then she nods and tugs the other eyelid taut and starts on that one.

"I feel stupid for not knowing that," I say.

"Why would you feel stupid? I guess I never mentioned it."

"But I never asked."

The worst part is when she does the bottom, because I have to hold my eyes open and the pencil goes right onto the edge, and I freaking hate it when things touch my eyes.

"Don't blink," says Abby.

"I'm trying not to."

Her tongue sticks out a little bit between her lips, and she smells sort of like vanilla extract and talcum powder.

"All right. Look at me."

"Am I done?" I ask.

She pauses, appraising me. "Basically," she says. But then

she attacks me like a ninja with powders and brushes.

"Whoa," says Brianna, passing through.

"I know," says Abby. "Simon, don't take this the wrong way, but you look kind of ridiculously hot."

Which leads to me almost getting whiplash from turning my head toward the mirror so fast.

"What do you think?" she says, grinning behind me.

"I look weird," I say.

It's a little bit surreal. I'm barely used to my face without glasses anyway, and with the eyeliner, the overall impression is: EYES.

"Wait till Cal sees," Abby says under her breath.

I shake my head. "He's not . . ."

But I can't finish the thought. I can't stop looking at myself.

The first performance of the day goes surprisingly smoothly, though most of the seniors use it as an opportunity to sleep in an extra two hours. But the freshmen are pretty geeked to be missing first and second period, which makes them the most wildly awesome audience ever. The exhaustion from the week falls away, and I'm carried forward by adrenaline, laughter, and applause.

We change out of our costumes, and everyone is really happy and amped up as Ms. Albright gives us notes. And then we're released for regular lunch with the non-theater civilians. I'm a little bit excited to be going to lunch with my stage makeup still intact. And not just because of my supposed ridiculous hotness. It's just kind of awesome to be marked as part of the ensemble.

Leah is obsessed with the eye makeup. "Holy fuck, Simon."

"Don't you love it?" says Abby.

I feel this tug of self-consciousness. It doesn't help that Cute Bram is looking at me.

"I had no idea your eyes were so gray," Leah says. She turns to Nick, incredulously. "Did you know?"

"I did not," Nick affirms.

"Like, they're kind of charcoal around the edges," she says, "and lighter in the middle, and then almost silver around the pupil. But dark silver."

"Fifty shades of gray," says Abby.

"Gross," Leah says, and she and Abby exchange smiles.

It's actually kind of a miracle.

We meet back in the auditorium after lunch so Ms. Albright can remind us how awesome we are, and then we head backstage to put our costumes back on for the first scene. It's a little rushed this time, but I think I kind of like that. The orchestra warms up again, and chatter rises in the auditorium as the sophomores and juniors file into the seats.

This is the one I'm excited about. Because it's my own class. Because Blue will be out there somewhere. And as pissed as I am at him, I still like the idea of him being in the audience.

I stand with Abby, peeking out at the audience through a crack in the curtains. "Nick's here," she says, pointing toward the left side of the auditorium. "And Leah. And Morgan and Anna are right behind them."

"Shouldn't we be starting soon?"

"I don't know," says Abby.

I turn to peek over my shoulder, where Cal is stationed at a desk in the wings. He wears headphones and a little microphone that curves down in front of his mouth, and at the moment, he's frowning and nodding. And then he stands up and walks out toward the auditorium.

I look back out into the audience. The houselights are still on, and people are hoisted up onto the backs of their chairs, yelling across the room to each other. A couple of people have crumpled their programs into balls, and are lobbing them toward the ceiling.

"Our audience awaits," says Abby, grinning into the semi-darkness.

And then there's a hand on my shoulder. It's Ms. Albright.

"Simon, would you come with me for a minute?"

"Sure," I say. Abby and I exchange shrugs.

I follow Ms. Albright to the dressing room, where Martin is flopped all over a plastic chair, winding the end of his beard around his finger.

"Go ahead and grab a seat." She shuts the door behind us. Martin shoots me a look like he's asking me what the hell this is all about.

I ignore him.

"So, something just happened," Ms. Albright says, slowly, "and I wanted to talk to you guys about it first. I think you have a right to know."

Right away, I get this sinking feeling. Ms. Albright stares past us for a second, and then she sort of blinks herself back into the moment. She looks completely exhausted. "Someone altered the cast list out in the atrium," she says, "and they changed the names of both of your characters to something inappropriate."

"To what?" asks Martin.

But I know immediately. Martin plays Fagin. I'm listed as "Fagin's boy." I guess some genius thought it would be hilarious to cross out a couple of "i"s and "n"s.

"Oh," he says, putting it together a moment later. We exchange glances, and he rolls his eyes, and for a moment, it's almost like we're friends again.

"Yup. And there was a drawing. Anyway," Ms. Albright says, "Cal's taking it down now, and in a minute, I'll step out there to have a quick chat with your lovely classmates."

"Are you canceling the show?" asks Martin, hands on his cheeks.

"Would you like me to?"

Martin looks at me.

"No. It's fine. Just—don't cancel it." My heart is pounding.

I feel—I don't know. I don't want to think about any of this. But the one thing I'm sure about is this: the thought of Blue not seeing the play is kind of devastating.

I wish it didn't matter.

Martin buries his face in his hands. "I'm so, so sorry, Spier."

"Just stop it." I stand up. "Okay? Stop."

I guess I'm getting a little fucking tired of this. I'm trying not to let it touch me. I shouldn't care if stupid people call me a stupid word, and I shouldn't care what people think of me. But I always care. Abby puts her arm around my shoulders, and we watch through the wings as Ms. Albright steps onto the stage.

"Hi," she says into the microphone. She's holding a notebook, and she's not smiling. Not even a little bit. "Some of you know me. I'm Ms. Albright, the theater teacher."

Someone from the audience whistles suggestively, and a few people giggle.

"So I know you're all here to see an exclusive sneak preview of a pretty awesome play. We've got a great cast and crew, and we're eager to get started. But before we get to that, I want to spend a couple of minutes reviewing Creekwood's bullying policy together."

Something about the words "review" and "policy" just shuts people down. There's this drone of quiet conversation and denim rustling against seats. Someone shrieks with laughter, and someone else yells, "QUIET!" So then a bunch of people start giggling.

"I'll wait," Ms. Albright says. And when the laughter dies down, she holds up the notebook. "Does anyone recognize this?"

"Your diary?" Some asshole sophomore.

Ms. Albright ignores him. "This is the Creekwood handbook, which you should have read and signed at the beginning of the year."

Everyone immediately stops listening. God. It's got to freaking suck to be a teacher. I sit cross-legged on the floor backstage, surrounded by girls. Ms. Albright keeps talking and reading from the handbook and talking some more. When she says something about zero tolerance, Abby squeezes my hand. The minutes just drag.

I feel so totally blank right now.

Eventually, Ms. Albright steps back into the wings, slamming the handbook down on a chair. "Let's do this," she says. There's this scary-intense look in her eyes.

The houselights start to dim, and the first notes of the overture rise up from the pit. I step out of the wings and onto the stage. My limbs feel really heavy. I kind of want to go home and crawl into bed with my iPod.

But the curtains start to open.

And I keep moving forward.

28

BUT LATER, IN THE DRESSING room, it hits me.

Martin Van Buren. Our eighth fucking president.

But there's no way. It's not possible.

My washcloth falls to the floor. All around me, girls tug hats off and let their hair down and scrub foamy soap onto their faces and zip up garment bags. A door bursts open somewhere, and there's a sudden shriek of laughter.

My mind is racing. What do I know about Martin? What do I know about Blue?

Martin is smart, obviously. Is he smart enough to be Blue? I have no idea if Martin is half-Jewish. I mean, he could be. He's not an only child, but I guess he could be lying about that. I don't know. I don't know. It doesn't make sense at all. Because Martin's not gay.

But then again, someone thinks he is. Though I probably shouldn't take anything on the authority of some anonymous asshole who called me a fag.

"Simon, no!" says Abby, appearing in the doorway.

"What?"

"You washed it off!" She stares at my face for a minute. "I guess you can still kind of see it."

"You mean the ridiculous hotness?" I say, and she laughs.

"Listen. I just got a text from Nick, and he's waiting for us in the parking lot. We're taking you out tonight."

"What?" I say. "Where?"

"I don't know yet. But my mom's up in DC this weekend, meaning the house and car are mine. So you're spending the night in Suso territory."

"We're sleeping at your house?"

"Yup," she says, and I notice that she's out of makeup and back in her skinny jeans. "So go drop off your sister. Whatever you have to do."

I look in the mirror and attempt to push down my hair. "Nora already took the bus," I say slowly. It's strange. The Simon in the mirror is still wearing contacts. Still almost unrecognizable. "Why are we doing this again?"

"Because we don't have rehearsal for once," she says, poking my cheek, "and because you've had a weird-ass day."

I almost laugh. She has no fucking idea.

All the way out to the parking lot, she talks and schemes,

and I let her words kind of wash over me. I'm a little stuck on this Martin situation. It's almost unfathomable.

It would mean that Martin wrote that post on the Tumblr back in August—the one about being gay. And that Martin's the one I've been emailing every day for five months. I can almost believe it, but I can't explain the blackmail. If Martin's actually gay, why bring Abby into it at all?

"I think we should spend the afternoon in Little Five Points," Abby says, "and then we're definitely going into Midtown."

"Sounds good," I say.

It just doesn't make sense.

But then I think about the afternoons at Waffle House and the late evening rehearsals, and the way I was actually starting to like him before things fell apart. Blackmail with a side of friendship. Maybe that was the whole point.

Except I never got the vibe that he liked me. Not even once. So it can't be that. Martin can't be Blue.

Unless. But no.

Because it can't be a joke. Blue can't be a joke. That's not even a possibility. No one could be that mean. Not even Martin.

I'm having trouble catching my breath.

It can't be a joke, because I don't know what I would do if it were a joke.

I can't think about it. God. I'm sorry, but I can't.

I won't.

◆ ◆ ◆

Nick's waiting in front of the school, and he and Abby bump fists when they see each other. "Got him," she says.

"So now what?" asks Nick. "We drive home and get our stuff, and then you pick us up?"

"That's the plan," says Abby. She swings her backpack around and unzips the smallest pouch, pulling out her car keys. Then she tilts her head to the side. "Did you guys talk to Leah?"

Nick and I look at each other.

"Not yet," Nick says. He kind of deflates. It's tricky, because as much as I love Leah, her presence changes everything. She'll be moody and snarly about Nick and Abby. She'll be weird about Midtown. And I don't know how to describe it, really, but her self-consciousness is contagious sometimes.

But Leah hates being excluded.

"Maybe just us three," Nick says, carefully, eyes shifting downward. I can tell he feels kind of shitty about this.

"Okay," I say.

"Okay," Abby says. "Let's go."

Twenty minutes later, I'm in the backseat of Abby's mom's car with a stack of paperbacks under my feet.

"Put them anywhere," Abby says, eyes flicking to meet mine in the rearview mirror. "She reads them when she's waiting to pick me up. Or if I'm driving."

"Wow, I get nauseous just from reading my phone in the car," says Nick.

"Nauseated," I say, and my heart twists.

"Well, listen to you, Mr. Linguist." Nick turns around in his seat to grin at me.

Abby eases onto 285 and merges with no difficulty whatsoever. She doesn't even appear tense. It occurs to me that she's easily the best driver out of all of us.

"Do you know where we're going?" I ask.

"I do," says Abby. And twenty minutes later, we pull into the lot for Zesto. I never go to Zesto. I mean, I almost never come into Atlanta proper. It's warm and noisy inside, full of people eating chili dogs and burgers and things like that. But I quite honestly don't give a shit that it's January. I get chocolate ice cream swirled with Oreos, and for the ten minutes it takes to eat it, I almost feel normal again. By the time we step back out to the car, the sun is beginning to set.

So then we go to Junkman's Daughter. Which is right next to Aurora Coffee.

But I'm not thinking about Blue.

We spend a few minutes poking around inside. I sort of love Junkman's Daughter. Nick gets caught up in a display of books about Eastern philosophy, and Abby buys a pair of tights. I end up wandering through the aisles, trying not to make eye contact with scary-looking pink mohawk girls.

I'm not thinking about Aurora Coffee, and I'm not thinking about Blue.

I can't think about Blue.

I really can't think about Blue being Martin.

It's dark but not late, and Abby and Nick want to take me to this feminist bookstore that evidently has a lot of gay stuff. So we look through the shelves, and Abby pulls out LGBT picture books to show me, and Nick shuffles around looking awkward. Abby buys me a book about gay penguins, and then we walk down the street for a little while longer. But it's getting chilly and we're getting hungry again, so we pile back into the car and drive to Midtown.

Abby seems to know exactly where we're going. She pulls into a side street and parallel parks like it's nothing. Then we walk briskly up to the corner and onto the main road. Nick shivers in only a light jacket, and Abby rolls her eyes and says, "Georgia boy." And then she puts her arm around him, rubbing her hand up and down his arm as they walk.

"Here we are," she says finally when we arrive at a place on Juniper called Webster's. There's a big patio strung with Christmas lights and rainbow banners, and even though the patio's empty, the parking lot is overflowing.

"Is this like a gay bar?" I ask.

Abby and Nick both grin.

"Okay," I say, "but how are we getting in?" I'm five seven, Nick can't grow facial hair, and Abby's wearing a wristful of friendship bracelets. There's no freaking way we pass for twenty-one.

"It's a restaurant," says Abby. "We're getting dinner."

Inside, Webster's is packed with guys wearing scarves and jackets and skinny jeans. And they're all cute and they're all overwhelming. Most of them have piercings. There's a bar in the back, and some kind of hip-hop music playing, and waiters turning sideways to squeeze through the crowd with pints of beer and baskets of chicken wings.

"Just the three of y'all?" asks the host, resting his hand on my shoulder for barely a second, but it's enough to make my stomach flutter. "Should be just a minute, hon."

We step off to the side, and Nick gets a menu to look through, and everything they serve here is an innuendo. Sausages. Buns. Abby can't stop giggling. I have to keep reminding myself this is just a restaurant. I accidentally make eye contact with a hot guy wearing a tight V-neck shirt, and I look away quickly, but my heart pounds.

"I'm going to the bathroom," I say, because I'm pretty sure I'm going to combust if I keep standing here. The bathrooms are down a little hallway past the bar, and I have to push through this crowd of people to get there. When I step out again, the crowd is even thicker. There are two girls holding beers and sort of dancing, and a group of guys laughing, and lots of people holding drinks or holding hands.

Someone taps my shoulder. "Alex?"

I turn around. "I'm not—"

"You're not Alex," says the guy, "but you have Alex hair." And then he reaches up to ruffle his fingers through it.

He's sitting on a barstool, and he looks like he's not much older than I am. He's got blond hair, much lighter than mine. Draco-blond. He's wearing a polo shirt and normal jeans, and he's very cute, and I think he might be drunk.

"What's your name, Alex?" he says to me, sliding off the barstool. When he stands, he's almost a head taller than me, and he smells like deodorant. He has extremely white teeth.

"Simon," I say.

"Simple Simon met a pie-man." He giggles.

He's definitely drunk.

"I'm Peter," he says, and I think: *Peter Peter pumpkin eater.*

"Don't move," he says. "I'm buying you a drink." He puts a hand on my elbow, and then turns to the bar, and all of a sudden I'm holding an honest-to-God martini glass full of something green. "Like apples," says Peter.

I take a sip, and it's not awful. "Thanks," I say, and the fluttery feeling takes over completely. I don't even know. This is so totally different from my normal.

"You have amazing eyes," Peter says, smiling down at me. Then the song changes to something with a heavy thumping bass. He opens his mouth to say something else, but the words get swallowed.

"What?"

He takes a step closer. "Are you a student?"

"Oh," I say. "Yes." My heart pounds. He stands close enough that our drinks are touching.

"Me too. I'm at Emory. I'm a junior. Hold on." He empties the rest of his glass in one big swallow, and then turns back to the bar. I crane my neck over the crowd and look for Nick and Abby. They've been seated at a table across the room, and they're watching me, looking uneasy. Abby sees me looking and waves frantically. I grin and wave back.

But then Peter's hand is on my arm again, and he hands me a shot glass filled with something bright orange, like that cold medicine. Like liquid Triaminic. But I'm only half done with my apple drink, so I sort of chug it, and hand the empty glass back to him. And then he clinks his shot of Triaminic against mine and makes it disappear.

I sip mine, and it tastes like orange soda, and Peter laughs and tugs at my fingertips. "Simon," he says. "Have you ever taken a shot before?"

I shake my head.

"Aww, okay. Tilt your head back, and just . . ." He demonstrates on his empty shot glass. "Okay?"

"Okay," I say, and that warm, happy feeling starts to creep in. I take the shot in two gulps, and I manage not to spit anything. And I grin at Peter, and he takes my glass away, and then he takes my other hand and laces his fingers through mine.

"Cute Simon," he says. "Where are you from?"

"Shady Creek," I say.

"Okay," he says, and I can tell he hasn't heard of it, but he smiles and sits back down on his barstool and pulls me closer. And his eyes are sort of hazel, and I sort of like this. And talking is just easier now, and it's easier than not talking, and everything I say is the right thing, and he nods and laughs and presses my palms. I tell him about Abby and Nick, who I'm trying not to look at, because every time I look at them, their eyes start yelling at me. And then Peter tells me about his friends, and he says, "Oh my gosh, you have to meet my friends. You have to meet Alex."

So he buys us each another Triaminic shot, and then he takes me by the hand and leads me to a big round table in the corner of the room. Peter's friends are a big group of mostly guys, and they're all cute, and everything is spinning. "This is Simon," Peter says, flinging his arm around me and hugging me sideways. He introduces everyone, and I forget their names instantly, except for Alex. Whom Peter presents by saying, "Meet your doppelgänger." But it's really a little baffling, because Alex doesn't look like me at all. I mean, we're both white. But even our famously similar hair is totally different. His is purposely messy. Mine is just messy. But Peter keeps looking back and forth between us and giggling, and someone sits on someone else's lap to clear a chair for me, and someone passes me a beer. I mean, drinks are just everywhere.

Peter's friends are loud and funny, and I laugh so hard I'm hiccupping, but I can't even remember what I'm laughing about. And Peter's arm is tight around my shoulders, and at one point out of nowhere, he leans over to kiss me on the cheek. It's this strange other universe. It's like having a boy-friend. And somehow I start telling them about Martin and the emails and how he actually freaking blackmailed me, and it's actually kind of a hilarious story, now that I think about it. And everyone is full-on belly laughing, and the one girl at the table says, "Oh my God, Peter, oh my God. He's adorable." And it feels amazing.

But then Peter leans toward me and his lips are close to my ear and he says, "Are you in high school?"

"I'm a junior," I say.

"In high school," he repeats. His arm is still around me. "How old are you?"

"Seventeen," I whisper, feeling sheepish.

He looks at me and shakes his head. "Oh, honey," he says, smiling sadly. "No. No."

"No?" I ask.

"Who did you come here with? Where are your friends, cute Simon?"

I point out Nick and Abby.

"Ah," he says.

He helps me up and holds my hand, and the room keeps lurching, but I end up in a chair somehow. Next to Abby and across from Nick, in front of an untouched cheeseburger. Cold, but totally plain and perfect with nothing green and lots of fries. "Good-bye, cute Simon," says Peter, hugging me, and then kissing me on the forehead. "Go be seventeen."

And then he stumbles away, and Abby and Nick look like they don't know whether to laugh or panic. Oh my God. I love them. I mean, I seriously love them. But I feel sort of wavy inside.

"How much did you have?" asks Nick.

I try to count it on my fingers.

"Forget it. I don't want to know. Just eat something."

"I love it here," I say.

"I can see that," says Abby, shoving a French fry into my mouth.

"But did you see his teeth?" I ask. "He had like the whitest freaking teeth I've ever seen. I bet he uses those things. The Crest things."

"Whitestrips," says Abby. She's got her arm around my waist and Nick's got his arm around my other waist. I mean my same waist. And my arms are around their shoulders, because I love them SO FREAKING MUCH.

"Definitely Whitestrips." I sigh. "He's in college."

"So we've heard," Abby says.

It's a perfect night. Everything is perfect. It's not even cold out anymore. It's a Friday night, and we're not at the Waffle House, and we're not playing *Assassin's Creed* in Nick's basement, and we're not pining for Blue. We are out and we are alive, and everyone in the universe is out here right now.

"Hi," I say, to somebody. I smile at everyone we pass.

"Simon. Good lord," says Abby.

"All right," says Nick. "You're taking shotgun, Spier."

"What? Why?"

"Because I don't think Abby needs your vomit in her mom's upholstery."

"I'm not gonna vom," I say, but as soon as the words come out, there's this ominous twist in my gut.

So, I take the front and crack the window, and the cold air feels sharp and refreshing on my face. I shut my eyes and lean my head back. And then my eyes snap open. "Wait, where are we going?" I ask.

Abby pauses to let some car pull ahead of her. "To my house," she says. "College Park."

"But I forgot my shirt," I say. "Can we stop at my house?"

"Total opposite direction," says Abby.

"Fuck," I say. *Fuck fuck fuck.*

"I can lend you an extra shirt," says Abby. "I'm sure we have some of my brother's stuff down here."

"Also, you're wearing a shirt," says Nick.

"Noooo. No. It's not to wear," I say.

"Then what's it for?" asks Abby.

"I can't wear it," I explain. "That would be weird. I have to have it under my pillow."

"Because that's not weird," says Nick.

"It's an Elliott Smith shirt. Did you know he stabbed himself when we were five? That's why I never made it to his shows."

I close my eyes. "Do you believe in an afterlife? Nick, do Jewish people believe in heaven?"

"All right," says Nick. He and Abby exchange some kind of look in the rearview mirror, and then Abby moves over to the right lane. She takes the turn for the highway, and when she merges on, I realize we're going north. Back to Shady Creek. Back to get my shirt.

"Abby, did I mention you are the absolute best person in the entire universe? Oh my God. I love you so much. I love you more than Nick loves you." Abby laughs, and Nick starts coughing, and I feel a little nervous because now I can't remember if it's a secret that Nick loves Abby. I should probably keep talking. "Abby, what if you became my sister? I need new sisters."

"What's wrong with your old sisters?" she says.

"They're terrible," I say. "Nora's never home anymore, and now Alice has a boyfriend."

"How is that terrible?" asks Abby.

"Alice has a boyfriend?" asks Nick.

"But they're supposed to be Alice and Nora. They're not supposed to be different," I explain.

"They're not allowed to change?" Abby laughs. "But you're changing. You're different than you were five months ago."

"I'm not different!"

"Simon. I just watched you pick up a random guy in a gay bar. You're wearing eyeliner. And you're completely wasted."

235

"I'm not wasted."

Abby and Nick look at each other again in the mirror and bust up laughing.

"And he wasn't a random guy."

"He wasn't?" says Abby.

"He was a random *college* guy," I remind her.

"Ah," she says.

Abby pulls into my driveway and puts the car in park, and I hug her and say, "Thank you thank you thank you." She ruffles my hair.

"Okay. One second," I say. "Don't go anywhere."

The driveway is a little lurchy, but not so bad. It takes me a minute to figure out my key. The lights in the entryway are off, but the TV is on, and I guess I thought my parents would be asleep by now, but they're tucked onto the couch wearing pajama pants with Bieber wedged between them.

"What are you doing home, kid?" asks my dad.

"I have to get a T-shirt," I say, but I think that might not sound right, so I try again. "I'm wearing a shirt, but I have to get a shirt to bring to Abby's house, because it's a certain shirt and it's not a big deal, but I need it."

"Okay . . . ," my mom says, and her eyes cut to my dad.

"Are you watching *The Wire*?" I ask. It's paused now. "Oh my God. This is what you do when I'm not home. You watch scripted TV." And now I can't stop laughing.

"Simon," says my dad, looking confused and stern and amused all at once. "Is there something you'd like to tell us?"

"I'm gay," I say, and I giggle. Giggles keep escaping around the edges.

"Okay, sit down," he says, and I'm about to make a joke, but he keeps looking at me, so I sit on the arm of the love seat. "You're drunk." He looks a little stunned. I shrug.

"Who drove?" he asks.

"Abby."

"Did she drink?"

"Dad, come on. No." He tips his palms up. "No! God."

"Em, do you want to . . ."

"Yup," my mom says, shifting Bieber off her legs. And then she gets off the couch and goes out through the entryway, and I hear the front door open and shut.

"She's going out there to talk to Abby?" I say. "Seriously? You guys don't even trust me?"

"Well, I don't know why we should, Simon. You show up at ten thirty, obviously drunk, and you don't seem to think that's a problem, so—"

"So you're saying the problem is I'm not trying to hide it. The problem is I'm not lying to you."

My dad stands up suddenly, and I look at him, and I realize he's really freaking pissed off. Which is so unusual that it makes me nervous, but it also makes me a little fearless, and so I say, "Do you like it better when I lie about things? It probably sucks for you now that you can't make fun of gay people anymore. I bet Mom won't let you, right?"

"*Simon,*" says my dad, like a warning.

I giggle, but it comes out too sharp. "That awkward moment when you realize you've been making gay jokes in front of your gay kid for the last seventeen years."

There's this awful, tense silence. My dad just looks at me.

Finally, my mom comes back in, and she looks back and forth between us for a minute. And then she says, "I sent Abby and Nick home."

"What? Mom!" I stand up too fast, and my stomach flips. "No. No. I'm just here to get my shirt."

"Oh, I think you're staying in tonight," says my mom. "Your dad and I need a minute to talk. Why don't you go get yourself a glass of water, and we'll be right in."

"I'm not thirsty."

"It's not a request," says my mom.

They have to be fucking kidding me. I'm supposed to sit here and drink my water, and they just get to talk about me behind my back. I slam the kitchen door shut.

As soon as the water hits my lips, I gulp it down so fast I almost forget to breathe. My stomach is churning. I think the water makes it worse. I pretzel my arms on the table and tuck my head into my elbow. I'm so freaking tired.

My parents come in a few minutes later and sit down next to me at the table. "Did you have water?" asks my dad.

I nudge my empty glass toward him without lifting my head.

"Good," he says. He pauses. "Kid, we've got to talk consequences."

Right, because things aren't shitty enough. People at school think I'm a joke, and there's a boy I can't seem to stop being in love with, and he just might be someone I can't stand. And I'm pretty sure I'm going to puke tonight.

But yeah. They want to talk consequences.

"We've discussed it, and—presumably this is a first offense?" I nod into my arms. "Then your mom and I have agreed that you'll be grounded for two weeks starting tomorrow."

I whip my head up. "You can't do that."

"Oh, I can't?"

"It's the play next weekend."

"Oh, we're well aware," says my dad. "And you can go to school and rehearsals and all of your performances, but you'll come straight home afterward. And your laptop is moving into the living room for a week."

"And I'll take your phone right now," says my mom, putting out her hand. All business.

"That's so effed up," I say, because that's what you say, but I mean, honestly? I don't even fucking care.

29

IT'S MLK WEEKEND, SO WE don't get back to school until
Tuesday. When I get there, Abby's waiting in front of my locker.
"Where have you been? I've been texting you all weekend. Are
you okay?"

"I'm fine," I say, rubbing my eyes.

"I was really worried about you. When your mom came
out . . . your mom is actually kind of terrifying. I thought she
was going to give me a Breathalyzer."

Oh God. "Sorry," I say. "They're really intense about driving." Abby steps aside, so I can twist in my locker combination.

"No, it was fine," she says. "I just felt bad leaving you. And
then when I didn't hear back from you all weekend . . ."

I click the latch open. "They took my phone away. And
my computer. And I'm grounded for two weeks." I dig around

for my French notebook. "So yeah."

Abby's face falls. "But what about the play?"

"No, that's fine. They're not messing with that." I push my locker closed, and the latch clicks dully.

"Well, good," she says. "But I'm so sorry. This is all my fault."

"What's your fault?" Nick asks, falling into step with us on the way to English.

"Simon's grounded," she says.

"It's not your fault at all," I say. "I'm the one who got drunk and paraded it in front of my parents."

"Not your best move," says Nick. I look at him. Something's different, and I can't quite pin it down.

Then I realize: it's the hands. They're holding hands. My head snaps up to look at them, and they both smile self-consciously. Nick shrugs.

"Well well well," I say. "I guess you guys didn't miss me too much Friday night, after all."

"Not really," says Nick. Abby buries her face in his shoulder.

I pry the story out of Abby during small group conversation practice in French class.

"So how did it go down? Tell me everything. *C'était un surprise*," I add as Madame Blanc makes her way up my row.

"*C'était* une *surprise*, Simon. *Au féminin*." You have to love French teachers. They make such a big freaking deal about

241

gender, but they always pronounce my name like *Simone*.

"Um, *nous étions . . .*" Abby smiles up at Madame Blanc, and then waits for her to move out of earshot. "Yeah, so we dropped you off, and I was kind of upset, because your mom seemed really mad, and I didn't want her to think I would drink and drive."

"She wouldn't have let you drive home if she thought that."

"Yeah, well," Abby says, "I don't know. Anyway, we left, but we ended up just parking in Nick's driveway for a while, just in case you were able to talk your parents into letting you come back out."

"Yeah, sorry. No dice."

"Oh, I know," she says. "I just felt weird leaving without you. We texted you, and then we waited for a little while."

"Sorry," I say again.

"No, it was fine," Abby says, and then she breaks into a huge grin. *"C'était magnifique."*

Lunch is actually amazing, because Morgan and Bram both had birthdays over the long weekend, and Leah's very strict about everyone getting their own giant sheet cake. Which means two cakes, both chocolate.

Except I don't know who brought the cakes today, because Leah never shows up for lunch at all. And now that I think about it, she wasn't in English or French.

I reach into my back pocket automatically, but then I remember my phone is in custody. So, I lean over toward Anna, who's wearing two party hats and eating a pile of straight-up icing. "Hey, where's Leah?"

"Um," says Anna, not meeting my eyes. "She's here."

"She's at school?"

Anna shrugs.

I try not to worry about it, but I don't see her all day, and then I don't see her the next day either. Except Anna says she's here. And her car's in the parking lot, which makes it so much weirder. And her car's still in the parking lot at seven, when we finally get out of rehearsal. I'm not sure what's going on.

I just want to make contact. Maybe there are missed texts from her on my phone that I don't even know about.

Or maybe not. I don't know. It just sucks.

But on Thursday afternoon, in that narrow window between school and rehearsal, I finally see her stepping out of the bathroom near the atrium.

"Leah!" I run over to her and catch her in a hug. "Where have you been?"

She stiffens in my arms.

I step back. "Um, is everything okay?"

She looks at me with jagged eyes. "I don't want to talk to you," she says. She tugs her shirt down and then folds her arms up under her chest.

"What?" I look at her. "Leah, what happened?"

"You tell me," she says. "How was Friday? Did you, Nick, and Abby have fun?"

There's this beat of silence.

"I don't know what you want me to say," I tell her. "I mean, I'm sorry."

"You sound really sorry," she says.

A couple of freshman girls scamper past us, shrieking and chasing each other and body slamming the door. We pause.

"Well, I am sorry," I say, once the door shuts behind them. "I mean, if this is about Nick and Abby, I don't know what to tell you."

"Right, this is all about Nick and Abby. I mean . . ." She laughs, shaking her head. "Whatever."

"Well, what? Do you actually want to talk about it," I ask, "or do you just want to be really sarcastic and not tell me what's going on? Because if you're just going to laugh at me—seriously—you're going to have to wait in line."

"Oh, poor Simon."

"Okay, you know what? Forget it. I'm going to go to my fucking dress rehearsal now, and you can find me whenever you're ready to not be an asshole." I turn around and start walking, trying to ignore the lump rising in my throat.

"Awesome," she says. "Have fun. Say hi to your BFF for me."

"Leah." I turn around. "Please. Just stop."

She shakes her head slightly, and her lips are pulled in, and she's blinking and blinking. "I mean, it's cool. But next time you guys decide to all hang out without me," she says, "text me some pictures or something. Just so I can pretend I still have friends."

Then there's this noise like an aborted sob, and she pushes past me, straight through the door. And all through rehearsal, all I can hear is that noise over and over again.

30

I GET HOME, AND ALL I want to do is walk somewhere. Anywhere. But as it stands, I'm not even allowed to walk my freaking dog. And I feel so restless and strange and unhappy.

I hate it when Leah's mad at me. Hate it. I'm not saying it doesn't happen a lot, because there's this hidden emotional subtext with Leah, and I'm always missing it. But this feels different and worse than our normal. She was just so mean about everything.

Also, it's the first time I've ever seen Leah cry.

Dinner is grilled cheese and Oreos, because my parents are still working and Nora's out again. And then I basically spend the evening staring at my ceiling fan. I don't have it in me to do my homework. No one's going to expect it from me anyway with the play opening tomorrow. I listen to music, and I'm bored and antsy and, honestly, miserable.

Then, around nine, my parents come in wanting to Talk. Just when I thought today couldn't get any better.

"Can I sit?" asks my mom, sort of hovering over the end of the bed. I shrug, and she sits, and my dad takes my desk chair.

I tuck my hands behind my head and sigh. "Let me guess. Don't get drunk."

"I mean, yeah," my dad says, "don't get drunk."

"Got it."

They look at each other. My dad clears his throat.

"I owe you an apology, kid."

I look up at him.

"What you said on Friday. About the gay jokes."

"I was kidding," I say. "It's fine."

"No," my dad says. "It's not really fine."

I shrug.

"Well, I'm just going to put this out there, in case the message got lost somewhere. I love you. A lot. No matter what. And I know it's got to be awesome having the cool dad."

"Ahem," says my mom.

"Excuse me. The cool parents. The hardcore, badass, hipster parents."

"Oh, it's awesome," I say.

"But rein us in if you need to, okay? Rein me in," he says. He rubs his chin. "I know I didn't make it easy for you to come out. We're very proud of you. You're pretty brave, kid."

"Thanks," I say. I pull myself up and lean against the wall, thinking it's a good time for hair ruffling and *sleep tight, kid* and *don't stay up too late*.

But they don't move. So I say, "Well, for the record, I knew you were kidding. That's not the reason I didn't want to come out."

My parents look at each other again.

"Can I ask you what the reason was?" says my mom.

"I mean, there wasn't like a specific reason," I say. "I just didn't want to have to talk about it. I knew it would be a big deal. I don't know."

"Was it a big deal?" says my mom.

"Well, yeah."

"I'm sorry," she says. "Did we make it a big deal?"

"Oh my God. Seriously? You guys make everything a big deal."

"Really?" she says.

"When I started drinking coffee. When I started shaving. When I got a girlfriend."

"That stuff is exciting," she says.

"It's not that exciting," I say. "It's like—I don't even know. You guys are so freaking obsessed with everything I do. It's like I can't change my socks without someone mentioning it."

"Ah," says my dad. "So, what you're trying to say is that we're *really creepy*."

"Yes," I say.

My mom laughs. "See, but you're not a parent yet, so you can't understand. It's like—you have this baby, and eventually, he starts doing stuff. And I used to be able to see every tiny change, and it was so fascinating." She smiles sadly. "And now I'm missing stuff. The little things. And it's hard to let go of that."

"But I'm seventeen. Don't you think I'm supposed to be changing?"

"Of course you are. And I love it. It's the most exciting time," she says. She squeezes the end of my foot. "I'm just saying I wish I could still watch it all unfold."

I don't quite know what to say.

"You guys are just so grown-up now," she continues, "all three of you. And you're all so different. I mean, even when you were babies. Alice was fearless, and Nora was so self-contained, and then you were this complete ham. I mean, everyone kept saying you were your father's son."

My dad grins, and I'm honestly a little bit speechless. I have never, ever thought of myself that way.

"I actually remember holding you for the first time. Your little mouth. You latched right onto my breast—"

"Mom."

"Oh, it was the most incredible moment. And your dad carried your sister in, and she kept saying, 'No baby!'" My mom laughs. "I couldn't take my eyes off you. I couldn't believe we were the parents of a boy. I guess we had gotten so used to thinking of ourselves as girl parents, so it was like this whole new thing to discover."

"Sorry I didn't turn out to be much of a boy," I say.

My dad spins the chair around to face me directly. "Are you kidding me?"

"Sort of."

"You're an awesome boy," he says. "You're like a ninja."

"Well, thank you."

"You're freaking welcome," he says.

There's this distant slam of the front door shutting and dog nails skittering across the hardwoods—Nora's home.

"Listen," says my mom, poking my foot again. "I don't want to cramp your style, but maybe you could just humor us? Keep us in the loop about stuff where you can, and we'll try not to be weird and obsessed."

"Fair enough," I say.

"Good," she says. They look at each other again. "Anyway, we have something for you."

"Is it another awkward anecdote about me breast-feeding?"

"Oh my God, you were all about the boob," my dad says. "I can't believe you turned out to be gay."

"Hilarious, Dad."

"I know I am," he says. Then he stands up and pulls something out of his pocket. "Here," he says, tossing it.

My phone.

"You're still grounded, but you get parole this weekend.

And you can get your laptop back after the play tomorrow if you remember all your lines."

"I don't have any lines," I say slowly.

"Then you don't have anything to worry about, kid."

But it's sort of funny, because even without any lines to mess up, I'm nervous. Excited and fluttery and amped up and nervous. As soon as the dismissal bell rings, Ms. Albright takes Abby, Martin, Taylor, and a few of the others to do an extra vocal warm-up in the music room, but the rest of us just sit there on the floor of the auditorium eating pizza. Cal's running around dealing with the tech people, and it's kind of a relief to just be hanging out with a bunch of random senior girls at the moment. No Calvin Coolidge or Martin Van Buren or any other confusing presidential boys. No Leah looking at me with weapons for eyes.

The show begins at seven, but Ms. Albright wants us fully in costume by six. I put in my contact lenses and get changed early, and then I sit around in the girls' dressing room waiting for Abby. It's five thirty by the time she gets there, and she's clearly in a weird mood. She barely says hello.

I pull my chair beside her and watch her apply her makeup.

"Are you nervous?" I ask.

"A little." She stares into the mirror, sort of dabbing a mascara wand against her eyelashes.

"Nick's coming tonight, right?"

"Yup."

These clipped, abrupt answers. She almost seems annoyed.

"When you're done," I say, "will you help me be ridiculously hot?"

"Eyeliner?" she asks. "Okay. One sec."

Abby brings over her makeup bag and pulls her chair across from mine. At this point, we're the only ones left in the dressing room. She uncaps the pencil and pulls my eyelid taut, and I try not to squirm.

"You're so quiet," I say, after a moment. "Is everything okay?"

She doesn't answer. I feel the pencil push across the edge of my lashes. Scritch scritch scritch.

"Abby?" I ask. The pencil lifts away, and I open my eyes.

"Keep them closed," she says. Then she starts my other eyelid. She's quiet for a minute. And then she says, "What was this whole thing with Martin?"

"With Martin?" I ask, and my stomach twists.

"He told me everything," she says, "but I'd sort of like to hear it from you."

I feel frozen in place. *Everything*. But what does that even mean?

"The blackmail thing?"

"Yeah," she says. "That. Okay, open them." She starts tracing the bottom lid, and I fight the urge to blink. "Why didn't you tell me?"

"Because," I say, "I don't know. I didn't tell anyone."

"And you just went along with it?"

"I didn't exactly have much of a choice."

"But you knew I wasn't attracted to him, right?" She caps the pencil again.

"Yeah," I say, "I did."

Abby leans back for a moment to examine me, before sighing and leaning forward again. "I'm going to even this out," she says. And then she's quiet.

"I'm sorry." Suddenly, it feels so important for her to understand. "I didn't know what to do. He was going to tell everyone. I really didn't want to help him. I barely did help him."

"Yeah."

"Which, you know, that's why he ended up even posting that thing on the Tumblr. Because I wasn't helping him enough."

"No, I get it," she says.

She finishes with the pencil, and then smudges everything with her finger. A moment later, I feel her run some poufy makeup brush all over my cheeks and nose.

"I'm done," she says, and I open my eyes. She looks at me and frowns. "It's just, you know. I get that you were in a difficult position. But you don't get to make the decisions about my love life. I choose who I date." She shrugs. "I would think you would understand that."

I hear myself inhale. "I'm so sorry." I hang my head. I mean, I wish I could just disappear.

"Well, you know. It is what it is." She shrugs. "I'm gonna head out there, okay?"

"Okay." I nod.

"Maybe someone else could do your makeup tomorrow," she says.

The play goes fine. I mean, it's better than fine. Taylor is perfectly earnest, and Martin is perfectly crotchety, and Abby is so lively and funny that it's almost like our conversation in the dressing room never happened. But after it's over, she disappears without saying good-bye, and Nick's gone by the time I get out of costume. And I have no idea if Leah was here at all.

So, yeah. The play's great. I'm the one who's miserable.

I meet my parents and Nora in the atrium, and my dad's carrying this giant bouquet of flowers that looks like something out of Dr. Seuss. Because even without a speaking part, I'm apparently God's gift to theater. And all the way home, they hum the songs and talk about Taylor's amazing voice and ask me if I'm friends with the hilarious kid with the beard. A.k.a. Martin. God, what a question.

I reunite with my laptop as soon as we get home. To be honest, I'm more confused than ever.

I guess it's not a huge surprise that Leah's pissed about last Friday. I think she's going a little overboard with it, but I get it. I probably had it coming. But Abby?

It honestly hit me out of nowhere. It's weird, because of

all the things I felt guilty about, it never occurred to me to feel guilty about Abby. But I'm a fucking idiot. Because who you like can't be forced or persuaded or manipulated. If anyone knows that, it's me.

I'm a shitty friend. Worse than a shitty friend, because I should be begging for Abby's forgiveness right now, and I'm not. I'm too busy wondering what exactly Martin told her. Because it doesn't sound like he mentioned anything other than the blackmail.

Which could mean he doesn't want to admit that he's Blue. Or it could mean he's not Blue at all. And the thought of Blue being someone other than Martin gives me this breathless, hopeful feeling.

Actually hopeful, despite the mess I've made. Despite the drama. Despite everything. Because even with all the shit that's gone down this week, I still care about Blue.

The way I feel about him is like a heartbeat—soft and persistent, underlying everything.

I log into my Jacques email, and when I do, something clicks. And it isn't Simon logic. It's objective, indisputable truth:

Every email Blue ever sent me is time-stamped.

So many of the emails were sent right after school. So many were sent when I was in rehearsal. Which means Martin was also in rehearsal, with no time to write and no wireless internet.

Blue isn't Martin. He's not Cal. He's just someone.

So, I go all the way back to the beginning, back to August,

and I read through everything. His subject lines. Every line of every email.

I have no idea who he is. No freaking clue.

But I think I'm falling for him again.

31

FROM: hourtohour.notetonote@gmail.com
TO: bluegreen118@gmail.com
DATE: Jan 25 at 9:27 AM
SUBJECT: Us.

Blue,

I've been writing and deleting and rewriting this email all weekend, and I still can't get it right. But I'm going to do this. So here we go.

I know I haven't written in a while. It's been a weird couple of weeks.

So, first I want to say this: I know who you are.

I mean, I still don't know your name, or what you look

like, or all the other stuff. But you have to understand that I really do know you. I know that you're smart and careful and weird and funny. And you notice things and listen to things, but not in a nosy way. In a real way. You overthink things and remember details and you always, always say the right thing.

And I think I like that we got to know each other from the inside out.

So, it occurred to me that I've been spending a lot of time thinking about you and rereading your emails and trying to make you laugh. But I've been spending very little time spelling things out for you and taking chances and putting my heart on the line.

Obviously, I don't know what the hell I'm doing here, but what I'm trying to say is that I like you. I more than like you. When I flirt with you, it's not a joke, and when I say I want to know you, it's not just because I'm curious. I'm not going to pretend I know how this ends, and I don't have a freaking clue if it's possible to fall in love over email. But I would really like to meet you, Blue. I want to try this. And I can't imagine a scenario where I won't want to kiss your face off as soon as I see you.

Just wanted to make that perfectly clear.

So, what I'm trying to say is that there's an extremely badass carnival in the parking lot of Perimeter Mall today, and it's apparently open until nine.

For what it's worth, I'll be there at six thirty. And I hope I see you.

Love,

Simon

32

I CLICK SEND AND TRY not to think about it, but I'm restless and punchy and jittery all the way to school. And cranking Sufjan Stevens at top volume doesn't solve anything, which is probably why people don't crank Sufjan Stevens. My stomach is apparently on a spin cycle.

First I put my costume on backward, and then I spend ten minutes looking for my contact lenses before remembering I'm wearing them. I've achieved Martin levels of twitchiness—Brianna has a ridiculous time putting on my eyeliner. And all through the bustle and pep talks and swelling of the overture, my mind is stuck on Blue Blue Blue.

I don't know how I make it through the performance. I honestly don't remember half of it.

Afterward, there's this big goopy scene onstage of people

hugging and thanking the audience and thanking the crew and thanking the orchestra. All the seniors get roses, and Cal gets a bouquet of them, and Ms. Albright's bouquet is off the freaking charts. My dad calls it the Sunday Matinee Tearfest, which quickly inspired the Sunday Afternoon Unavoidable Golf Conflict. I don't even blame him.

But then I think about Ms. Albright making it her life's mission to get those in-tha-butt guys suspended. And how pissed off and determined she looked, slapping the handbook down on that chair backstage.

I wish I had brought her another bouquet or a card or a freaking tiara. I don't know. Something just from me.

Then we have to get dressed again. And we have to strike the set. Everything takes forever. I never wear a watch, but I pull my phone out again and again and again to check the time. 5:24. 5:31. 5:40. Every part of me twists and flips and screams with anticipation.

At six, I leave. I just walk out the door. And it's so warm outside. I mean, it's warm for January. I want to be less excited, because who the hell knows what Blue is thinking, and who the hell knows what I'm setting myself up for. But I can't help it. I just have a good feeling.

I keep thinking about what my dad said. *You're pretty brave, kid.*

Maybe I am.

The carnival is basically our cast party, and everyone's

driving straight from school to the mall. Except for me. I make a left at the light and drive home. Because I don't care if it's January. I want the T-shirt.

It's under my pillow, soft and white and neatly folded, with its wall of red and black swirls, and a picture of Elliott standing in front. Black and white, except for his hand. I pull it on quickly and grab a cardigan to throw over it. At this point, I have to haul ass to the mall if I'm going to make it by six thirty.

Except there's something stiff and pokey between my shoulder blades, in that exact spot you can never quite scratch. I slide my arm underneath the hem and up through the bottom. A piece of paper is taped to the fabric inside. I catch it and tug it out.

It's another note on blue-green construction paper, and it starts with a postscript. My fingers tremble as I read it.

P.S. I love the way you smile like you don't realize you're doing it. I love your perpetual bed head. I love the way you hold eye contact a moment longer than you need to. And I love your moon-gray eyes. So if you think I'm not attracted to you, Simon, you're crazy.

And underneath that, he's written his phone number.

There's a tingling feeling that radiates outward from a point below my stomach—wrenching and wonderful and almost unbearable. I've never been so aware of my heartbeat. Blue and his vertical handwriting and the word "love" repeated over and over again.

Not to mention the fact that I could call him right this second and know who he is.

But I think I won't call. Not yet. Because, for all I know, he's waiting for me. For real. In person. Which means I have to get to the mall.

It's almost seven by the time I get there, and I'm kicking myself for being so late. It's already dark, but the carnival is noisy and lit and alive. I love these pop-up carnivals. I love that a parking lot in January can be transformed into summer at Coney Island. I see Cal and Brianna and a couple of the seniors standing in line to get tickets, so I make my way toward them.

I'm worried that it's too dark. And I'm worried, of course, that Blue has come and gone. But it's impossible to know when I don't know who I'm looking for.

We all buy tons of tickets, and then we ride everything. There's a Ferris wheel and a carousel and bumper cars and flying swings. We fold our legs up into the baby train and ride that, too. And then we all get hot chocolate, and drink it sitting on the curb near the concession stand.

I stare at everyone walking, and every time someone looks down and makes eye contact, my heart goes haywire.

I spot Abby and Nick sitting in front of the games, holding

hands and eating popcorn. Nick has a holy buttload of stuffed animals lined up around his feet.

"There's no way he won all of these for you," I say to Abby. I feel nervous as I walk up to her. I'm not sure we're on speaking terms.

But she smiles up at me. "Not even. I won these for him."

"It's that crane game," says Nick. "She's a total boss. I think she's cheating." He nudges her sideways.

"Keep thinking that," says Abby.

I laugh, feeling shy.

"Sit with us," she says.

"Are you sure?"

"Yeah." She scoots closer to Nick to make room. Then she leans her head against my shoulder for a moment and whispers, "I'm sorry, Simon."

"Are you kidding me? I'm sorry," I say. "I'm so sorry."

"Eh, I've thought about it, and you definitely get a pass when you're being blackmailed."

"Oh, really?"

"Yup," she says. "And because I can't stay mad when I'm deliriously happy."

I can't see Nick's face, but he taps the toe of his sneaker against her ballet flat. And they seem to shift closer to each other.

"You guys are going to be a really gross couple, aren't you?" I say.

"Probably," says Nick.

Abby looks at me and says, "So, is that the shirt?"

"What?" I ask, blushing.

"The shirt that Drunky McDrunkbutt made me drive all the way across town for."

"Oh," I say. "Yeah."

"I'm guessing there's a story behind it."

I shrug.

"Does it have to do with the guy you're looking for?" she asks. "This is about a guy, right?"

I almost choke. "The guy I'm looking for?"

"Simon," she says, putting her hand on my arm. "You're obviously looking for someone. Your eyes are everywhere."

"Hmph," I say, burying my face.

"You know, it's okay to be kind of romantic," she says.

"I'm not romantic."

"Right." Abby laughs. "I forgot. You and Nick are so cynical."

"Wait, what did I do?" asks Nick.

Abby leans into him, but looks up at me. "Hey. I hope you find him, okay?" she says.

Okay.

But it's eight thirty, and I still haven't found him. Or he hasn't found me. It's hard to know what to think.

He likes me. I mean, that's basically what the note said. But the note was written two weeks ago. It almost kills me. Two weeks with the shirt under my freaking pillow, and I had no idea what was tucked away inside of it. I know it's been said, but I'm a monumental idiot.

I mean, in two weeks, he could have changed his mind about me.

The carnival shuts down in half an hour, and my friends have all gone home. I should go, too. But I have another couple of tickets, so I blow most of them on midway games and save my last one for the Tilt-A-Whirl. I figure it's the last place I'll find Blue, so I've been avoiding it all night.

There's no line at all; I walk straight onto the ride. The Tilt-A-Whirl has these metal pods with domed tops, and there's a metal wheel in the middle that you can turn to make your pod spin. And then the ride itself whirls around quickly, and the whole point is just to get you dizzy. Or maybe the point is to empty your head.

I'm alone in my seat, with the seat belt pulled as tight as I can make it. A couple of girls squeeze into the pod next to mine, and the operator walks over to latch the gate. Almost all the other pods are empty. I lean back and shut my eyes.

And then someone slides in beside me.

"Can I sit here?" he asks, and my eyes snap open.

It's Cute Bram Greenfeld, of the soft eyes and soccer calves.

I loosen the seat belt to let him in. And I smile at him. It's impossible not to.

"I like your shirt," he says. He seems nervous.

"Thanks," I say. "It's Elliott Smith."

The operator reaches over us and pulls the guardrail down, locking us in.

"I know," says Bram. There's something in his voice. I turn to him, slowly, and his eyes are wide and brown and totally open.

There's this pause. We're still looking at each other. And there's this feeling in my stomach like a coil pulled taut.

"It's you," I say.

"I know I'm late," he says.

Then there's a grinding noise and a jolt and a swell of music. Someone shrieks and then laughs, and the ride spins to life.

Bram's eyes are clenched shut and his chin is locked down. He's perfectly silent. He cups his hands over his nose and mouth. I hold the metal wheel in place with both hands, but it keeps pulling into a clockwise rotation. It's like the ride wants to spin. And it spins and it spins.

"Sorry," he says, when it finally stops, and his voice is stretched thin, and his eyes are still closed.

"It's okay," I say. "Are you okay?"

He nods and exhales and says, "Yeah. I will be."

We step off the ride and make it to the curb, and he leans all the way forward, tucking his head between his knees. I settle in beside him, feeling awkward and jittery and almost drunk.

"I just got your email," he says. "I was sure I was going to miss you."

"I can't believe it's you," I say.

"It's me," he says. His eyes slide open. "You really didn't know?"

"Not a clue," I say. I study his profile. He has these lips that meet just barely, like the slightest touch would coax them open. His ears are slightly big and there are two freckles on his cheekbone. And his eyelashes are more dramatic than I've ever noticed.

He turns toward me, and I look away quickly.

"I thought I was so obvious," he says.

I shake my head.

He stares straight ahead. "I think I wanted you to know."

"Then why didn't you just tell me?"

"Because," he says, and his voice sort of shakes. And I'm aching to touch him. Quite honestly, I've never wanted anything so badly in my life. "Because, if you had been looking for it to be me, I think you would have guessed it yourself."

I don't quite know how to respond to that. I don't know if it's true or not.

"But you never gave me clues," I say finally.

"I did," he says, smiling. "My email address."

"Bluegreen118," I say.

"Bram Louis Greenfeld. My birthday."

"Jesus. I'm an idiot."

"No, you're not," he says softly.

But I am. I'm an idiot. I was looking for him to be Cal. And

I guess I assumed that Blue would be white. Which kind of makes me want to smack myself. White shouldn't be the default any more than straight should be the default. There shouldn't even be a default.

"I'm sorry," I say.

"For what?"

"For not figuring it out."

"But it would be completely unfair of me to expect that," he says.

"You guessed it was me."

"Well, yeah," he says. He looks down. "I kind of guessed a long time ago. Except I thought maybe I was just seeing what I wanted to see."

Seeing what he wanted to see.

I think that means Bram wanted it to be me.

There's this twist in my stomach, and my brain feels hazy. I clear my throat. "I guess I should have shut up about who my English teacher is."

"Wouldn't have helped."

"Oh no?"

He smiles slightly, and turns away. "You sort of talk the way you write."

"No freaking way."

I'm kind of hardcore grinning now.

In the distance, they begin shutting down the rides and turning off lights. There's something beautiful and eerie about a darkened, unmoving Ferris wheel. Beyond the carnival, the lights turn off in the doorways of the department stores. I know my parents expect me home.

But I scoot closer to Bram, until our arms are almost touching, and I can feel him twitch just slightly. Our pinkie fingers are maybe an inch apart, and it's as if an invisible current runs between them.

"But how are you a president?" I ask.

"What?"

"The same first name as a former president."

"Oh," he says, "Abraham."

"Ohhh."

We're quiet for a moment.

"And I can't believe you rode the Tilt-A-Whirl for me."

"I must really like you," he says.

So I lean in toward him, and my heart is in my throat. "I want to hold your hand," I say softly.

Because we're in public. Because I don't know if he's out.

"So hold it," he says.

And I do.

33

IN ENGLISH CLASS ON MONDAY, my eyes find Bram immediately. He sits on the couch beside Garrett, wearing a collared
shirt under a sweater, and he's so freaking adorable that it
almost hurts to look at him.

"Hi, hi," I say.

He smiles like he's been waiting for me, and he scoots over
to make room.

"Good job this weekend, Spier," says Garrett. "Pretty frig-
gin' funny."

"I didn't know you were there."

"I mean," he says, "Greenfeld made me go three times."

"Oh, really?" I say, grinning at Bram. And then he grins
back, and I'm giddy and breathless and kind of unraveled.
And I didn't sleep at all last night. Not even for a second. I've

basically been picturing this moment for ten hours, and now that it's here, I don't have a clue what I'm supposed to say. Probably something awesome and witty and not school-related.

Probably not: "Did you finish the chapter?"

"I did," he says.

"I didn't," I say.

Then he smiles and I smile. And then I blush and he lowers his eyes, and it's like this entire pantomime of nervous gestures.

Mr. Wise comes in and starts reading aloud from *The Awakening*, and we're supposed to follow along in our own copies. But I keep losing my place. I've never been so distracted. So, I lean in to look on with Bram, and his body shifts toward me. I'm perfectly attuned to every point of contact between us. It's like our nerve endings have found a way to slip through fabric.

And then Bram stretches his legs forward and pushes his knee into mine. Which means the rest of the period is pretty much devoted to staring at Bram's knee. There's a place where his jeans are fraying, and a tiny patch of brown skin is barely visible between the fibers of the denim. And all I want to do is touch it. At one point, Bram and Garrett both turn to look at me, and I realize I've just sighed out loud.

After class, Abby hooks an arm around my shoulders and says, "I didn't realize you and Bram were such good friends."

"Hush," I say, and my cheeks burn. Freaking Abby never misses a freaking thing.

I'm not expecting to see him again until lunch, but he

materializes at my locker right before. "I think we should go somewhere," he says.

"Off campus?"

Technically, only the seniors are allowed, but it's not like the security guards know we're not seniors. So I imagine.

"Have you done this before?"

"Nope," he says. And he presses his fingertips softly against mine, just for a moment.

"Me neither," I say. "Okay."

So, we walk out the side door and briskly through the parking lot with as much confidence as we can muster. The air is sharply cold from an hour or two of early morning rain.

Bram's Honda Civic is old and comfy and meticulously neat, and he cranks up the heat as soon as we get inside. An auxiliary cable strings out from the cigarette lighter, attached to an iPod. He tells me to pick the music. I'm not sure if Bram knows that handing me his iPod is like handing me the window to his soul.

And of course his music selection is perfect. A lot of classic soul and newer hip-hop. A surprising amount of bluegrass. A single guilty pleasure song by Justin Bieber. And, without exception, every album or musician I've ever mentioned in my emails.

I think I'm in love.

"So, where are we going?" I ask.

He glances at me and smiles. "I have an idea."

So I lean back against the headrest, spinning through Bram's music list as the heater revives my fingers. It's beginning to rain again. I watch the droplets slide in tapering diagonals across the window.

I make a decision and press play, and Otis Redding's voice comes quietly through the speakers. "Try a Little Tenderness." I turn up the volume.

And then I touch Bram's elbow. "You're so quiet," I say.

"Now or in general?"

"Well, both."

"I'm quiet around you," he says, smiling.

I smile back. "I'm one of the cute guys who gets you tongue-tied?"

He squeezes the steering wheel.

"You're *the* cute guy."

He pulls into a shopping center not far from school, and parks in front of Publix.

"We're going grocery shopping?" I ask.

"It looks like it," he says, with a spark of a smile. Mysterious Bram. We cover our heads with our hands as we run through the rain.

As we step into the brightly lit entryway, my phone buzzes through my jeans. I've missed three text messages, all from Abby.

R u coming to lunch?
Um, where r u?

Bram's gone too. How strange. ;)

But there's Bram, carrying a grocery basket, and his curls are damp and his eyes are luminous. "Twenty-seven minutes until the end of lunch," he says. "Maybe we should divide and conquer."

"You got it. Where to, boss?"

He directs me to the dairy aisle for a pint of milk.

"So what did you get?" I ask, when we reconvene at the checkout.

"Lunch," he says, tilting his basket toward me. Inside, there are two plastic cup containers of miniature Oreos and a box of plastic spoons.

I almost kiss him right there in front of the U-Scan.

He insists on paying for everything. The rain has picked up, but we make a break for it, falling breathlessly into the seats and letting the doors slam shut. I rub my glasses against my shirt to dry them. Then Bram twists the ignition, and the heat kicks back on, and the only sound is the tap of raindrops against the window. He looks down at his hands, and I can see he's grinning.

"Abraham," I say, trying it out, and there's this soft ache below my stomach.

His eyes flick toward me.

And the rain makes a kind of curtain, which is probably for the best. Because all of a sudden, I'm leaning over the gear stick, and my hands are on his shoulders, and I'm trying to keep breathing. All I can see are Bram's lips. Which fall gently open the moment I lean in to kiss him.

And I can't even describe it. It's stillness and pressure and rhythm and breathing. We can't figure out our noses at first, but then we do, and then I realize my eyes are still open. So I shut them. And his fingertips graze the nape of my neck, in constant quiet motion.

He pauses for a moment, and my eyes flutter open, and he smiles, so I smile back. And then he leans in to kiss me again, sweet and feather-soft. And it's almost too perfect. Almost too Disney. This can't actually be me.

Ten minutes later, we're holding hands and eating Oreo mush, and it's the perfect lunch. More Oreos than milk. And I never would have remembered spoons, but he did. Of course.

"So now what?" I ask.

"We should probably go back to school."

"No, I mean, us. I don't know what you want. I don't know if you're ready to be out," I say, but he taps along the creases in my palm with his thumb, and it makes me lose focus.

His thumb stops tapping, and he looks at me, and then he twines his fingers through mine. I lean back, tilting my head toward him.

"I'm all in, if you are," he says.

"All in?" I say. "Like what? Like boyfriend?"

"I mean, yeah. If that's what you want."

"That's what I want," I say. My boyfriend. My brown eyed,

grammar nerd, soccer star boyfriend.

And I can't stop smiling. I mean, there are times when it's actually more work not to smile.

That night, as of 8:05, Bram Greenfeld is no longer Single on Facebook—a.k.a. the best thing that has ever happened in the history of the internet.

At 8:11, Simon Spier is no longer Single either. Which generates about five million Likes and an instantaneous comment from Abby Suso: *LIKE LIKE LIKE*.

Followed by a comment from Alice Spier: *Wait—what?*

Followed by another comment from Abby Suso: *Call me!!*

I text her and tell her I'll talk to her tomorrow. I think I want to keep the details to myself tonight.

Instead, I call Bram. I mean, I almost can't believe I didn't have his number until yesterday. He picks up right away.

"Hi," he says, quickly and softly. Like the word belongs to us.

"Big news on Facebook tonight." I sink backward onto my mattress.

His quiet laugh. "Yeah."

"So what's our next move? Do we keep it classy? Or do we blast everyone's newsfeeds with kissing selfies?"

"Probably the selfies," he says. "But just a couple dozen a day."

"And we have to shout out our anniversary every week. Every Sunday."

"Well, and every Monday for our first kiss."

"And a couple dozen posts every night about how much we miss each other."

"I do miss you, though," he says.

I mean, Jesus Christ. What a week to be grounded.

"What are you doing right now?" I ask.

"Is that an invitation?"

"I wish it was."

He laughs. "I'm sitting at my desk, looking through my window, and talking to you."

"Talking to your boyfriend."

"Yeah," he says. I can hear him smiling. "Him."

"All right." Abby accosts me at my locker. "I'm about to lose it. What the heck is going on with you and Bram?"

"I'm, uh." I look at her and smile as a wave of heat rises in my cheeks. She waits. And I shrug. I don't know why it's so weird talking about this.

"Oh my gosh. Look at you."

"What?" I ask.

"Blushing." She pokes my cheeks. "I'm sorry, but you're so cute, I can't even stand it. Just go. Keep walking."

Bram and I have English and algebra together, which basically amounts to two hours of staring longingly at his mouth and five hours of longingly imagining his mouth. Instead of lunch, we sneak into the auditorium, and it's strange seeing the stage stripped of the set for *Oliver!* The school talent show is on Friday, and someone's already hung spangled gold tassels in front of the curtains.

We're alone in the theater, but it feels too big, so I take Bram by the hand and pull him into the boys' dressing room.

"Aha," he says as I fiddle with the latch. "This is a doors-locked kind of activity."

"Yup," I say, and then I kiss him.

His hands fall to my waist, and he pulls me in closer. He's only a few inches taller than me, and he smells like Dove soap, and for someone whose kissing career began yesterday, he has seriously magical lips. Soft and sweet and lingering. He kisses like Elliott Smith sings.

And then we pull out chairs, and I twist mine around sideways so I can rest my legs across his lap. And he drums his hands across my shins, and we talk about everything. Little Fetus being the size of a sweet potato. Frank Ocean being gay.

"Oh, and guess who was apparently bisexual," Bram says.

"Who?"

"Casanova."

"Freaking Casanova?"

"For real," he says. "According to my dad."

"You're telling me," I say, kissing his fist, "that your dad told you Casanova was bisexual."

"It was his response to me coming out."

"Your dad is amazing."

"Amazingly awkward."

I love his wry smile. I love watching him relax around me. I mean, I love this. Everything. He leans forward to scratch his ankle, and my heart just twists. The golden brown skin on the nape of his neck.

Everything.

I float through the rest of the day, and he's all I can think about. And then I text him as soon as I get home. *Miss you sooooo much!!!*

I mean, it's a joke. Mostly.

He texts back immediately. *Happy two day anniversary!!!!!!*

Which makes me cackle at the kitchen table.

"You're in a good mood," says my mom, walking in with Bieber.

I shrug.

She shoots me this curious half smile. "All right, well, don't feel like you have to talk about it, but I'm just saying. If you wanted to . . ."

Freaking psychologists. So much for not being weird and obsessed.

I hear a car pull into the driveway. "Nora's home already?" I ask. It's funny, but I've gotten used to her being gone until dinner.

I look out the window and do a double take. I mean, Nora's home. But the car. The driver.

"Is that Leah?" I ask. "Driving Nora?"

"Appears to be."

"Okay, yeah. I have to go out there."

"Oh no," she says. "Too bad you're grounded."

"Mom," I say.

She tips her palms up.

"Come on. Please." Already, Nora's opening the car door.

"I'm open to negotiating," she says.

"For what?"

"One night of parole in exchange for ten minutes of access to your Facebook."

Jesus Christ.

"Five," I say. "Supervised."

"You got it," she says. "But I want to see the boyfriend."

So yeah. At least one of my sisters is about to get murdered.

But first: Leah. I sprint out the door.

Nora's face whips toward me in surprise, but I run straight past her, panting, as I reach the passenger side door. Before Leah can object, I pull it open and climb inside.

Bram's car is old, but Leah's car is a Flintstones relic. I mean, it has a tape deck and crank windows. There's a line of plush anime characters on the dashboard, and the floor is always littered with papers and empty Coke bottles. And there's that floral grandmother smell.

I actually sort of love Leah's car.

Leah looks at me in disbelief. I mean, waves of stink-eye

roll off of her. "Get the hell out of my car," she says.

"I want to talk."

"Okay, well, I don't."

I click in my seat belt. "Take me to Waffle House."

"You're fucking kidding me."

"Not even a little bit." I lean back into the seat.

"So you're carjacking me."

"Oh," I say, "I guess so."

"Fucking unbelievable." She shakes her head. But a moment later, she starts driving. She stares straight ahead with her mouth in a line, and she doesn't say a word.

"I know you're pissed at me," I say.

Nothing.

"And I'm sorry about Midtown. I really am."

Still.

"Will you just say something?"

"We're here." She puts the car in park. The lot is almost empty. "You can get your fucking waffle or whatever."

"You're coming with me," I say.

"Um, yeah, no."

"Okay, then don't. But I'm not going in without you."

"Not my problem."

"Fine," I say. "We'll talk here." I unlatch my seat belt and turn toward her.

"There's nothing to talk about."

"So, what? That's it? We're just not going to be friends anymore?"

She leans back and shuts her eyes. "Aww. Maybe you should go cry about it to Abby."

"Okay, seriously?" I say. "What the hell is your problem with her?" I'm not trying to raise my voice, but it comes out booming.

"I don't have a problem with her," Leah says. "I just don't know why we're suddenly best friends with her."

"Well, because she's Nick's girlfriend, for one thing."

Leah whips her head toward me like I've slapped her.

"That's right. Keep making this about Nick," she says, "and we can all just fucking forget that you're obsessed with her, too."

"Are you kidding me? I'm gay!"

"You're platonically obsessed with her!" she yells. "It's cool, though. She's such a fucking upgrade."

"What?"

"Female best friend four-point-fucking-oh. Now available in the prettiest, perkiest package ever!"

"Oh, for the love of God," I say. "You're pretty."

She laughs. "All right."

"Seriously, just stop it. I'm so fucking tired of this." I look at her. "She's not an upgrade. You're my best friend."

She snorts.

"Well, you are. Both of you. And Nick. All three of you," I say. "But I could never replace you. You're Leah."

"Then why did you come out to her first?" she says.

"Leah," I say.

"Just—whatever. I don't have the right to give a shit."

"Stop saying that. You can give all kinds of shits."

She's quiet. And then I'm quiet. And then she says, "It was just so, I don't know. It was obvious that Nick liked her. None of that's been a fucking surprise. But when you told her first, it was like, I didn't even see that coming. I thought you trusted me."

"I do," I say.

"Well, apparently you trust her more," she says, "which is awesome, because how long have you known her? Six months? You've known me for six years."

And I don't know what to say. There's a lump in my throat.

"But whatever," she says. "I can't—you know. It's your thing."

"I mean." I swallow. "Yeah, it was easier to tell her. But it's not about trusting her more or you more or anything like that. You don't even know." My eyes prickle. "It's like, yeah. I've known you forever, and Nick even longer. You guys know me better than anyone. You know me too well," I say.

She grips the steering wheel and avoids my eyes.

"I mean, everything. You know everything about me. The wolf T-shirts. The cookie cones. 'Boom Boom Pow.'"

She cracks a smile.

"And no, I don't have that kind of a history with Abby. But that's what made it easier. There's this huge part of me, and I'm still trying it on. And I don't know how it fits together. How I fit together. It's like a new version of me. I just needed someone who could run with that." I sigh. "But I really wanted to tell you."

"Okay."

"It's just, it got to the point where it was hard to bring it up."

I stare at the steering wheel.

"I mean, I get that," she says finally. "I do. It's like the longer you sit with some shit, the harder it is to talk about."

We're both silent for a moment.

"Leah?"

"Yeah?"

"What happened with your dad?" My breath hitches.

"My dad?"

I turn my head toward her.

"Well, it's kind of a funny story."

"Yeah?"

"Um. Not really. He hooked up with this hottie nineteen-year-old at his work. And then he left."

"Oh." I look at her. "Leah, I'm so freaking sorry."

I spent six years not asking that question.

God, I'm such an asshole.

"Stop blinking like that," she says.

"Like what?"

"Don't you dare cry."

"What? No way."

Which is the moment I lose it. Full-on, puff-eyed, snot-faucet crying.

"You're a mess, Spier."

"I know!" I sort of collapse into her shoulder. Her almond shampoo smell is so perfectly familiar. "I really love you, you know? I'm so sorry about everything. About the Abby thing. All of it."

"It's fine."

"Really. I love you."

She sniffs.

"Um, did you get something in your eye, Leah?"

"No. Shut up. You did."

I wipe my eyes and laugh.

34

FROM: marty.mcfladdison@gmail.com
TO: hourtohour.notetonote@gmail.com
DATE: Jan 29 at 5:24 PM
SUBJECT: sorry doesn't even begin to cover it

Hey Spier,

I'm assuming you hate me, which would make absolute sense under the circumstances. I don't even know where to begin with all of this, so I guess I'll just start by saying I'm sorry. Even though I know that sorry is a completely inadequate word, and maybe I should be doing this in person, but you probably don't even want to look at me, so I guess it is what it is.

Anyway, I can't stop thinking about our conversation in the parking lot and what you said about what I took from you. And I really feel like I took something enormous. It's like I didn't let myself see it before, but now that I see it, I can't believe the things I did to you. All of it. The blackmail, and you're right, it was actually blackmail. And the Tumblr post. I don't know if you realize, but I took the post down myself before the mods could even deal with it. I know that doesn't really make it better, but I guess I want you to know that. I just feel sick with guilt about the entire thing, and I'm not even going to ask you to forgive me. I just want you to know how sorry I am.

I don't even know how to explain it. I'll try, but it's probably going to sound stupid, most likely because it is in fact stupid. You should know first that I'm not homophobic and I honestly think gay people are awesome or normal or whatever you prefer. So that's all good and everything.

Anyway, my brother came out over the summer, right before he went back to Georgetown, and it's been this huge deal with my whole family. My parents are trying to turn it into this big awesome thing, and so now our house is like this gay utopia. But it's so totally weird, because Carter's not even home, and he never actually talks about it even when he is home. My parents and I marched in the Pride Parade this year, and he wasn't even there, and when I told him about it, he said, "Um, okay, cool," like maybe it was a bit much. And maybe it was. And that was the weekend before I logged into your email. I guess I was in kind of a weird place.

But I'm probably just making excuses, because maybe it was all about me having a crush on a girl and feeling desperate. And me being jealous of how a girl like Abby could move here and choose to befriend you out of everyone, and you have so many friends already, and I don't think you even get what a big deal that is. I don't mean to call you out or insult you or anything. I'm just saying that it seems like it's so easy for you, and you should know you're actually really lucky.

So I don't even know if that makes any sense at all, and you probably stopped reading this ages ago, but I'm just putting all of it out there. And for what it's worth, I'm so incredibly, impossibly sorry. Anyway, word on the street is that you are now deliriously happy in gay love with one Abraham Greenfeld, and I want you to know that I'm way beyond happy for you. You deserve it completely. You're an awesome dude, Spier, and it was cool getting to know you. If I could do it again, I would have blackmailed you into being my friend and left it at that.

Extremely sincerely,

Marty Addison

35

THE TALENT SHOW STARTS AT seven, and Nick and I arrive just as they're dimming the lights. Bram and Garrett are supposed to be sitting in the back toward the middle, with two seats saved. My eyes find him immediately. He's twisted all the way around in his chair, watching the door, and he smiles when he sees me.

We squeeze through the row, and I sit beside Bram, with Nick and Garrett on either side of us. "Is that a program?" Nick asks, leaning over me.

"Yup. Want it?" Garrett asks, passing down an already-worn cylinder of paper.

Nick scans through the list of acts, and I know he's looking for Abby.

"Bet she comes on first or last," I say.

He smiles. "Second to last." And then the houselights shut off.

The audience chatter tapers off as the stage lights come up, and Student Council Maddie steps up to the microphone. I lean closer to Bram. And because it's so dark, I slide a hand onto his knee. I feel him shift quietly as he laces his fingers through mine. He lifts them and presses his lips to the edge of my palm.

He pauses, holding them there. And there's this fluttery yank below my navel.

Then he lets our intertwined hands fall back onto his lap. And if this is what it's like having a boyfriend, I don't know why in God's name I waited so long.

Onstage, it's one girl after another. All in short dresses. All singing songs by Adele.

And then it's Abby's turn, and she emerges from the wings, dragging a skinny black music stand to the edge of the stage. My eyes cut to Nick, but he doesn't see me. He's staring raptly forward, with straight posture and a smile edging his lips. A blond sophomore girl steps out with a violin and sheet music. Then she tucks the violin beneath her chin, and looks at Abby. Who nods at her and inhales, visibly. And the violinist starts to play.

It's a strange, almost mournful version of "Time After Time." Abby's movements convey every note. I've never watched anyone dance solo before, beyond the awkward showboating that happens when people circle up at bar mitzvahs. At first,

I have no point of reference. In a group, you can look for synchronicity. But Abby controls her own motion; and yet, every movement and gesture feels rich and deliberate and true.

I can't help but look at Nick as he watches. He smiles quietly into his fist the entire time.

Abby and her violinist finish to surprised, appreciative applause, and then the curtains close partially while the stage is set for the final act. They pull out a drum set, so I guess it's some kind of band. Maddie takes the mic and makes a bunch of announcements about various ways you can give the student council money. There are a few experimental twangs and booms from behind the curtain as the instruments are plugged in and tested.

"Who is this?" I ask Nick.

He checks his program. "They're called Emoji."

"Cute."

The curtain opens on five girls with instruments, and the first thing I notice is the colors. They're all wearing different patterned fabrics, and the colors are so bright that it's weirdly punk rock. And then the drummer kicks in with a fast twitchy beat.

Which is when I notice that the drummer is Leah.

I'm actually speechless. Her hair hangs past her shoulders, and her hands move impossibly quickly. And then she's joined by the other instruments—Morgan on the keyboard and Anna on the bass. Taylor on vocals.

And my sister Nora on lead guitar, looking so relaxed and confident that I almost don't recognize her. I mean, I'm gobsmacked. I didn't even know she was playing guitar again.

Bram looks at me and laughs. "Simon, your face."

They cover Michael Jackson's "Billie Jean," and I'm not even kidding. It's absolutely electric. Girls are getting up and dancing in the aisles. And then they transition straight into the Cure's "Just Like Heaven." Taylor's voice is sweet and high and effortless, and it's somehow perfect. But I'm still so stunned. I can barely process it.

Bram was right: people really are like houses with vast rooms and tiny windows. And maybe it's a good thing, the way we never stop surprising each other.

"Nora's not bad, right?" says Nick, leaning toward me.

"You knew about this?"

"I've been working with her for months. But she told me not to tell you."

"Seriously? Why?"

"Because she knew you'd make it a big deal," he said.

I mean, that's my family. Everything's a freaking secret, because everything's a big deal. Everything is like coming out.

"My parents are going to go nuts about missing this."

"Nah, I got them here," Nick says, pointing across the aisle, where I can see the backs of their heads a couple of rows up. They're leaning toward each other with their heads together. And then I notice the messy knot of dark blond hair sitting next to my mom. It's funny, but it almost looks like it could be Alice.

Nora smiles her tiny smile, and her hair is loose and wavy, and there's actually kind of a lump in my throat.

"You look so proud," whispers Bram.

"Yeah, it's weird," I say.

Then Nora's hand stills against the body of the guitar, and Taylor stops singing, and everyone stops playing, except Leah, who gets this pissed-off, determined look on her face. And then she launches into the most freaking awesome, badass drum solo I've ever heard. Her eyes are focused and her cheeks are flushed, and she really looks so pretty. She'd never believe me if I told her.

I turn to look at Bram, but he's turned the other direction, facing Garrett, and I can see from his cheeks that he's grinning. And Garrett shakes his head and smiles, and says, "I don't want to hear it, Greenfeld."

The song ends, and people yell and cheer as the house-lights come on. There's a swell of movement out the back to the atrium, and we let it pass us. Abby comes out and finds us directly. And then a guy with brown hair and a short red beard slides into the empty row in front of us and smiles at me.

"You're clearly Simon," he says.

I nod, confused. He looks familiar, too, actually, but I can't quite place him.

"Hi. I'm Theo."

"Theo, like . . . Alice's Theo?"

"Something like that," he says, grinning.

"Is she here? What are you doing here?" My eyes flick automatically to where my parents had been sitting, but their row is already empty. "It's nice to meet you," I add.

"Likewise," he says. "So, Alice is in the lobby, but she sent me in with a message for you and, uh, Bram."

Bram and I exchange glances, while Nick, Abby, and Garrett look on with interest.

"Okay," he says. "She wanted me to tell you that your parents are about to invite you to some place called The Varsity, and you're supposed to say you can't go. And the magic words are that you need to catch up on homework."

"What? Why?"

"Because," Theo says, nodding, "apparently, it takes half an hour to get down there, and half an hour to get back, plus all the time spent ordering and eating."

"Which is completely freaking worth it," I inform him. "Have you had their Frosted Orange?"

"I have not," Theo says. "Though, in fairness, I've spent a lifetime sum total of five hours in Atlanta. So far."

"But why doesn't she want me there?"

"Because she's giving you two hours at home unsupervised."

"Oh." My cheeks are burning. Nick snorts.

"Yup," Theo says, grinning briefly at Bram. "So, I guess I'll see you guys out there." He heads toward the atrium.

I look at Bram, and his eyes are lit with mischief. It's very un-Bram-like.

"Oh, were you in on this?"

"No," he says, "but I stand in support."

"I mean, it's a little creepy having my sister orchestrate the whole thing."

He smiles, biting his lip.

"But kind of awesome," I admit.

So, we head out to the atrium, and I make a beeline for Alice. Bram hangs back, standing with Nick, Abby, and Garrett.

"I can't believe you're here."

"Well," she says, "little Nick Eisner clued me in that something big was happening. But I'm sorry I missed the play last week, bub."

"It's fine. I met Theo," I say, lowering my voice. "He's cool."

"Yeah, yeah." She smiles self-consciously. "Which one's yours?"

"Gray zippy sweater, next to Nick."

"I'm lying. I've been stalking him on Facebook," she says, hugging me. "He's adorable."

"I know."

And then the side door swings open, and the girls of Emoji step into the atrium. Nora actually yelps when she sees us.

"Allie!" she says. She launches toward her. "What are you doing here? Why aren't you in Connecticut?"

"Because you're a rock star," Alice says.

"I'm not a rock star," Nora says, beaming.

My parents have a majorly Seussish bouquet for her, and

they spend about five minutes gushing about her guitar skills. And then they want to gush about the rest of the band and Abby, so we sort of converge into one big group. And Nora is talking to Theo, and my parents are shaking hands with Bram, and Taylor and Abby are randomly hugging. It's a surreal, wonderful scene.

I walk over to Leah, and she grins and shrugs. So I give her this crushing hug. "You are a freaking boss," I tell her. "I had no idea."

"They let me borrow some of the school drums. I've been teaching myself."

"For how long?"

"About two years."

I just look at her. She bites her lip.

"I guess I'm awesome?" she says.

"YES," I say. And I'm sorry, but I just have to hug her again.

"All right," she says, squirming a little. But I can tell she's smiling.

So I kiss her on the forehead, and she turns unbelievably red. When Leah blushes, it's so hardcore.

And then my parents walk over to propose a celebratory trip to The Varsity.

"I should probably catch up on homework," I tell them.

"You sure, kid?" asks my dad. "Want me to bring you back a Frosted Orange?"

"Or two," says Alice. And then she grins.

Alice tells me to keep my phone on, so she can text me when they're on the way home.

"And you won't forget the Frosties."

"Simon. I believe this is known as having your cake and eating it, too."

"Large ones," I say. "Souvenir cups."

There are probably a hundred people still walking toward the parking lot. I'm riding back with Bram. It's too public to hold hands. This being Georgia. So, I walk next to him, leaving a space between us. Just a couple of guys hanging out on a Friday night. Except the air around us seems to crackle with electricity.

Bram is parked in the raised area of the parking lot, on the top level. He unlocks his car from the top of the stairs, and I walk around to the passenger side. Then the car next to me comes noisily to life, startling me. I wait for it to pull out before opening my door, but the driver doesn't move. And then I look into the window and see that it's Martin.

We lock eyes. I'm surprised he's here, because he wasn't in school today. Which means I haven't seen him since he emailed me.

He rakes his hand through his hair, and his mouth sort of twists.

And I just sort of look at him.

I haven't written back to his email. Not yet.

I don't know.

But it's chilly outside, so I slide into the car, and then watch through the window as Martin backs out.

"Are you warm enough?" Bram asks. I nod. "So, I guess we're going to your place."

He sounds nervous, and it makes me nervous. "Is that okay?"

"Yeah," he says, eyes flicking to me. "I mean, *yeah.*"

"Okay. Yeah," I say. And my heart pounds.

Stepping into the entryway with Bram is like seeing it for the first time. The random painted wood dresser against the wall, overflowing with catalogs and junk mail. A creepy, framed drawing of Alvin and the Chipmunks that Nora made in kindergarten. There's the muffled thud of Bieber jumping off the couch, followed by jangling and clicking as he skitters toward us.

"Well, hi," Bram says, practically crouching. "I know who you are."

Bieber greets him passionately, all tongue, and Bram laughs in surprise.

"You have that effect on us," I explain.

He kisses Bieber on the nose and follows me into the living room. "Are you hungry?" I ask. "Or thirsty?"

"I'm fine," he says.

"We probably have Coke." I very badly want to kiss him,

and I don't know why I'm stalling. "Do you want to watch something?"

"Sure."

I look at him. "I don't."

He laughs. "So, let's not."

"Do you want to see my room?"

He smiles his mischievous smile again. So maybe it is Bram-like. Maybe I'm still figuring him out.

Framed photographs line the wall by the staircase, and Bram pauses to look at each one. "The famous trash can costume," he says.

"Nora's finest hour," I say. "I forgot you knew about that."

"And this is you with the fish, right? So obviously thrilled."

In the picture, I'm six or seven, sun-flushed, my arm extended as far away from my body as possible, dangling a caught fish from a piece of twine. I look like I'm about to burst into horrified tears.

"I've always loved fishing," I say.

"I can't believe how blond you were."

When we reach the top of the stairs, he takes my hand and squeezes it. "You're really here," I say, shaking my head. "So, this is it."

I open the door, and try to kick some of the clothes aside as we walk in. "Sorry about . . . all of this." There's a dirty-clothes pile next to the empty hamper, and a clean-clothes pile next to the empty dresser. Books and papers everywhere. An empty bag of Goldfish crackers on the desk, next to a nonfunctioning Curious George alarm clock, my laptop, and a plastic robotic arm. Backpack on the desk chair. Framed vinyl album covers hanging askew on the walls.

But my bed is made. So that's where we sit, leaning against the wall with our legs stretched forward.

"When you email me," he says, "where are you?"

"Usually here. Sometimes at the desk."

"Huh," he says, nodding. And then I lean over and kiss him softly on the neck, just below his jaw. He turns to me and swallows.

"Hi," I say.

He smiles. "Hi."

And then I kiss him for real, and he kisses me back, and his hands fist my hair. And we're kissing like it's breathing. My stomach flutters wildly. And somehow we end up horizontal, his hands curved up around my back.

"I like this," I say, and my voice comes out breathless. "We should do this. Every day."

"Okay."

"Let's never do anything else. No school. No meals. No homework."

"I was going to ask you to see a movie," he says, smiling. When he smiles, I smile.

"No movies. I hate movies."

"Oh, really?"

"Really, really. Why would I want to watch other people kissing," I say, "when I could be kissing you?"

Which I guess he can't argue with, because he pulls me in closer and kisses me urgently. And suddenly, I'm hard, and I know he is, too. It's thrilling and strange and completely terrifying.

"What are you thinking about?" Bram says.

"Your mom."

"Noooo," he says, laughing.

But I actually am. Specifically, her Every Time Including Oral rule. Because it only now occurs to me that the rule might apply to me. At some point. Eventually.

I kiss him briefly on the lips.

"I really do want to take you out," he says. "If you didn't hate all movies, what would you want to see?"

"Anything," I say.

"But probably a love story, right? Something Simonish, with a happy ending."

"Why does no one ever believe I'm a cynic?"

"Hmm." He laughs.

I let my body relax on top of his, my head tucked into the crook of his neck. "I like no endings," I say. "I like things that don't end."

He squeezes me tighter and kisses my head, and we lie there.

Until my phone buzzes in the back pocket of my jeans. Alice. *Exiting the highway. Be ready.*

Roger that. Thanks, Paul Revere. I rest my phone on Bram's chest while I type.

Then I kiss him again quickly, and we both stand up and stretch. And then we each spend some time in the bathroom. But by the time my family gets home, we're sitting on the love seat in the living room with a pile of textbooks between us.

"Oh, hi," I say, looking up from a work sheet. "How was it? Bram came over to study, by the way."

"And I'm sure you were very productive," my mom says. I press my lips together. And Bram quietly coughs.

I can tell from her expression that a conversation is coming. Some kind of awkward discussion about ground rules. Some kind of big deal.

But maybe this is a big deal. Maybe it's a holy freaking huge awesome deal.

Maybe I want it to be.

Acknowledgments

There are so many people who left beautiful fingerprints all over this book, and who deserve more thanks and recognition than I can possibly express. I am forever grateful to . . .

. . . Donna Bray, my genius editor, who completely gets Simon's sense of humor, and who knows this story inside and out. Thank you for adoring and embracing Simon from day one. I was so blown away by the depth, texture, and wisdom of your feedback. It strengthened this book to a degree I didn't imagine was possible.

. . . Brooks Sherman, the extraordinary agent who was the first to believe in this book, and who sold it in four days like a ninja. You are part oracle, part editor, part psychologist, and part living proof that Slytherins are wonderful people. Thanks for being such a tremendous champion for my work, such an all-around badass, and such an amazing friend.

. . . Viana Siniscalchi, Emilie Polster, Stef Hoffman, Caroline Sun, Bethany Reis, Veronica Ambrose, Patty Rosati, Nellie Kurtzman, Margot Wood, Alessandra Balzer, Kate Morgan Jackson, Molly Motch, Eric Svenson, and the rest of the team at B+B and Harper, for your endless enthusiasm and incredibly hard work (and for Suman Seewat, for championing me so hard at Harper Canada!). Many thanks, too, to Alison Klapthor and Chris Bilheimer, for the cover of my dreams.

. . . the awesome and amazingly collaborative team at the Bent Agency, especially Molly Ker Hawn and Jenny Bent. Thanks, too, to Janet Reid and the gang at FinePrint—plus Alexa Valle, who got the ball rolling. Also so grateful for my wonderful publicist, Deb Shapiro.

. . . my brilliant and incredibly supportive team at Penguin/Puffin UK, including Jessica Farrugia Sharples, Vicky Photiou, Ben Horslen, and especially Anthea Townsend (with extra whoops). Wildly thankful, too, to all of my foreign publishing teams for believing in this book and working so hard to bring it to life overseas.

. . . Kimberly Ito, my very first reader and my platonic Blue. I'll never be able to thank you enough for your wisdom, support, and sense of humor.

. . . Beckminavidera (which includes the following geniuses: Adam Silvera, David Arnold, and Jasmine Warga). Worming my way into your cult was the smartest thing I ever did. How would I have survived without our epic email threads, Oreo debates, and collective Elliott Smith worship?

. . . Heidi Schultz, for supplying endless sisterly wisdom and making me crave all the desserts.

. . . the Atlanta Writers Club for the opportunity to attend your extraordinary conference and critique groups—especially George Weinstein and the hilarious, brilliant minds of Team Erratica: Chris Negron, Emily Carpenter, and Manda Pullen.

. . . the Fearless Fifteeners and my many other friends in the writing community who laughed with me, supported me, advised me, and kept me sane. Many thanks, too, for the incredible librarians, bloggers, publishing professionals, and booksellers who have blown me away with their support—with extra Oreos for Diane Capriola! Thanks for making me feel so welcome in this community from day one.

. . . my heroes, Andrew Smith, Nina LaCour, Tim Federle, and Alex Sanchez, who slayed me with their books, and then slayed me again by blurbing mine.

. . . the brilliant teenagers, kids, adults, and families I've worked with during my years as a practicing psychologist. Thanks in particular to the students at Kingsbury, who never let me get away with being old and out of touch.

. . . the extraordinary teachers I've had over the years, especially Molly Mercer, for being more than moderately badass, and for being the best, most important teacher of my life.

. . . my Riverwood High School theater friends, whose

influence on my life and on this book cannot be overstated (especially Sarah Beth Brown, Ricky Manne, and Annie Lipsitz). Thanks, too, to the many other friends who inspired and supported me more than they even know: Diane and the entire Blumenfeld family, Lauren Starks, Jaime Hensel and the entire Hensel family, Jaime Semensohn, Betsy Ballard, Nina Morton, the Binswangers, the Shumans, and so many others— and to the Takoma Mamas, who saved my life in five million tiny ways.

. . . My family: Molly Goldstein, Adele Thomas, Curt and Gini Albertalli—plus so many more Goldsteins, Albertallis, Thomases, Bells, Bermans, Wechslers, Levines, and Witchels. Thanks, too, to Gail McLaurin and Kevin Saylor for ongoing support. Finally, huge thanks to my stepmother, Candy Goldstein, and my stepbrothers, William Cotton and Cameron Klein.

. . . Eileen Thomas, my mom, who has always treated my life like a holy awesome big deal; to Jim Goldstein, the original badass, hardcore, hipster dad; to my sister, Caroline Goldstein, who rocked the trash can costume for Purim and knows about Coke bottle mouth; and to my brother, Sam Goldstein, whose preschool-era Pokémon stories are better (and more vulgar) than anything I could ever write.

. . . my sons, Owen and Henry Albertalli, whom I love wholly and ridiculously. Learning who you are and watching you grow are the greatest privileges of my life.

. . . my husband, Brian Albertalli, who is my absolute best friend and partner in crime, and who owns the other half of my brain. There wouldn't be a book without you. You are my shore worth swimming to. You are my big deal.

. . . Edgardo Menvielle, Cathy Tuerk, Shannon Wyss, and the many other clinicians and volunteers who change lives daily through the CNMC Gender and Sexuality program. Thanks for all that you do, and thanks for welcoming me with open arms.

. . . and to the extraordinary LGBT and gender-nonconforming children and teens in my life (and your extra-ordinary families): you blow me away with your wisdom, humor, creativity, and courage. You probably already guessed this, but I wrote this book for you.

#SIMON VS

'*You've Got Mail* for a YA audience. Achingly romantic and effortlessly diverse. Your heart will smile for Simon and Blue'
Jess Hearts Books @JessHeartsBooks

'Albertalli spins a tale of love and growing into who you want to be. *Simon Vs* is an amazing coming-of-age story'
Sondra, SorceryInTheBookshelves.com, @RunYouCleverBoy

'Funny, heartwarming and utterly compelling – *Simon Vs* is a very genuine and innovative exploration of LGBTQIA + life'
Georgina Howlett, BritishBiblioholic, @thereadurrent

'Emotionally gripping and tackles strong yet sensitive issues that face a large percentage of teenagers today! #SimonVs'
Daniel, The Bloggers Bookshop, @theBlogbookshop

'#SimonVs is a truly wonderful book. Funny, thoughtful and a brilliant read all round' Lee Farnell, @leefarnell

'Everybody should read this book. Not because it is diverse, not because it is different. Simply because it is good'
Eline Berkhout, @TheBookaneers29

The Very First  Emails

FROM: bluegreen118@gmail.com
TO: hourtohour.notetonote@gmail.com
DATE: Aug 23 at 8:12 PM
SUBJECT: I've never done this before

Dear anonymous person on the internet,

I don't really know where to begin. To be honest, I'm not sure this is a real email address, and I'm also not sure you're a real person. But in case you are real, hello! I'm the original poster from the creeksecrets thread about the vast houses and tiny windows and shore worth swimming to. I'm rereading what I wrote there and I can't stop cringing, so I'll start by apologizing for that. I'm not usually such an abuser of similes and metaphors.

Anyway, I'm not sure how to interpret your comment, but it sounds like you identify with part of what I wrote. Maybe? Even if not, I'm glad you commented. It made me feel less like I was shouting into the void, so thanks for that. And since you left your email address, I assume you're okay with me writing back. Though, I can't believe I'm actually writing you—I really didn't think I would. But it's been a week, and I haven't been able to stop thinking about your comment.

I guess I'm thinking it could be nice to talk with someone who can relate to how I'm feeling. No pressure, of course, but feel free to write back if you want to. I don't want to use my real name, but you can call me Blue.

FROM: hourtohour.notetonote@gmail.com
TO: bluegreen118@gmail.com
DATE: Aug 24 at 9:56 PM
SUBJECT: Re: I've never done this before

Hi, Blue!

Wow, I'm actually kind of flipping out right now, because I seriously didn't think I'd hear from you. I'm so glad I checked this email account!! Wow. Okay. First of all, thanks for your email and also for your Tumblr post. I really liked it, Blue, and it wasn't cringey at all, I promise.

So do you go here (here meaning CHS)? I do, I'm a

junior. And I'm a guy (are you a guy?). Anyway, I could relate a lot to your post. Like, pretty much all of it, but especially the part about being gay. I'm not out yet, either. I guess a part of me wants to be, but a part of me's like . . . no. It's hard to explain. I don't know. Maybe you get it.

So, yeah—it's really nice to meet you! This is kind of cool, right? Even writing this email makes me feel eleven times less alone.

—Jacques (not my real name, bwahahaha—two can play at this game)

FROM: bluegreen118@gmail.com
TO: hourtohour.notetonote@gmail.com
DATE: Aug 26 at 7:46 PM
SUBJECT: Re: I've never done this before

Jacques,

Eleven times less alone? That's oddly specific. ☺ But I know exactly what you mean.

Anyway, wow. Hi. You wrote back. I'm really glad you liked my post. Now I'm actually happy I put it out there. I have to admit, it's strange to be writing a somewhat personal email to you when we don't know each other's identities. Though, in a way, I guess that makes it easier.

I am a guy, and I'm also a junior at Creekwood. I think you're actually the first other gay guy I've met here. It's pretty surreal to be talking to you (in a good way, though). I wonder if we know each other in real life.

I think I understand what you mean. I feel like I'm constantly going back and forth about wanting to come out. I have these moments where I'm almost bursting to tell people—of course, that's where I was when I posted the thing on the Tumblr. But I always feel so weird about it a few hours later, and sometimes I'm intensely relieved no one knows yet. What about you?

—Blue

FROM: hourtohour.notetonote@gmail.com
TO: bluegreen118@gmail.com
DATE: Aug 27 at 10:12 PM
SUBJECT: Re: I've never done this before

I mean, let's be real, eleven is the best number, which is perfect, because we're both in eleventh grade. WOW. And I can't believe we're both juniors. I bet we do know each other, which is weird to think about. What if we're actually enemies in real life? Do you have enemies? I don't think I do, not really. Though I guess various random people low-key annoy me. It's not even their fault. Some people just have really punchable faces. (FYI, I'm actually a really nonviolent person. Or more like I'm a violent person who at the same time doesn't want to hurt anyone, so I have to resort to fantasizing about punching people. It's very complicated. To be honest, usually I just eat my feelings.)

It's funny, for me, it's actually not so much that I go back and forth about wanting to come out. It's like I simultaneously do and don't want to be out. Which is pretty freaking exhausting, honestly. Like I'm in this constant state of JUST SAY IT and NO NEVER. Do you think that ever ends? I don't know, maybe I'm just a really indecisive person.

So what kind of stuff do you like to do after school and everything?

—Jacques

FROM: bluegreen118@gmail.com
TO: hourtohour.notetonote@gmail.com
DATE: Aug 29 at 9:13 PM
SUBJECT: Re: I've never done this before

I don't think I have any enemies, but now I'm definitely wondering if I'm the guy with the punchable face. How do you know if you have a punchable face? I've never been punched, so hopefully that's a good sign. I will say, I'm definitely with you on the issue of eating your feelings. I'm that person who has never smoked a cigarette or gotten drunk or anything like that, but I once ate five full jars of Nutella in one sitting. I do not recommend.

And I'm indecisive, too, in some ways. Okay, full disclosure: I was really conflicted when you replied to my post. I kept going back and forth about whether I should email you. I was (and am) definitely intrigued, but I guess I was also a little bit paranoid. It's just that you could have been anyone, and it's hard to know sometimes if someone's being a jerk or if they're being sincere. But I'm really glad I decided to email you.

So, you're probably going to think I'm ridiculous, but I'd rather not answer your last question. It's just . . . I think I like being anonymous for now. Is that okay?

—Blue

FROM: hourtohour.notetonote@gmail.com
TO: bluegreen118@gmail.com
DATE: Aug 30 at 3:47 PM
SUBJECT: Punchability

Oh, Blue, you have so much to learn about the rules of punchability, starting with the fact that it is completely impossible for you to have a punchable face. Rule number one: cute guys who make metaphors about the ocean between people are automatically unpunchable. Rule number two: there is no rule number two, it's just the one rule, so memorize it. BOOM.

Also, five jars of Nutella in one sitting is the most WTF idea I've ever heard in my life. Challenge accepted.

I don't think you're ridiculous, Blue. I totally understand why you don't want to tell me about your extracurricular activities (I'm guessing interpretive dance, though, you seem like the type). But seriously, I get it. It's this weird contradiction, right? It's so much easier to be open with someone who doesn't know you at all.

Anyway, I'm really glad you decided to email me, too. ☺

—Jacques

FROM: bluegreen118@g mail.com
TO: hourtohour.notetonote@gmail.com
DATE: Aug 31 at 10:20 AM
SUBJECT: Re: Punchability

Jacques,

I am so glad I qualify for exception to punchability per the terms of the first rule. Whew! But I'm confused, because I heard there was actually a second punchability exception for cute guys with French names and very poor judgment re: Nutella, despite being warned. And everyone else can catch these fists. Or is it catch these hands? This would probably be more intimidating if I actually knew the right phrasing.

And how did you know about my interpretive dance skills? Though I don't really think of that as an extracurricular activity. It's more of a calling. Also, I know exactly, exactly what you mean about it being easier to be open with someone who doesn't know you. We've been emailing for, what, a week? Already, you know things about me that I've never even told my best friend. I guess it makes you think about what it really means to know someone.

—Blue

FROM: hourtohour.notetonote@gmail.com
TO: bluegreen118@gmail.com
DATE: Sep 1 at 7:14 PM
SUBJECT: Re: Punchability

Hmm . . . I believe the phrase you're looking for is "catch these mittens." But uh-oh, what if my name's not actually French? And what if my judgment's not actually poor (seriously, I'm so confused, what about five jars of Nutella makes you think I have poor judgment)?? Also, how am I the one with poor judgment when YOU'RE THE ONE WHO ATE THE NUTELLA, BLUE. You. That was you.

But wow. I can relate so much to everything you're

saying. I already feel like I can tell you things I haven't told my best friend. Or my other best friend. Or my other best friend (I have a lot of best friends). I do think a big part of it is the anonymity. But it's not just that. It's weird, but I feel like you get me in some way. Which is probably why I jumped all over your original Tumblr post like the fanboy I am.

I think you're lonely, right? Me too.

—Jacques

FROM: bluegreen118@gmail.com
TO: hourtohour.notetonote@gmail.com
DATE: Sep 3 at 6:36 PM
SUBJECT: Catch these mittens

I mean, I don't want to belabor the point with the Nutella, but I'll just say this: it's one thing to innocently eat five jars of Nutella the night before the seventh-grade dance, resulting in four zits and some deeply, deeply uncomfortable moments doing the Cupid Shuffle. It's another thing entirely to go into it with eyes wide open. Poor. Judgment. (But also, enjoy! I'm dying to hear how it goes.)

Oh, wow. I'm kind of nervous about the idea of you fanboying over my post. Not in a bad way. I'm just not used to people noticing me like that. I'm really glad you liked it, though. I wrote it really quickly. Have you ever had that experience where you're writing something and it just pours out of you with no effort? It's so strange when that happens. It almost feels like the words already exist, and you're just transcribing them.

I do think I'm a little bit lonely. But I was lonelier two weeks ago.

—Blue

FROM: hourtohour.notetonote@gmail.com
TO: bluegreen118@gmail.com
DATE: Sep 5 at 12:14 AM
SUBJECT: Re: Catch these mittens

Okay, but real talk—is the Cupid Shuffle ever NOT deeply, deeply uncomfortable? Even realer talk: Why do seventh-grade dances even exist? Why do teachers do this to themselves? And I'm sorry, but high school dances are even worse. Not that I've actually been to one. But okay, you'll probably remember when Mila Odom and Adam Arnold left the homecoming dance and got to third base in Ms. Knight's office. Her freaking office! OF ALL PLACES. Belly of the beast. That was some A++ Tumblr content. Oh, creeksecrets, you fountain of beauty and wisdom.

So I kind of ALWAYS have the experience of writing

with no effort? I don't think we're talking about the same thing, though. I'm not really a writer, so I just kind of roll with whatever words pop into my head. I used to write a little bit. I just don't think I'm really good at it.

I was lonelier two weeks ago, too. It's funny—my mom even commented that I've been in a good mood lately. I told her it was because Taylor Swift has a new album. Not sure she believed me. ☺

—Jacques

FROM: bluegreen118@gmail.com
TO: hourtohour.notetonote@gmail.com
DATE: Sep 6 at 1:44 PM
SUBJECT: Re: Catch these mittens

Jacques,

I absolutely remember the Mila Odom/Adam Arnold handjob. Not that I was physically present for that iconic moment. But I do remember it being all over creeksecrets.

Side note: What are your thoughts about creek-secrets? I have mixed feelings. On one hand, it led me to you, which is nice. On the other hand, the second-hand embarrassment gets so real, I literally have to stop reading sometimes. I can't believe the things people are willing to share about themselves. AND THE

PHOTOGRAPHS. Why would I want to see a picture of pubic hair on a toilet seat? Who is the intended audience for that?

I don't think of myself as a writer, really, but I love to read. What about you? Do you have a favorite book? It's strange—there are so many things I can't ask you or tell you, or else we'll probably be able to figure out each other's identities. Like I don't want to tell you my favorite sport, for reasons. I guess I could tell you my least favorite sport (football). Do you have a least favorite sport? I'm sorry if these are awkward questions. I'm kind of an awkward person.

—Blue

FROM: hourtohour.notetonote@gmail.com
TO: bluegreen118@gmail.com
DATE: Sep 7 at 5:23 PM
SUBJECT: but I like awkward people

Okay, Blue, I guess I'll start with your adorably awkward questions. Favorite book: obviously Harry Potter. But I like basically everything except what we have to read in English class (a.k.a. old white guy shiterature). My least favorite sport is all sports. I don't know, maybe we should ask each other questions that are less grounded in day-to-day life. Like what's your favorite memory of all time? Other than getting to see a picture of pubic hair—obviously nothing could compete with that.

Now I'm trying to think of mine. Maybe it was the day we got our dog. Blue, you don't even know. We got him when he was like nine weeks old, and I almost died because he was so freaking cute. We have these family friends in Alabama, and their dog had a whole litter of babies. I was like ten at the time. Anyway, we drove to Alabama right after they were born, and they were these tiny squeaky beans, so precious and cute. So we picked our favorite little pupper, and he was such a mush. But he was too little to come home with us yet, so we went back to get him a few weeks later. And that whole time, I was so hyped, I couldn't even sleep. This went on for weeks. And then we got there, and he ran right to me. He totally remembered me. He slept in my lap on a towel for the whole ride home, and I fell asleep holding him, and I think that was the best moment of my life. All downhill from there.

—Jacques

FROM: bluegreen118@gmail.com
TO: hourtohour.notetonote@gmail.com
DATE: Sep 9 at 8:11 PM
SUBJECT: I'm glad you like awkward people

Okay, I have to confess that I like some old white guy shiterature, but I like a lot of other stuff, too. I've been really into graphic novels lately. Anyway, you're probably right—it's probably safer to avoid any of the details. My favorite memory. Hmm.

Okay. I don't know if this counts, because it's not really a specific memory (also, it's really nerdy. Like, REALLY nerdy. Brace yourself). So, in elementary school, I used to really love the first day of school. You know how you were so excited to get your puppy, you couldn't even sleep? That was me on the last night of summer, every single year. I'm pretty sure the excitement was 99 percent school supply–related. I love school supplies so much, Jacques. They are so crisp and hopeful, and they always make me feel like THIS is going to be my year.

But Jacques, your dog story is so ridiculously cute. I can totally picture it. I'm thinking beagle, right? A TINY SLEEPY BEAGLE PUPPY? Now I just want to hold him and maybe wrap him up in a blanket and feed him one kibble of dog food at a time. I love dogs so much. I've never had one, but I've wanted one my whole life. So, I guess your dog must be six or seven now? Give him a hug from me, okay?

—Blue

FROM: hourtohour.notetonote@gmail.com
TO: bluegreen118@gmail.com
DATE: Sep 11 at 12:02 AM
SUBJECT: I'm glad you're glad that I like awkward people

Well, Blue, I don't want to assume anything here, but I'm kind of getting the vibe you were one of those kids who sniffs school supplies. No judgment, though. School supplies are so crisp and hopeful, it's true. It's such a shame we have to ruin them with school. Okay, I'm calling it. Best school supply: the compass. Remember those? The circles I drew with that thing were round as hell.

Not a beagle! But I guess I shouldn't tell you what kind of dog he actually is, with the anonymity thing and everything. Not that I really expect people to know my dog, but you never know. I'll just say he's bigger than a Chihuahua and smaller than a Great Dane. That should narrow it down, right? I'll definitely give him a hug from you, though he is solidly passed out and snoring. On my bed, too. What a jerk. I'm gonna go spoon with him now.

—Jacques

FROM: bluegreen118@gmail.com
TO: hourtohour.notetonote@gmail.com
DATE: Sep 11 at 10:51 PM
SUBJECT: I do NOT sniff school supplies . . . often

Jacques,

Your dog sleeps in your bed, and I am so jealous. I think my vision for the perfect future is basically a king-sized bed with a husband and a dog. Anyway, I'm not usually up this late (I'M A NERD. SHH. I KNOW THIS), so this will be a quick email. I'm sorry! But I just wanted to write back today. Also, I have another question for you. Most embarrassing moment. Go.

—Blue

FROM: hourtohour.notetonote@gmail.com
TO: bluegreen118@gmail.com
DATE: Sep 12 at 9:08 PM
SUBJECT: you asked for this

Blue,

I mean, I actually have approximately fifty gazillion most embarrassing moments, but this one is the literal worst. And I'm going to take you at your word that you're up for hearing this. Just remember: I warned you. Dun dun dunnnnnnn.

So, I think I was about six years old, and we were at the pool. It was a super-hot day, and it was really crowded. And—I actually remember this—I felt like I had to fart, so I just went for it. BUT THIS WAS NO MERE FART. It was . . . yeah. So, at the time, I figured it was just a turd, and therefore not a big deal, so I kind of shook it out of my bathing suit and kept swimming. (Yes, I was THAT kid.)

Anyway, OF COURSE someone saw it, and everyone freaked out, and it was this huge commotion. We all had to get out of the pool so they could disinfect it, and everyone was standing around in their towels trying to figure out who did it. I honestly remember thinking, "Hoooooly fuck." (Okay, I was six, so it was probably more like "heck" and "dang." But seriously: FUUUUUUCK.) I was just like, "Dear God, do not let these people find out it was me."

Everything ended up taking so long that my dad decided to just bring us home. And I was actually relieved. Like, I was just so ready to get the fuck out of there, and so glad no one had ID'd the turd. I couldn't believe I'd gotten away with it.

But in the car on the way home, my dad starts singing: *turd, turd, the turd is the word.* And then we get to a red light, and he turns around and gives me this huge fucking wink.

HE KNEW.

drops mic

(Please still be my friend, Blue. I'm so much less gross these days.)

—Jacques

FROM: bluegreen118@gmail.com
TO: hourtohour.notetonote@gmail.com
DATE: Sep 13 at 7:15 PM
SUBJECT: Re: you asked for this

THAT WAS YOU?!

No, don't worry—I didn't even live in Atlanta when we were six. ☺ That is tragically funny, Jacques. Though, now I'm worried you're going to be disappointed when I tell you mine.

So, I used to be really into Barney (the alleged "dinosaur sensation"). I had this really gross stuffed animal I carried around and slept with at night, and I used to chew on its hands when I was nervous. And, according to my mom, I spent the entire ride to kindergarten every day crying and begging her to let me bring Barney to school.

Well, one morning, I think she gave up, and she told me to just bring him. I remember hugging Barney in the car, feeling really victorious. When I got to school,

I carried him all the way down the hall to my classroom, and then it suddenly hit me that this was the world's worst idea. Like, I was standing there in the doorway with everyone looking at me, and that was the moment I knew: Barney is the worst.

So, I did the only thing I could think of in that moment: I started gnawing on Barney's hand.

One thing I really love about moving here is that no one calls me Dinosucker anymore.

—Blue

P.S. I did finally stop sleeping with Barney when I was about thirteen.

P.P.S. No, I'm kidding. I was eleven.

P.P.P.S. And a half.

P.P.P.P.S. You still think I'm cool, right?

Becky's Movie Set Scrapbook

Friend and fellow author Adam Silvera with Becky on the van to set, ready for their Halloween party cameo.

Becky with Greg Berlanti, the director who's bringing Simon to life.

Becky in Simon's perfectly Simon-ish room (Oreos were EVERYWHERE).

Angie Thomas, another friend and author, hangs out with Becky and their shared producer, Wyck Godfrey, of Temple Hill Entertainment.

Becky with Josh Duhamel, the ultimate hipster dad in the film.

Becky snuggling up with puppy Bieber.

Nick Robinson and Keiynan Lonsdale as Simon and Bram, featuring art by a real-life Creekwood student named Max.

Becky and Katherine Langford (Leah) casually reading *The Upside of Unrequited* on set at Creekwood High School.

Becky fangirling hard for Tony Hale, who plays the principal of Creekwood High.

Becky and Jorge Lendeborg, who plays Nick Eisner and is your newest crush.

Drew Starkey and Keiynan Lonsdale as Garrett and Bram, bromance of the century.

Photos from the author's private collection.

Becky Albertalli
in conversation with

Adam Silvera (author of *They Both Die at the End*)
and Angie Thomas (author of *The Hate U Give*)
July 12, 2017, Orlando, Florida

AS: All three of us have this really deep friendship now that goes beyond our books, but ultimately was born because of our books. It's weird to think that if we didn't write our books and they didn't publish them at a very serendipitous time, we would be losing a very important source of support. Becky and I read each other's books early on, we read *The Hate U Give* very early on as well, and had the tremendous honor of blurbing that book.

AT: Thank you!

BA: Oh, we were like begging to blurb it.

AS: It's just very cool to be part of a special edition for *Simon*. Personally, that book has meant so much to me. I've read it four times, and by the time this is printed, there will probably be another couple of times thrown in there—but the first time I read it, I was like, wow, this is the book that I would have appreciated at sixteen years old. I read it at age twenty-three for the first time, and I was a gay boy from the South Bronx who didn't have any literature or TV where I saw myself represented. And then I met Simon, who was this very geeky, Harry Potter–loving gay boy who wasn't disturbed by his sexuality, but was still kind of on the fence about coming out, because he wasn't sure what that would mean. And that's how I always felt. I never hated myself for being gay, but I still wasn't ready to make that leap just yet. But I'd like to think that if I'd had *Simon* in my hands when I was sixteen, I would have felt comfortable coming out sooner. So it's very special to be able to participate in a special edition as we approach the movie.

AT: Oh, Becky looks like she's about to cry!

BA: I know! We talked earlier today about what our favorite emojis are, and I mentioned one of my favorites is that monkey who's covering her mouth with her hands, and that's kind of how I feel right now?

AS: This year's been very special, because you also got to visit the *Simon* set, and I'm sure you had many of those monkey-emoji moments—

BA: Do you want to talk about the movie or something, Adam?

AS: Segue. I mean, I'd love to hear how that experience has been for you—everything from seeing Nick Robinson inhabit Simon for the first time . . .

BA: Oh my gosh—okay, so you guys are the perfect people to do this interview with, because you have been to the set, and Adam was there when I found out Nick would be playing Simon.

AS: Literally sitting one foot away from you.

BA: I'm going to keep the Nick Robinson crush stuff to a minimum in this interview, but everyone knows by now that I adore Nick Robinson, and I adore him as Simon. Seeing him in that role was very, very surreal. My impression of Nick was that he's a little bit soft-spoken and a little reserved, but also very funny, and if you tell him a joke—of course I'm the one who's there trying to tell jokes to Nick Robinson from the second I met him. Actually, the first time I met him, I stepped on his foot.

AT: Oh no!

BA: We were just off to a great start. I know. And the second time I met him, I told him to enjoy his boner.

AS: Uh, should we explain the context of that?

AT: Yeah, that needs a little more context.

BA: So they were filming a boner scene, and I really wanted to watch it, but I also had to drive home and hang out with my kids, which makes this story next-level inappropriate. I did end up choosing my children over the boner, so I had to leave, and I'm in this room, and Nick and Keiynan Lonsdale, who plays Bram, were just hanging out in there. And I'm making my grand exit. This was my first day on set, and my heart is so full, so I just told Nick, "Enjoy your boner."

AS: Perfect.

BA: It was memorable.

AS: And what was it like observing Greg Berlanti, the director?

BA: One of the things that I loved about Greg Berlanti directing this was that some of the things that Simon goes through in this story are things that Greg has lived through, and he brings nuances to the story that I couldn't bring to the book. I'll never forget watching Greg direct the scene where Simon comes out to his family. And he comes out to his family on Christmas, and it's very similar to the scene in the book. As it was being filmed, Greg was checking in with each actor in the room: Nick Robinson as Simon, Jennifer Garner as his mom, Josh Duhamel as his dad, and Talitha Bateman as Nora. Alice is not in the movie. She's . . .

AS: She's there in spirit.

AT: She's in our hearts.

BA: She went to college . . . really far away.

AT: And never came back.

BA: But Greg was just picking up these emotional beats that were so subtle but added so much, and you could see the actors playing around with that. And of course, they brought so much—their interpretation of his direction, and where it went after those conversations and what that collaboration turned into—was just so amazing. Greg understands not only what Simon was feeling in those moments, but he also has the perspective to have at least some understanding of what each member of that family was feeling in that moment, and also, he knew what Simon needed to hear, and what Simon wasn't hearing from them. It was just absolutely beautiful, what he brought to the table.

AS: It's a very different project for him as well, since Greg is known for big DC properties like *Supergirl* and *The Flash*. When I got to visit the set, it was really cool to see him take on something that didn't have that superhero pace, but tripled in heart.

AT: You could tell, when I went to set and watched, that this is a passion project for him. You could tell this is close to his heart and it's important to him to get this story right, which is the best thing you could ask for.

AT: And you got that vibe from everybody, even the people bringing the drinks to set and the van drivers. You could tell.

BA: I could feel it. And, you know, I got to know a lot of the people in the crew and people who were connected to the production in some way, and that's what I heard from so many people. The extras, even. You know, a lot of Simon's story starts with the fact that he perceives himself to be one of the only gay kids in his school, and that's also the story that plays out in the movie—but there's this whole added dimension to it, because so many of the extras are *Simon* readers, and several are gay kids and trans kids and bi kids, and a whole mix of many different identities in that community, and I'm like . . . that's my new headcanon! Just this beautifully diverse Creekwood High School. So much better than I could have written it. And I just love the idea that Simon's walking around this school, and he has no idea that he's surrounded by friends and by people who understand his perspective. There are a lot of people who were drawn to this project because they come from the same broad community that Simon comes from.

AS: And was there any scene you were most excited to see adapted?

BA: Yeah! And—it's funny—I had read the script before it was filmed, and I'm just so in love with it. It's written by Isaac Aptaker and Elizabeth Berger, who write for *This Is Us*, and some of the new stuff they put in there is spot-on. They know these characters so well, and it's absolutely flawless. One scene that I was really excited to see filmed was the Halloween party. One small difference between the book and the movie is that in the book, Simon gets tipsy at the Halloween party and gets super drunk at the gay bar. In the movie, it's reversed, so he has one drink at the gay bar but gets drunk at the party. So, not only did I get to see the Halloween party, but I got to see drunk Simon, who's my favorite Simon. Can I say that?

Okay, so they had a whole cameo role for me in the carnival scene, but then they had to switch the days because of the weather that week. I was going to be on book tour, so the only scene I could be in was the Halloween party. But I still wanted a cameo role, and the problem with the party is that . . .

AS: We . . . don't look like teenagers anymore.

BA: And you know what's funny about high school kids is that they don't invite their teachers to their boozy parties— even Bram Greenfeld doesn't invite his teachers to parties. So they had us in Halloween costumes with our faces out—

AS: And they had us in hair and makeup—

BA: But they took one look at us, and they were like, "Yeah, we're going to put you guys in masks." I think I was looking just a little bit too . . . thirty-four.

AT: So what kind of mask did they put on you?

BA: Well. So, I was a bunny, because they gave me a bunny mask, BUT. Don't you think there's this amazing meta kind of thing, where it's an Easter egg . . .

AT: You were the Easter egg.

BA: And I'll let Adam explain his costume.

AS: So, it's a pink unicorn costume—

BA: Like a onesie—

AS: A pink unicorn onesie, and it was a fine fit, but there was still the problem of my face not being concealed. So they gave me a smiling emoji mask. So it was a very odd combo, but I'm there.

BA: I think it was the grimace, like the one that's on the cover of *Upside*. Oh, and I also want to talk a little bit about my favorite moment from the day Angie came to set.

AT: Oh my gosh.

BA: I'm guessing you're thinking about what I'm thinking with the van . . .

AT: With the van—yeah. That was so funny. It was awesome, because that was the first day Becky got to see Jennifer Garner in action. And so we were already geeking out. They introduced you to her, right, but it was kind of brief.

BA: Yeah, it was kind of in between takes.

AT: They introduced Becky to Jennifer, and she was so sweet, and it was quick, but we were like, that was great, though. Nobody's complaining.

BA: We can always say for the rest of our lives that we met Jennifer Garner. We were done.

AT: So, that's it. And we were getting ready to leave the set, and they had the vans come to take us to base camp—

BA: Well, first we told Jennifer to enjoy her boner.

AT: And then they told her, "Hey, Angie has a movie coming out, too," and Jennifer was like, "I could play the mom in that!" And I was like, "Ummmm . . ." I'm probably the first person to turn Jennifer Garner down. It's no shade, Jennifer. It's just, it would not work. I'm sorry. That was the last thing I said to her, too, before—I feel so bad.

AS: That Angie Thomas is so mean.

AT: But we were cool, apparently, later, because we got in the van to go back to base camp, and there's Jennifer Garner coming toward us. And we're like, no way are they putting Jennifer Garner in this van. Yeah, it's a Mercedes van, but there's no way they're putting Jennifer Garner in this van. Jennifer Garner gets in the van. And she sits right next to Becky. And I, along with Jennifer Garner, made Becky into a sandwich. She's on one side, and I'm on the other, and she just starts chatting with us about stuff. I think you showed her a picture of your kids.

BA: Oh, she and I on a later date talked about our kids, and I'm nodding along, trying to pretend like I don't know the names of her kids already. . . . I don't even know how I know them! I haven't even read those kinds of magazines in years.

AT: I know them, too.

BA: So, my husband had just picked up the kids from school and taken them to the park, and we're sitting in the van with Jennifer. And he sends me a text, and it's a picture of my children, who, at the time of filming, were four and two. And they're playing at the park. And I don't even have to text him any words at all. I just text him—immediately—the selfie of me, Angie, and Jennifer Garner—

AT: That Jennifer Garner took because our arms were too short and hers were long enough to get all three of us.

BA: So, that's my advice to you guys. Just have short arms and celebrities will offer to take your pictures for you.

AS: Just on the Jennifer Garner note, too, the night I was leaving set, my Lyft driver asked me what was going on there, and I was like, "Oh, they're filming a movie." I was telling her what it was about and who was starring in it, and when I said

Jennifer Garner, she almost stopped the car. I really thought she was going to leave me on the side of the road so she could go back and find Jennifer Garner.

BA: So right now, I haven't seen the movie yet, I haven't even seen the trailer. It's all anticipation, which is a great place to be. I really think it's going to be so amazing. It's going to be like those classic teen movies I loved when I was a teen.

AS: It's going to be incredible to see a major motion picture revolving around a gay boy's coming out. It's going to be huge to so many people, and it's already meant so much to your readers. I'm just so excited and proud and ready for the maximum visibility for this book and Simon's story that will reach readers once that trailer drops and this movie's in theaters and we're all having Netflix binge parties once it goes up.

AT: And I'm excited, because the cast is so diverse, too. That's a huge thing you don't see enough of in teen movies. I think back to when I was a teen, and a lot of the time, teen movies were white. You know, you may have the funny black girl or the jock black boy, but that was it.

BA: But just one.

AT: Right! And they only get one line, and if it was a horror movie, they were the first to get killed. You know. So, it's great to see such a diverse cast for this movie. I'm so excited for multiple reasons, but that's a huge one. It's great to know that *Simon* is that teen movie that's going to break so many barriers in so many ways. That's amazing!

BA: Anyway, I guess the very last question here—

AS: The most important—

BA: The one I'm sure you've been skimming the rest of this interview trying to get to this part—and I hope you realize what a brave thing it is for me to bring this question up when I'm in hostile territory here . . . the Oreo issue.

AT: You make it sound so political. The Oreo issue.

BA: This sounds like NPR.

AT: Or like we're at a political debate.

BA: So let me just say my piece about classic Oreos, which are easily the best Oreos—

AS: Fake news.

AT: Fake news.

BA: So Golden Oreos—I'm sure they're fine just as a cookie, but they're not Oreos. It's just illogical that you would call them Oreos—

AT: But—

BA: And that's all the time we have here for today!

Turn the page for a sneak peek from

LEAH ON THE OFF BEAT

In this sequel to the acclaimed *Simon vs. the Homo Sapiens Agenda*, we follow Simon's BFF Leah as she grapples with changing friendships, first love, and senior year angst.

I DON'T MEAN TO BE dramatic, but God save me from Morgan picking our set list. That girl is a suburban dad's midlife crisis in a high school senior's body.

Case in point: she's kneeling on the floor, using the keyboard stool as a desk, and every title on her list is a mediocre classic rock song. I'm a very tolerant person, but as an American, a musician, and a self-respecting human being, it is both my duty and my privilege to blanket veto that shit.

I lean forward on my stool to peer over her shoulder. "No Bon Jovi. No Journey."

"Wait, seriously?" says Morgan. "People love 'Don't Stop Believin'.'"

"People love meth. Should we start doing meth?"

Anna raises her eyebrows. "Leah, did you just—"

"Did I just compare 'Don't Stop Believin' ' to meth?" I shrug. "Why, yes. Yes I did."

Anna and Morgan exchange a capital-L Look. It's a Look that says *here we go, she's about to dig her heels in.*

"I'm just saying. The song is a mess. The lyrics are bullshit." I give a little tap on the snare for emphasis.

"I like the lyrics," Anna says. "They're hopeful."

"It's not about whether they're hopeful. It's about the gross implausibility of a midnight train going, quote unquote, *anywhere.*"

They exchange another Look, this time with tiny shrugs. Translation: *she has a point.*

Translation of the translation: *Leah Catherine Burke is an actual genius, and we should never ever doubt her music taste.*

"I guess we shouldn't add anything new until Taylor and Nora are back," Morgan concedes. And she's right. School musical rehearsals have kept Taylor and Nora out of commission since January. And even though the rest of us have been meeting a few times a week, it sucks rehearsing without your singer and lead guitarist.

"Okay," Anna says. "Then I guess we're done here?"

"Done with rehearsal?"

Welp. I guess I should have shut up about Journey. Like, I get it. I'm white. I'm supposed to love shitty classic rock. But I kind of thought we were all enjoying this lively debate about music and meth. Maybe it went off the rails somewhere, though, because now Morgan's putting the keyboard away and Anna's texting her mom to pick her up. I guess that's game over.

My mom won't be here for another twenty minutes, so I hang around the music room even after they leave. I don't really mind. It's actually nice to drum alone. I let my sticks take the lead, from the bass to the snare and again and again. Some fills on the toms. Some *chhh chhh chhh* on the hi-hat, and then the crash.

Crash.

Crash.

And another.

I don't even hear my phone buzzing until it pings with a voice mail. It's obviously my mom. She always calls, only texts as a last resort. You'd think she was fifty or a million years old, but she's thirty-five. I'm eighteen. Go ahead and do the math. I'm basically your resident fat Slytherin Rory Gilmore.

I don't listen to the voice mail, because Mom always texts me after—and sure enough, a moment later: So sorry to do this, sweetie. I'm swamped here—can you catch the bus today?

Sure, I write back.

You're the best. Kissy emoji.

Mom's boss is an unstoppable robot workaholic lawyer, so this happens a lot. It's either that, or she's on a date. It's not even funny, having a mom who gets more action than I do. Right now, she's seeing some guy named Wells. Like the plural of *well*.

He's bald and rich, with tiny little ears, and I think he's almost fifty. I met him once for thirty minutes, and he made six puns and said "oh, fudge" twice.

Anyway, I used to have a car, so it didn't matter as much—if I beat Mom home, I'd just let myself in through the garage. But Mom's car died last summer, so my car became her car, which means I get to ride home with thirty-five freshmen. Not that I'm bitter.

We're supposed to clear out of the music room by five, so I take apart the kit and carry it into the storage closet, drum by drum. I'm the only one who uses the school kit. Everyone else who plays has their own set in the finished basements of their personal mansions. My friend Nick has a customizable Yamaha DTX450K e-kit, and he *doesn't even drum*. I could never afford that in a billion years. But that's Shady Creek.

The late bus doesn't leave for another half hour, so I guess I'll be a theater groupie. No one ever cares if I wander into rehearsal, even though the show opens on Friday. Honestly, I crash rehearsal so often, I think people forget I'm not in the play. Most of my friends are—even Nick, who'd never auditioned for anything in his life until this. I'm pretty sure he only did it to spend time with his sickeningly adorable girlfriend. But since he's a true legend, he managed to snag the lead role.

I take the side hallway that leads directly backstage, and slip through the door. Naturally, the first person I see is the peanut himself, my number one bro, demolisher of Oreos: Simon Spier.

"Leah!" He's standing in the wings, half in costume, surrounded by dudes. No clue how Ms. Albright talked so many guys into auditioning this year. Simon shrugs away from them. "You're just in time for my song."

"I planned that."

"You did?"

"No."

"I hate you." He elbows me, and then hugs me. "No, I love you."

"I don't blame you."

"I can't believe you're about to hear me sing."

I grin. "The hype is real."

Then there's a whispered command I can't quite hear, and the boys line up in the wings, amped and ready. Honestly, I can't even look at them without laughing. The play is *Joseph and the Amazing Technicolor Dreamcoat*, and all of Joseph's brothers are wearing these fluffy fake beards. I don't know, maybe it's in the costume notes of the Bible or something.

"Don't wish me luck," Simon says. "Tell me to break a leg."

"Simon, you should probably get out there."

"Okay, but listen, don't take the bus. We're going to Waffle House after this."

"Noted."

The boys shuffle onstage, and I step deeper into the wings. Now that the flock has cleared, I can see Cal Price, the stage manager, stationed at a desk between the curtains. "Hey, Red."

That's what he calls me, even though I'm barely a redhead. It's fine—Cal's a cinnamon roll—but every time he does it, there's this hiccup in my chest.

My dad used to call me Red. Back when he used to call me.

"Have you seen this one?" Cal asks, and I shake my head. He nudges his chin toward the stage, smiling, so I take a few steps forward.

The boys are lurching. I don't know any other way to describe it. The choir teacher bangs out some French-sounding song on the piano, and Simon steps forward, hand on his heart.

"Do you remember the good years in Canaan . . ."

His voice is shaking, just a little, and his French accent's a disaster. But he's funny as hell up there—sinking to his knees, grasping his head, moaning—and I don't want to oversell it or anything, but this just may be the most iconic performance of all time.

Nora sidles up to me. "Guess how many times I've heard him sing this in his bedroom."

"Please tell me he has no idea you can hear him."

"He has no idea I can hear him."

Sorry, Simon, but you're too precious. If you weren't gay and taken, I'd totally marry you. And let's be honest, marrying Simon would be amazing—and not just because I had a sad, secret crush on him for most of middle school. It's more than that. For one thing, I'm totally up for being a Spier, because that family is literally perfect. I'd get Nora as my sister-in-law, plus an awesome older sister in college. And the Spiers live in this huge, gorgeous house that doesn't have clothes and clutter on every surface. I even love their dog.

The song ends, and I slip out and around to the back row of the auditorium, known among the theater kids—aspirationally—as Makeout Alley. But I'm all alone back here, and only halfway participating. Surveying the action from across the room. I've never been in a play, even though Mom's always trying to get me to audition. But here's the thing. You can spend years drawing shitty fan art in sketchpads, and no one has to see it. You can drum alone in the music room until you're decent enough for live shows. But with acting, you don't really get to spend years stumbling along in private. You have an audience even before there's an audience.

A swell of music. Abby Suso steps forward, wearing a giant beaded collar and an Elvis wig. And she's singing.

She's amazing, of course. She doesn't have one of those limitless voices like Nick or Taylor, but she can carry a tune, and she's funny. That's the thing. She's a straight-up goofball onstage. At one point, Ms. Albright actually guffaws. Which is saying something—not just because who knew guffawing was an actual thing people did, but because you know Ms. Albright has seen this thing a thousand times already. Abby's just that good. Even I can't take my eyes off her.

When the show ends, Ms. Albright herds the cast onstage

for notes. Everyone drapes themselves all over the platforms, but Simon and Nick scoot to the end of the stage, next to Abby. Of course.

Nick slides his arm around her shoulders, and she tucks up closer to him. Also of course.

There's no Wi-Fi in here, so I'm stuck listening to Ms. Albright's notes, followed by an unsolicited ten-minute monologue from Taylor Metternich about *losing yourself* and *becoming your character.* I have a theory that Taylor literally gets off on the sound of her own voice. I'm pretty sure she's having tiny secret orgasms right before our eyes.

Ms. Albright finally shuts it down, and everyone streams out of the auditorium, grabbing backpacks on the way—but Simon, Nick, and Abby wait in a cluster near the orchestra pit. I stand and stretch and head down the aisle to meet them. And a part of me wants to spew praise all over them, but something stops me. Maybe it's just too painfully sincere, a little too fifth-grade Leah. Not to mention that the thought of fangirling over Abby Suso makes me want to vomit.

I high-five Simon. "You killed it."

"I didn't even know you were here," Abby says.

Hard to know what she means by that. Maybe it's a secret diss. Like, *why are you even here, Leah?* Or maybe: *I didn't even notice you, you're so irrelevant.* But maybe I'm overthinking this. I've been known to do that when it comes to Abby.

I nod. "I heard you guys were going to Waffle House?"

"Yeah, I think we're just waiting for Nora."

Martin Addison walks by. "Hey, Simeon," he says.

"Hey, Reuben," says Simon, looking up from his phone. Those are their characters' names. And yes, Simon plays a guy named Simeon, because I guess Ms. Albright couldn't resist. Reuben and Simeon are two of Joseph's brothers, and I'm sure this would all be adorable if it didn't involve Martin Addison.

Martin keeps walking, and Abby's eyes flash. Honestly, it's pretty hard to piss Abby off, but Martin does it just by existing. And by going out of his way to talk to Simon, like last year didn't happen. It's so fucking audacious. Simon doesn't even talk to Martin that much, but I hate that he does at all. Not that I get to dictate who Simon talks to. But I know—I can just tell—that it bugs Abby as much as it bugs me.

Simon turns back to his phone, clearly texting Bram. They've been dating for a little over a year, and they're one of those vomitously happy couples. I don't mean that in the PDA sense. They actually barely touch each other in school, probably because people are prehistoric dickwads about gay stuff. But Simon and Bram text and eyefuck all day long, like they can't even go five minutes without contact. To be totally honest, it's hard not to be jealous. It's not even just about the true-love-heart-eyes-get-a-room-dudes fairy-tale magic. It's the fact that they went for it. They had the balls to say *fuck this, fuck Georgia, fuck all of you homophobic assholes*.

"Are Bram and Garrett meeting us there?" Abby asks.

"Yup. They just got out of soccer." Simon smiles.

I end up in Simon's passenger seat, with Nora in the back, digging through her backpack. She's wearing rolled-up jeans, covered in paint, and her curls are tied back in a messy knot. One ear is pierced all the way to the top, and she has a tiny blue nose stud she got last summer. That girl is honestly too adorable. I love how much she looks like Simon, and I love that they both look like their older sister. They're a total copy-paste family.

Finally, Nora's hand emerges from her backpack, holding a giant unopened bag of M&M's. "I'm starving."

"We're literally driving to Waffle House. Right now," Simon says, but he stretches his hand back to take some. I take a handful, and they're perfectly melted—which is to say, they're not quite melted. Just a little soft on the inside.

"So, it wasn't too much of a shitshow, right?" Simon asks.

"The play?"

He nods.

"Not at all. It was awesome."

"Yeah, but people are still messing up their lines, and we open on Friday. And freaking Potiphar screwed up a whole song today. God, I need a waffle."

I pull out my phone and check Snapchat. Abby's posted this epically long story from rehearsal, and it's like a montage from a rom-com. A snap of Nick and Taylor singing onstage. A mega close-up selfie of Abby and Simon. An even closer one of

Simon's face where his nostrils look so big, Abby stuck a panda graphic inside one of them. And Abby and Nick, over and over.

I stick my phone back in my pocket. Simon turns onto Mount Vernon Highway. I feel antsy and strange—like I'm bothered by something, but I can't remember what. It's like a tiny pinprick in the back of my mind.

"I can't figure out what song you're doing," Nora says.

It takes me a moment to realize she's talking to me, and a moment after that to realize I've been drumming on the glove compartment.

"Huh. I have no idea."

"It's like this," Nora says, tapping a straight one-two beat on the back of my seat. *Boom-tap-boom-tap.* All eighth notes, quick and even. My mind fills in the rest of it immediately.

It's "Don't Stop Believin'." My brain is an asshole.

Also by Becky Albertalli:

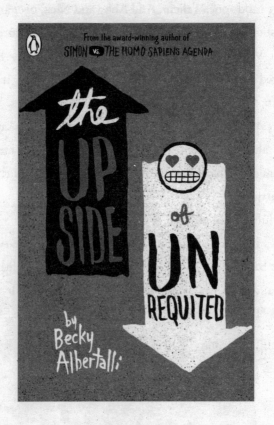

AVAILABLE NOW

'I have such a crush on this book. Not only is this
one a must-read, but it's a must-reread'
Julie Murphy, *New York Times* bestselling author of *Dumplin'*

'Heart-fluttering, honest and hilarious'
Stephanie Perkins, *New York Times* bestselling
author of *Anna and the French Kiss*